When **Virginia Heath** was a little girl, it took her ages to fall asleep, so she made up stories in her head to help pass the time while she was staring at the ceiling. As she got older the stories became more complicated, sometimes taking weeks to get to the happy ending. Then one day she decided to embrace the insomnia and start writing them down. Over twenty books and three Romantic Novel of the Year Award nominations later, and it still takes her for ever to fall asleep.

ONLY AN HEIRESS WILL DO

Virginia Heath

MILLS & BOON

First published in Great Britain 2025
by Mills & Boon, an imprint of HarperCollins*Publishers* Ltd,
1 London Bridge Street, London, SE1 9GF

www.harpercollins.co.uk

HarperCollins*Publishers*, Macken House, 39/40 Mayor Street Upper, Dublin 1, D01 C9W8, Ireland

Only an Heiress Will Do © 2025 Susan Merritt

ISBN: 978-0-263-34505-6

02/25

This book contains FSC™ certified paper and other controlled sources to ensure responsible forest management.

For more information visit www.harpercollins.co.uk/green.

Printed and Bound in the UK using 100% Renewable Electricity at CPI Group (UK) Ltd, Croydon, CR0 4YY

For my fellow collaborators
on this **A Season to Wed** series

Lucy Morris, Sarah Rodi and Ella Matthews

Chapter One

Lady Bulphan's Ball,
May 1816

Major Adam Mayhew wasn't normally a man for lists.

He wasn't usually a man for plans either, apart from his one enduring and lofty career plan which had, today, been thoroughly blown to smithereens yet again. Something he could not help feeling was oddly fitting despite the current dire circumstances as he probably didn't deserve to hope for more than he had already received anyway. The infinite powers of the universe had seen fit to spare him so many times from certain death on the brutal Napoleonic battle-fields and taken so many others instead, that expecting any more from life seemed…selfish. Especially now that the war was over and he was home safe and sound with barely a scratch to commemorate his six years on the very front of the front line.

And now fate was going to cruelly and unfairly snuff out one more life he cared about and there wasn't a damn thing Adam could do to stop it despite wishing with all his heart that he could swap places with his brother and die in his stead. After all, he had no wife or children who loved and needed him to live—and Phillip did. It stood to reason, surely, that it would be better all round if fate would answer his prayers and simply let them swap places? But alas, fate was cruel and the best it would allow Adam to do was make his beloved older brother's final months as bearable as possible. Finally free of all the hideous debts that had burdened him for so long and reassured that his family would always have a roof over their heads. Something that none of them would have very soon if the bailiffs had their way.

He stared across the crowded ballroom and the sea of bejewelled, befeathered and, occasionally, beautiful ladies present and then subtly glanced at the names on his list. Despite the many balls, parties and soirées he had been obliged to attend since his return, he still had no idea who any of these women were.

No idea of their characters or compatibility.

No idea of their ages or whether they were pretty or not.

Six years out of the ranks he was born into but had left before he was old enough to properly join meant that he was clueless about who was really who in the ton. Clueless and completely out of step with most of them too.

But thanks to his wretched father's gross mismanagement, his brother's wretched circumstances and the wretched piece of paper in his hand, Adam now knew how much each of these listed ladies' dowries were worth and somehow had to convince one of them to marry him before this month was out.

A stark, new reality which made him sick to his stomach.

'Some champagne, sir?' A passing footman proffered a tray.

'Why not.' Some Dutch courage was definitely needed tonight. Especially as the floor beneath Adam's feet had been whipped away and his entire world upended by a single dire conversation. 'I don't suppose you can point me in the direction of...' He glanced quickly at the list, written in a hurry after a frantic scour of the gossip columns this afternoon. 'Miss Arabella Westfield?' If money was the goal, he might as well start with the one who came with the most of it.

'Of course, sir.' He could tell by the footman's bland gaze that the fellow knew exactly what he was up to and judged him for it. Adam didn't blame him. He was disgusted at the mercenary task he had to do now too. Marrying for money was not the philanthropic and selfless civilian career he had intended to repay the benevolent but fickle universe with when he had finally ripped off his wretched cavalry uniform and burned the damn thing. 'She's over there in that alcove. Surrounded by all her other eager suitors.'

The footman sailed away and, already thoroughly ashamed of himself, Adam took a long swig of his drink while he steeled himself to join Miss Westfield's clearly already busy entourage. Thankfully, being charming was one of the pointless things he excelled at, so he was confident he could worm his way into her inner circle. He had weaselled his way into all manner of situations while on a mission before and done so with such effortless and convincing aplomb that those he had infiltrated rarely questioned why he was there.

Flirtation too, was a particular forte. Something he had done regularly for his own amusement from the moment he had discovered girls, and once or twice for King and country when the need had arisen. And he did not feel guilty for any of that. He did, however, feel unclean at the prospect tonight. But how else was he supposed to convince an heiress to marry him in record speed unless he charmed her into falling in love with him?

Another thing about this awful situation that made him feel sick to his stomach.

He would feel so much better about it all if he could simply be honest. Lay all his cards on the table so that he didn't have to pretend to feel anything or be anything other than what he was—a man who no longer had a purpose in life nor a pot to piss in but who needed funds fast.

In return—because his conscience and his moral compass insisted this transaction be a quid pro quo— he would uphold every single one of his vows as penance for luring her down the aisle under false pretences. He would be a decent and supportive husband and, hopefully, he would learn to love her as she deserved. She would be saving his family from destitution, and that in itself would gratefully render him beholden to her for life.

But all those truths were hardly wooing material and these were all coveted ladies who knew their worth. If they were sensible at least. If any were too stupid to realise that then Adam dreaded spending eternity with them. He knew beauty was only skin-deep so had no issue with a plain woman or a plump one. Or one who was all skin and bones for that matter. Whatever the package he was determined, as penance for his mercenary motive, to find and cherish all the things they had in common and try to love her regardless. However, although beggars could not be choosers, and being in no position to be picky, he hoped the universe would toss him a bone seeing as it was determined to rob him of his brother.

What would he and a vacuous bride talk about, for goodness' sake? He knew that he likely didn't deserve the fanciful sort of marital bliss his romantic heart had held out for, but he at least wanted to be able to tolerate the company of the woman he had to shackle himself to for all eternity.

He glanced up at the painted cherubs on Lady Bulphan's ostentatious ceiling and silently prayed for divine intervention even though he knew he had already used up all of his luck and some. *Please make Miss Westfield, or Miss Gower or Miss Wynne-Stanley or Miss Whoever-I-Have-To-End-Up-With have half a brain.*

That pathetic plea done, Adam drained his glass. No sooner had it left his lips and it was topped up. But not with champagne.

'Smuggled Scottish single malt,' mumbled his best friend Hawk and fellow former cavalry officer as he pocketed the flask. 'I figured we'd all need the good stuff to survive tonight.'

'I'm surprised to see you here. I thought you'd avoid this like the plague What with this being the biggest social occasion of the season and all.' You could always rely on Hawk to bravely fight beside you on the battlefield, and he had on more occasions than Adam could count, but he would usually run for the hills and leave you to the vultures in a ballroom.

'A wager is a wager and I lost. Unfairly because you all ganged up against me but unlike the rest of my so-called friends, I have principles.' Hawk shuffled uncomfortably with a scowl that would curdle milk. 'I'll happily desert this hell as soon as your co-conspirators have seen me fulfil my nonsensical obligation.' By co-conspirators, Hawk meant Ash and Ezra, the remaining pair of their tight-knit band of brothers who were yet to arrive. They had met at university, and all joined the army together on a whim the day they graduated. They had gone to hell and back daily in the Peninsular until they laid down their weapons straight after Waterloo. Now, still struggling to find their way in civilian life, they played whist every Wednesday at White's while they put the world to rights. 'But lessons have been learned and in all future card games, unless the stakes involve money or property, I won't bet on one again. I am shocked that I fell for that foolhardy bet in the first place.' He slanted Adam a glance. 'And on the subject of shock, I'm stunned that you haven't found some chit to flirt the night away with yet. You're slipping, Adam. You've normally swept one off her feet by ten. It's almost eleven and nobody is hanging off your dandified arm.'

Adam chuckled as he was supposed to at the friendly jibe even though this time it hit too near the knuckle to do anything but make him queasier. 'I've got my eyes on a few.' His list of potential victims seemed to burn inside his pocket. 'I'm simply weighing up my options before I weigh in.' Which was exactly the sort of flippant comment Hawk would expect from a man so perennially glib and outwardly super-ficial as he pretended to be. Except he found nothing funny now. 'What about you?' He changed the subject on purpose. As close as he was with his three friends, he couldn't quite bring himself to tell them what he was up to yet. It was all too fresh. All too awful. All so hideously unfair. 'See anyone you fancy?'

Hawk's scowl deepened as he scanned the room, typically more for trouble than enjoyment. 'If a woman chooses to waste her time here amongst all these brainless, gossip-fuelled fools then I can assure you I'd find nothing attractive about her. Besides, women cause nothing but problems and I...' He stilled sud-denly then grunted. 'They're here.' And here indeed Ash and Ezra were, although how his friend had spied them amongst the thronging masses spilling through the doorway on the other side of the packed dance floor was a mystery. But that was Hawk, who appar-ently had been born with eyes in the back of his head because he never missed a thing.

Half of London had to be here tonight. It was such a crush Adam could barely breathe. Or perhaps the dis-tinct lack of oxygen in his lungs was caused by all the tangled emotions strangling his innards? Fear, guilt, despair and desperation weren't the ideal combination for an evening of necessary wooing.

Hawk started towards their friends, eager to be done with his obligation, but when an overwhelmed

Adam remained rooted to the spot, he stopped. 'You not coming?'

As tempting as it was to spend an hour lamenting his latest catastrophic problem with his friends, Adam was a man on a quest so shook his head. 'There's someone I need to urgently flirt with first.' Unconsciously, he drained his glass in one desperate gulp and the generous measure of neat whiskey took his breath away.

Hawk's brows arched in surprise. 'Bloody hell. Like that, is it?'

Adam nodded.

'Then take this.' Hawk pressed the flask into his hand. 'Looks like you need my Scotch more than I do.'

Adam watched his friend barge through the crowds and then forced his feet to skirt the dance floor to get to the alcove to do what had to be done.

As the footman had promised, Miss Westfield wasn't hard to find. She was a petite and attractive blonde and was, thanks largely he presumed to her extremely wealthy father and her purported twenty-thousand-pound dowry, surrounded by men. The sort of men he would usually condemn as odious and self-centred scoundrels who shamelessly hunted down a woman with money like baying hounds after a fox. Except now he was one of them and in no position to judge.

A sobering thought he was forced to push to the

back of his mind as he loitered against a pillar while he did his reconnaissance. Miss Westfield appeared to enjoy their attentions and had a couple of favourites amongst the pack. The first was a tall and lanky fellow with a loud brocade waistcoat, which put Adam's scarlet silk one to shame, and who kept making private and obviously droll asides that made her laugh. The second was a tall and not so lanky gentleman who had decided to wordlessly anticipate her every need. He was currently in the midst of passing her a glass of champagne, his fingers brushing hers with just enough boldness to declare his passionate interest. She was certainly interested enough to turn away from the suitor entertaining her to stare at the one attempting to seduce her and to offer him a half-smile before her attention was pulled away.

Then a third gentleman caught her eye and she batted hers back at him as he regaled her with some story or other, his narrow chest pumped out like a peacock's parading in front of a potential mate. He was tall too. And oddly familiar. Toby Someone from Adam's Oxford days and, if his memory served, heir to some minor baronetcy somewhere.

So what could he conclude from all that?

That Miss Westfield was thoroughly enjoying being the centre of attention. That she was definitely on the market to be wooed. That she had a penchant for gentlemen of above average height, which Adam and his six feet and three inches definitely was. She liked a man with a sense of humour, which he had in spades. Liked to flirt too, which was just as well because so did he. And she—or more likely her new-monied father—was after someone who had run out of old money but still came with an ancient title.

Which Adam would also soon have.

Despite wishing with all his heart that he wouldn't.

That was when the grief slammed into him again. Sharp, visceral and so overwhelming tears pricked his eyes as he remembered every single detail of the utterly devastating news that had blindsided him only this morning.

Before he made a spectacle of himself and wept right there in the middle of Lady Bulphan's ballroom at the sheer, bloody heinousness of it all, Adam darted towards the nearest door so he could pull himself back together in private.

Gwen almost lost her balance as her feet hit the floor but managed to save herself from falling by grabbing a nearby tree branch. Clambering over a six-foot wall in a ball gown in the dark was not something she made a habit of, but in this case it had been unavoidable. When you were *persona non grata* as far as the ton was concerned, the only way to get into one of the grandest balls of the season was to sneak in the back way. Balls did not come much bigger and so well attended as Lady Bulphan's, so with any luck, she would find out all she needed to know here and never have to do this again as seven and twenty was much too old for wall scaling. Especially when you were a successful businesswoman on a quest to restore your shattered reputation!

Thank goodness she hadn't been seen and the garden and terrace were deserted as she made her way to the open French doors where the ball was already in full swing.

Good.

She was a woman with a mission and she had both the motivation and the means to make it happen, so she absolutely could not let her past get in the way of it.

It was a bold move to open an enormous store in Piccadilly. Bolder still to plan on calling it Trym's when Miss Gwendolyn Trym was still a scandalous social pariah as far as society was concerned.

But, putting her scandal to one side, no matter how personally infamous she was, Trym's as a brand was synonymous with quality furniture that still supplied the great and the good despite her shocking personal reputation. It existed entirely separate from her scandal and had done for thirty years. Therefore, using that name made sound business sense. Piccadilly was also the busiest shopping street in the land and served the wealthiest clientele. That was why it made sound business sense to put it there and she had been convinced for quite some time that opening a grand shop was the only way to expand the thriving business that her father had created from scratch.

Dear Papa had always been an ambitious visionary and he had passed that trait on to his daughter. After all, why just sell people chairs, tables, sofas and beds from a catalogue like every other furniture maker in the land when you could have the samples ready-made in a store to tempt them? And while you were about it, why not quadruple your profits with wallpapers, curtains and linens, lamps, tableware, rugs and even decorative knick-knacks? All available to purchase under one gloriously specialised and luxurious roof. It was a genius idea that nobody else had thought of and too good not to act upon before someone else did. Which was why Gwen had already purchased the building and was about to commence the massive renovation it needed to make it suitable for her vision.

Exciting times!

But also troubling times.

If she did not do things correctly when her scandal inevitably reared its ugly head again, the very people she hoped to lure into Trym's could boycott it altogether once they realised she was behind it. And there would be little chance of concealing that here in the viper's den called Mayfair where gossip was rife, and everybody knew everybody else's business. Mayfair wasn't as egalitarian as Cheapside but she could hardly continue to hide there when her business was expanding here! And frankly, nor did she want to. She had spent the last decade in purgatory and was thoroughly sick and tired of it. For the last year she had also felt…unfulfilled and burying herself in her work wasn't filling that empty void inside her like it always had. Therefore, she was in dire need of a new challenge to occupy her. Never mind that Trym's deserved to grow.

Obviously, she could brazen it out, open her shop in the heart of the ton and be damned, but she was too canny a businesswoman to do that. For forty years, Trym's had maintained a sterling reputation and she had no intention of tarnishing that. However, with her reputation more tarnished than a rusty bucket, Gwen knew that if she stood any chance of the new shop being the unmitigated, instant success it deserved to be, she had to become respectable to the ton long before it opened. Unfortunately, the only viable, reliable and rapid way to do that was to marry into the very society that had shunned her, and well enough that it couldn't shun her any longer.

Hence she was here.

Dressed in the most inconspicuous evening gown she could find and determined to do her darndest to blend into the wallpaper.

She slipped into the ballroom and loitered for several minutes with a cup of punch near the refreshment table while she got her bearings, taking great solace in the fact that not a single person had yet recognised her. Buoyed by that temporary miracle, because she'd likely be escorted out on the arms of a pair of burly footmen if she was, she surreptitiously slipped her notebook from her subtly beaded reticule to peruse one of the many important lists contained within. In particular, the one that detailed the criteria she required in a husband. Which, after much consideration and refinement, she had narrowed down to five key points.

He must be of noble birth or have connections impressive enough or useful enough to Trym's to compensate for his lack of title.

There could be no beating around the bush. If Gwen stood any chance of redemption here, she had to marry a respected man from the aristocracy. The ton had long memories when it came to a scandal, especially when it was caused by someone not from their ranks. They did however, have the often proven capacity to turn a blind eye if a transgressor was one of them. There had been several scandalous titled ladies in living memory, like the infamous Duchess of Devonshire for example, who had done far worse than Gwen but who was still embraced by society because her roots run deep within it. Therefore, an earl or viscount would make the perfect husband as the rank-obsessed ton would have to accept her once she too had a title. A marquess or duke would obviously be the dream because then she would outrank almost everyone here. Nobody dared disrespect a duchess! No matter how loose they perceived her morals to be! However, she had to be pragmatic and accept the fact that dukes were rare creatures, even here, and a penniless one in need of a wealthy wife was even rarer.

That was why she had a contingency plan. If the lack of destitute dukes, marquesses, earls or viscounts meant she had to shackle herself to a lesser blue blood, at least having a husband and a different surname would go some way to making her respectable again. Or at least tolerated. After ten years banished to the social wilderness, that was not to be sniffed at!

A fortune-hunter.

While most ladies would balk at the prospect, and she should most of all after her narrow escape all those years ago, Gwen had long outgrown the silly, romantic notions of her youth. She did not want hearts and flowers. Did not want her heart involved in the arrangement in any way at all, in fact, after it had been bludgeoned so badly that she had thought it would never heal. So she was going to consider this wholly as a business decision. She knew that even with her damaged reputation, her wealth was her trump card here on the marriage mart. She also knew that a man with no money would be easier to control. Especially as she had no intention of allowing him to get any control of hers. She could afford decent lawyers and already knew of several ways that the Trym bank balance could be protected from England's archaic marital laws. The easiest way to do that, of course, was to get him to sign away his claim, which led neatly on to the next point on the list. Her perfect groom needed to be:

All show and no substance (preferably brainless).

This attribute was paramount. The aristocratic fortune-hunter she had almost married at the tender age of seventeen had been a very clever and conniving man who would have taken everything before he cast her aside. She could not afford to marry one of those now. Instead, she wanted a husband who was dense enough or self-absorbed enough not to understand how the world of finance really worked and desperate enough for money that he would rub his hands together at the twenty thousand pounds immediate cash sum he would be given the second he signed. That lump sum would be followed by a generous annual stipend of ten thousand a year and a house once she was done with him. What self-absorbed, penniless and brainless dandy would turn down that? But—for her own sake—he also had to be:

A fine, fertile physical specimen with good teeth, preferably under the age of forty.

As a woman edging ever closer towards thirty, before she fully embarked on the next stage of Trym's expansion, she was only too aware her fertile years were diminishing. She needed to have a child—preferably a daughter—to leave her business to. Someone to nurture and love as, thanks to her shocking reputation, that aspect of her life was as barren as a desert. Increasingly, as her feelings of unfulfilment had grown, she had also felt lonely. An overwhelming ache that something was missing and a child of her own would fill that gap. Seven and twenty was the optimal age to have a baby before her womb shrivelled into an aging husk and, by hook or by crook, she was jolly well going to do that before this year was out. Killing two birds with one stone was always the most efficient use of her time. Especially when her time was always so strictly limited.

According to her diary, a February baby would be perfect. The business was always at its quietest in the cold months after Christmas, so she could even squeeze in a short confinement if it became necessary in the latter months of her pregnancy where she could work from home without doing much damage. A February baby would also give her over a year to become respectable again and a good six months to readjust to motherhood before the Trym Furniture Company's new shop would be ready to open its doors in the following August. That meant that the clock was ticking in more ways than one, so she needed to find herself a suitable husband immediately to get everything done in time.

As it might take several attempts to make a baby, her husband needed to be the sort of man she could bear to lie with. As unpleasant a prospect as that already was, if she had to put up with unpalatable huffing and puffing, she was not prepared to also endure sagging flesh and horrendous halitosis. She wanted a man—albeit temporarily—with enough vim and vigour to do the job well. And frankly, the faster the better. Ideally, a randy and healthy specimen who would take minutes, rather than hours, to do the necessary.

Which brought her to the final specification—

A man who preferably has a wandering eye or some other unsavoury hobby which would ensure that I have ample excuse to insist upon a quiet separation once he ceased being useful (hopefully within three to four months).

Gwen wasn't stupid after all.

At least not any more. The fresh-faced, green girl who had fallen head over heels in love and run away to Gretna Green with a predator before she caused the mother of all scandals was a savvy businesswoman now. One who understood how the cut-throat world worked and how to make it work in her favour, even if she did have to hide in the periphery of it. Married couples lived happily separate lives in the ton all the time and nobody blinked an eyelid so long as they didn't try to divorce. Her husband could live how he saw fit in his household while she lived in Cheapside with her daughter, and they would only ever have to collide if they absolutely had to for appearances.

She closed the notebook and scanned the room with a wry smile, pleased that she had chosen this ball to infiltrate. If she was going to find her ideal candidate anywhere, she was going to find him here. She had genuinely never seen as many pompous, lazy, useless, vacuous wastrels in all her life.

Gwen took a leisurely wander around the edge of the room, watching and learning. From the clusters of gentlemen hovering around a select few young ladies, it wouldn't be hard to work out who the current crop of fortune-hunters were. One lady in particular seemed to have more than her fair share and was holding court in an alcove, so Gwen headed there.

'It would be my honour to claim any dance.' A fawning young buck with slightly buck teeth craned over his rivals from the back of the melee to practically shout that at the pretty blonde who was basking in all the attention. 'Please leave a space for me.'

'I have one country dance left, Lord Fletcher.' The blonde, who was clearly on the lookout for the right sort of husband too, sent him a simpering smile. 'I shall pencil you in.'

The young buck simpered back with pathetic delight. 'Thank you, Miss Westfield.'

Westfield? That had to be William Westfield's daughter then. The tea importer. The one so desperate to become part of the aristocracy he'd hung a twenty-thousand-pound price tag around his eldest daughter's neck and then crowed the size of her dowry from the rooftops. She was obviously the fortune-hunters' catch of the season!

How marvellous!

Gwen had stumbled upon a gold mine without even trying.

She edged a little closer, pretending to rifle in her reticule to make it appear as if she wasn't just an eavesdropper.

'...you do make me laugh, Lord Jerrick.' Miss Westfield's attention was now on another chap. A tall, sandy-haired and surprisingly handsome man. 'But despite your ironic disdain for picnics and parlour games, I rather enjoy a house party. Do tell me more, Lord Vincent, and maybe you can convince me to attend.' Her short attention wandered to a third fellow, who also looked to be a promising specimen.

'My family's estate is in Hertfordshire and...'

Gwen lingered for as long as she could on the outskirts of Miss Westfield's gaggle of suitors without it looking odd, and then darted out of the ballroom, rummaging for her pencil as she went. She needed to record her findings in her notebook straight away or she would forget all the names. Six money-grabbing lords in a row and all in less than ten minutes!

Definite no's were Lord Fletcher (too young), Lord Trent (who made too much spittle in the corners of his mouth as he talked) and Lord Digby (who she would wager was as clever and calculated a predator as the snake she had fled to Gretna with!). Possibles were Lord Jerrick (although while he physically appealed, he was too witty to be as lacking in intelligence as she would like) and Lord Vincent (a good-looking future earl with a crumbling estate in need of funds).

Needing quiet and space to think, Gwen pushed open a random door as she deliberated which ones to approach with a proposal and almost crashed into a gentleman.

A tall, dark and handsome gentleman in a dandy's crimson waistcoat.

Who smelled of whiskey and spicy cologne as he pointed at her with a swaying flask.

'I don't suppose you're an heiress, are you?' It did not take a genius to work out that he was far from sober. 'Only I need to marry one straight away. Ideally before the week is out.'

Chapter Two

Gwen had one last scan of the hastily gathered documentation littering the opposite seat of her carriage to check she hadn't missed anything pertinent. There was no denying that it all made for interesting reading.

Very interesting reading indeed.

He might not have a title of his own—which did not make him ideal—but Major Adam Mayhew was both the brother of a viscount, a war hero and quite the charming social butterfly. Three things she could definitely leverage to get her foot back in the door of society.

Despite his lack of title, Major Mayhew appeared to be on every hostess's guest list since his return too—thanks to one intrepid feat of derring-do. On his own and against orders, he had done something both brave and reckless in the lead-up to Waterloo that had saved the lives of thirty of his fellow cavalry soldiers. Something that had been splashed all over the papers at the time and earned him a personal audience and commendation from the Regent.

However, impressive valour aside, recklessness seemed to be a common theme in his life according to his army records, which she had obtained after a significant bribe was given to a clerk at the War Office. His military conduct was, to put it mildly, a mixed bag. One that showed a man who frequently disobeyed orders and often got into trouble. Amongst the several commendations for gallantry and near constant mentions in dispatches were also many notations of concern. In his six years in uniform, which she had no doubt he had worn as rakishly well as he had that flamboyant waistcoat, were some serious reprimands for disobedience and conduct unbecoming and at least two demotions. Drunken brawls, insubordination, and a whole heap of ridiculous shenanigans while off-duty—including one night in the brig after the theft of a donkey—painted a picture of a man who leaned towards the hedonistic.

All of which matched her criteria for a husband well.

Yet interspersed with all that was some worryingly admirable stuff. Heroic stuff and, if she was reading between the lines correctly, the distinct possibility that he had been entrusted by the top brass to do some very important things during the wars with Napoleon. Things which were clearly too secret and covert to note down in any detail in his file, but which suggested that he was both well-thought-of and well-connected. Things, she reasoned, which could well work in her favour.

He had purchased a commission into the Thirteenth Light Dragoons at twenty-one and had resigned it straight after Napoleon's defeat at Waterloo.

In the year since, he did not appear to have done much beyond attend the odd ball or party. He had no career and no purpose and seemed content with that. He was, as she had witnessed herself three nights ago, a man who paid particular attention to his wardrobe and who had a penchant for purchasing colourful silk waistcoats at his tailor's in Jermyn Street. All traits that hinted at the sort of self-absorbed and superficial vanity she was looking for. He also liked to play cards, if the doorman at White's was to be believed, and played them every Wednesday with the same bunch of dubious cronies who had hauled him out of Lady Bulphan's ball three nights ago. Singing—out of tune—at the top of his lungs.

Yet despite his hedonistic love of all things wine, women, waistcoats and song, he did not appear to have any personal debts—at least not that she could find. He also apparently paid his bills on time and appeared to live within the limited means of his army pension, which wasn't the least bit hedonistic at all.

She wasn't sure what she felt about that beyond

hoping that those unsettling facts were indeed quite wrong.

His family, however, was another matter. His brother, Viscount Fobbing, had inherited a crumbling, unentailed estate on the outskirts of London which had long been sold to pay historic debts racked up by their deceased father and grandfather. The viscount now lived in a smart Mayfair townhouse that had also been mortgaged to the hilt by the father. Lord Fobbing had enjoyed some success speculating on the stock exchange and had made some real dents in paying back his inherited debts. But all that had mysteriously stopped early last year, and like his father before him, he had fallen woefully behind on the many mortgages. Enough that there was a very real risk of foreclosure as even the sale of the house would not cover the debts secured upon it.

Major Mayhew and his brother were very close, which led her to presume that his need to marry an heiress in haste was linked to the decline in his brother's fortunes. If that was the case, and she needed to investigate a little further to be sure, it made Major Mayhew a rather likeable fortune-hunter because his money-grabbing intentions were honourable.

She wasn't sure what she felt about that either.

All her plans involved basic toleration of her husband in the short term, not actually liking him in any way, shape or form at all in the long, so she sincerely hoped she would find more things about him that grated. Liking her husband was an unnecessary risk she wasn't prepared to take, especially as she had no plans to keep him for more than a few months.

However, those unfortunate likeable traits aside, he was also, an incredibly handsome fortune-hunter and that was rather handy too. Some short-term physical attraction in the bedchamber was preferable to complete repulsion, as it would ensure making a baby with him wasn't more of the onerous chore that she already knew it to be. If what lay under his well-fitting coat was as good as how well that coat fitted, then the residual youthful reckless and passionate part of her personality which refused to die was intrigued to see it.

It certainly gave him the edge over the other contenders as none of them had physically appealed anywhere near as much.

At least so far.

Should she hold out a bit longer for an actual title or was Major Mayhew the one?

On paper he seemed to be but, as her father always used to say, it was always best to look a man in the eyes to gauge his character before any contracts were signed. She sincerely hoped Major Mayhew's were sober this time as she wasn't sure how she felt about being shackled, even temporarily, to a drunkard. But then again, a man who liked his drink would also be easier to control and then justifiably get rid of, so perhaps she should see it as a positive if he received her deep in his cups again?

The carriage slowed as it turned onto Gilbert Street and inconvenient butterflies suddenly fluttered in her tummy. Gwen laid a palm on her middle to try to calm them as her compact carriage came to a sedate stop by the curb. Thankfully, there seemed to be nobody about on this quiet back street in Mayfair despite it being noon, so she darted out and knocked on the door of Major Mayhew's lodgings.

A stern-faced matron opened it, took in Gwen's attire and the smart carriage parked behind and decided she appeared respectable enough to be polite. 'Can I help you?'

'I wish to speak to Major Mayhew.'

That made the matron's polite mask melt into a scowl. 'Then I suggest you arrange to meet him somewhere that isn't here. I keep a respectable house for bachelors and *ladies* are not allowed to visit under any circumstances.' Her expression made no secret of the fact that she thought Gwen's motives immoral, which she supposed they were in the grand scheme of things. She intended to purchase a husband and the sire of her future daughter, after all, and that was a rather unconventional thing for a woman to do.

'Firstly, my visit is business and not pleasure. Secondly, that business will be concluded in less than ten minutes which will not require tea and thirdly...'

She rifled in her reticule for some money. 'I am prepared to pay you generously for the inconvenience, Mrs Wendell.' She enjoyed how the landlady's eyes widened in surprise at the use of her name. Then widened some more as she jiggled a fat purse in front of the woman's face. 'Will a shilling a minute suffice?' It was an offer only an idiot would refuse and, from what she already knew about the former bawdy house owner Mrs Wendell, she was a long way from stupid.

'Come in.'

'Thank you.'

'Who shall I tell him is calling?'

'I would prefer not to say.'

'Suit yourself.' With a disdainful sniff, Mrs Wendell showed Gwen into a neat but fussy parlour stuffed with too many mismatched chairs of substandard quality. The sort that would never be sold by Trym's.

Left alone, she decided not to sit and paced instead to try to banish some of the uncharacteristic nerves that irritated her. Especially when this was, technically, a business meeting—albeit an unusual one— and she had attended at least two business meetings a day since long before her father had passed four years ago. Yet despite how prepared she had thought she was to discuss the terms of this carefully considered transaction, she suddenly didn't feel the slightest bit prepared for it.

What if he turned her down? Then turned her into

a laughing stock by publicising her undeniably scandalous offer? What if that created yet another scandal? There would be no point going to all the expense of building her grand new shop if none of the great or the good would dare to cross its threshold. Perhaps she should simply leave and have a rethink before she bared her cards? Why the devil hadn't she thought to send someone to make some subtle, preparatory enquiries before she revealed her identity? That would have been the most sensible course of action and now she was kicking herself for her impetuousness and haste to get this—

The turn of the doorknob made her jump and she had barely composed herself when it opened and revealed a perplexed Major Mayhew. He was this morning, as he had been the evening they had met, impeccably turned out and so effortlessly handsome it took her breath away. Today's silk waistcoat was cornflower blue, another bold choice, but it did wonders for his eyes which were an almost identical shade. The navy coat showcased impressive shoulders and his buff breeches hugged his muscular thighs like a second skin, announcing better than anything possibly could that he had been on active duty in the cavalry for many years.

'Do I know you?' Clearly, she had made no impression on him whatsoever the other evening in the five minutes they had conversed, which galled when he had made enough of one on her that she was here.

Determined to keep the upper hand, she stared at him levelly with enough of a hint of reproach to let him know that he was dealing with an intelligent and not easily impressed woman. 'We met briefly at Lady Bulphan's ball, although I dare say you were too inebriated to remember.'

'We did?' He scrutinised her warily, winced, then sighed as he raked a hand through his dark hair and, somehow, the slight dishevelment suited him even more than the sublime neatness did. 'My sincerest apologies if I said anything—' Gwen cut him off with a raised palm, eager to stick to her carefully prepared script before she completely lost her nerve.

A combination of his breeches and his eyes had turned her fluttering butterflies into flapping seagulls. Something peculiar was also going on with her tongue because it felt cumbersome and three times its usual size as she choked out her purpose.

'My name is Miss Gwendolyn Trym. I am the owner of the Trym Furniture Company which currently trades out of substantial premises in Cheapside. You may have heard of us because we have furnished many a house here in Mayfair.' She paused, expecting some recognition of her well-respected brand but it was met with only a blank look.

'I am not currently in the market for any furniture, Miss Trym.'

'I am not here to sell you any, Major Mayhew.'

'Then you have me at a loss as to why you are here.'

Oddly, after all her dogged preparation, she felt much the same. It was one thing to meticulously plan for a future on your terms and another to action it. She could tell herself that this was simply a business transaction all day long, but it didn't feel like one in this precise moment. If this man did fit all her criteria to her satisfaction as he did on paper, then shortly he would be her husband and they would be intimate. He would climb into her bed, stick his tongue in her mouth, squash and twist her breasts hither and thither and then he would insert the pertinent part of his big and rather splendid body into hers and pound her with it until he collapsed.

Suddenly, with him and his pertinent part so close, that prospect dominated her thoughts and did odd things to her insides despite her complete aversion to bedsport.

'Sh-shall we sit, Major?' She wasn't sure which unsettled her the most—the wobble in her voice, the wobble in her knees or the peculiar wobbly feeling in her womb. Or perhaps it was the situation. Or just him. Whatever it was, confident, all-business Gwendolyn had disappeared. 'Only I might have a proposition for you.'

'Might?'

She wished he would stop interrupting her script. 'Let us sit while I go through all the details.'

He waited for her to pick a chair before he lowered himself into one, all the while watching her with an expression of bewilderment. She couldn't blame him. It wasn't the done thing for a lady to call upon a gentleman at his bachelor lodgings. Just this visit would be considered scandalous in the extreme if it leaked out. Or at least it would if she wasn't already ruined. But if he found the boldness of her visit surprising, she was about to blindside him with the rest of her speech. Which by hook or by crook she was determined to finish no matter how much it now made her toes curl inside her sensible half-boots.

'As I just said, since my father's passing four years ago, I am the owner of the Trym Furniture Company. He left the company with an exemplary reputation and in an excellent financial position which I have built upon. Our furniture has been likened in both quality and craftsmanship to that of the great Thomas Chippendale and, as a result, many of our designs grace the great houses around the country. We class many of the aristocracy as our clients.' She was rushing a bit. Her practised words, carefully chosen to impress, tumbled over one another in her hurry to get them all out. 'We are currently building our new shop which will open on Piccadilly next year. It is my intention to make Trym's a household name for all things interiors in the same way that Fortnum and Mason is to grocery, so, like Fortnum's, Trym's will occupy one entire huge corner of Piccadilly and will be on three floors.'

'And what has any of that got to do with me?' Major Mayhew's brows were furrowed and, worryingly, he did not look the slightest bit impressed. Instead, he appeared impatient to be shot of her. 'Would you kindly put me out of my misery and get to the point, Miss Trym. Only I do have somewhere to be imminently.' He gestured to his outfit, which was undeniably too smart for simply staying at home, but that only drew attention to his body and made her jumbled mind think about what it might look like unclothed.

Hurried and flustered, Gwen was forced to abandon the rest of her speech, which increased her nervousness tenfold. This wasn't going at all as planned and he wasn't behaving at all how she had envisaged. With only one chivvying sentence and a splendid pair of shoulders he had somehow taken control of this conversation and gained the upper hand and she had to rectify that. 'You mentioned, in your hideously drunken state, that you needed to marry an heiress and fast.' She enjoyed the way his blue eyes widened at his slip. 'And I am one, Major Mayhew.' She paused to allow that to sink in. 'If you can answer a couple of questions that I still have about your suitability to my complete satisfaction, I might be convinced to marry you at your earliest convenience.'

Adam was rarely lost for words, but he had none.

He was so shocked by the forthright Miss Trym's matter-of-fact but out-of-the-blue proposal he couldn't even muster the wherewithal to hoist his jaw back up from the floor where he feared it lolled.

By the smug look on her lovely face, she took great pleasure in his shock. 'Obviously, I have conducted a thorough investigation into your background, so my additional queries shouldn't take long.' She pulled out a notebook from her reticule, opened it to a page somewhere in the middle and then, pencil poised, asked him something intensely personal to prove it. 'How much money does your brother owe?'

'Er...' Outrage at the sheer cheek of the bloody woman warred with relief that apparently the miracle he was desperate for seemed to have occurred. 'I'm sorry...could we go back a little.' Because none of this made any sense. 'We've met?' He flapped his hand between them, staggered that he had absolutely no recollection of her as she was the sort of woman it was impossible to forget.

Her abrupt manner aside, she was much too attractive, for a start. Not pretty in the conventional sense. Her features were too strong. Her mouth too large. Her hair too dark. Almost as black as a raven's wing and, when the nation was obsessed with tight ringlets, wore it, refreshingly, as straight as a die. Striking was how he would describe her.

Alluring even. Phenomenally so.

Her eyes were an unusual shade of brown. Dark but enlivened with copper flecks which he knew would shimmer under candlelight, but which currently held his with the bold intensity of a woman who was used to being in charge. He estimated that she was his age or thereabouts and, as a result, she carried herself with a maturity that none of the heiresses he had seen in Lady Bulphan's ballroom had. And her body...

Even if he had forgotten her striking face, there was no way he would have forgotten that!

Miss Trym was a neat package of overt womanly curves in all the right places which were more than enough to make any man's mouth water. All incongruously encased in an expensive but plain pelisse and matching dress in sensible dove-grey when she seemed better suited to something more bold and seductive. He could picture her in a tight-fitting scarlet evening gown surrounded by a crowd of men fawning all over her. Or on the stage being admired by hundreds. Or even dressed as a tavern wench singing bawdy songs around a piano.

But what he absolutely could not picture her as was a woman who supposedly sold tables and chairs to the gentry.

The unsettled feeling that he had experienced ever since he had stepped into her presence intensified as suspicion surfaced. 'Who put you up to this? Ash? Ezra? Surely not Hawk?' Because one of his friends had to be playing a prank on him. Any fool knew that when an offer seemed too good to be true it usually was and when his world was imploding, this joke really wasn't funny. He must have poured out all his problems to them while drunk at Lady Bulphan's and they had hired an actress to tease him—except that did not ring true either.

His friends would never do that.

'I have no idea who those people are and can assure you that I am here in all seriousness.' She tapped her notebook with the tip of her pencil, reminding him of his crotchety theology lecturer from his Oxford days. 'Your brother's total debts are?'

'None of your damn business, madam!'

She rolled her eyes. 'They very much will be if I have to settle them, and I will be able to do that on the day of our wedding if I am apprised of them all accurately in advance. I have a rough idea, of course, and estimate fifteen thousand as that is all he has mortgaged but there are bound to be more because there are always incidentals here and there. Then there are your debts too, although I could not find any, and it is always prudent to build in a contingency. Would eighteen thousand do it?'

Adam had no clue how she knew, almost to the penny, how much it would take to keep the roof over his nieces' heads for the rest of their lives. 'Am I to suppose you just happen to have eighteen thousand lying around? Sequestered amongst your petticoats or in your reticule perhaps?'

'I do, Major Mayhew. Significantly more than eighteen thousand as a matter of fact. Although I prefer to keep my money in the bank where it will earn me interest rather than recklessly store it about my person. I can also produce the paperwork to prove it should it be inconceivable to you that someone who wears a petticoat is capable of running a successful business.' She stared at him levelly, her generous lips flattened as if he was being tiresome, her bloody pencil still poised, and for some inexplicable reason he believed her. In truth, it would be a brave soul that didn't. Whatever else she was, it was clear that the humourless, unsmiling and formidable Miss Trym was not a lady to be trifled with. 'What caused your brother to fall on hard times after so many years of solvency?'

'A tumour,' he found himself admitting while touching his abdomen, his voice catching as the bombshell was still so raw. 'In his stomach.' One so big it had felt like an apple beneath Adam's fingers when his brother had informed him that that was the cause of his persistent illness the other day.

'Oh...' Her face instantly filled with sympathy,

proving that she possessed some feelings despite all her sharpness and hard edges. 'I am so very sorry. His prognosis?'

'Is dire.' Bile churned in his gut at that because he could still barely accept it. Although ten years older, his brother Phillip had always been such a constant and reassuring presence in his life. Always so hale and hearty. Always so full of life—even when clearly he wasn't. To think of him dying—to have to powerlessly watch him die—was as inconceivable as it was unbearable. 'There is nothing more that can be done. At the moment he has more good days than bad, but that will not be the case for long.'

'I see.' She jotted something down. 'Your haste to marry now makes perfect sense. I presume, as his heir, the expectation is that you will be the one to provide for his family?'

It was probably the word "expectation" that annoyed him. That and the dismissive "your haste to marry now makes perfect sense" combined with the way she frantically scribbled in her little book as if he wasn't capable of stepping up and providing at all. 'I consider that solemn duty an honour and a privilege, Miss Trym, and not in any way a chore!'

Her gaze flicked up. 'I did not suggest that you did, I am merely factoring it into my calculations because that changes them significantly.' Her nose wrinkled as she tapped her blasted pencil against her lips.

'Suddenly, this isn't just about settling your brother's debts—it is also about maintaining two households and his family's lifestyle for as long as is necessary. In this case, either until your nieces marry or your sister-in-law remarries.'

Now she had crossed a line. 'Firstly, my only motive in marrying an heiress with all haste is to find the funds to ensure that the bank does not foreclose on my family before I am in a position to take over their financial responsibility. I am not without skills, Miss Trym, and am quite capable of earning my own living.' Although now that his original plan to study for the bar so that he could be a soldier for justice had had to be abandoned, again, he had no earthly clue how he was going to do that with the speed he needed to. He could hardly indulge himself in the final two and a half years of his three-year pupillage when he had to fund all of it and his army pension wasn't going to keep Abigail and his nieces in the manner they were accustomed to for long. 'And secondly, while my brother still lives, you will do him the courtesy of not planning his widow's next wedding as if she is a mild inconvenience to you and your blasted calculations!'

She bristled momentarily and then sighed. 'You are right. I apologise.' Her teeth worried her bottom lip and she looked contrite. 'For the record, I did not mean that to sound quite as blunt as it did. I was brought up to always consider things with a budget in mind and I spoke my thoughts aloud.' She tapped her head with her pencil. 'In a very clumsy and thoughtless way, I was trying to say that eighteen thousand would not be anywhere near enough now that I know all the details. And so I was re-evaluating my estimate based on a number of potential eventualities to ensure that I was being fair. But it was a poorly considered and unfeeling comment that definitely should have remained a private thought.'

'It very much should.' Good grief! Would wonders never cease? She possessed some self-awareness mixed in amongst all that...assertiveness. 'But thank you for the apology.'

'Thank you for accepting it.' She almost smiled. It hovered on the edges of her mouth for a moment before she gave up and jotted something else down. 'You have the reputation as a bit of a ladies' man, so I have to ask—do you have any acknowledged offspring I need to be apprised of?' And just like that she crossed another line.

'If I did, I can assure you that I would be married to their mother.'

'Any nasty diseases like the French Pox or Gonorrhoea?'

He shook his head because he was stunned at her blunt temerity, but she took that as a denial and ticked something off in her bloody little book.

'And finally, to quote the marriage vows, any just

cause or impediments that would prevent you from marrying straight away? No foreign wives left on the campaign trail, for instance?'

'Precisely what sort of despicable rogue do you think I am, Miss Trym?'

'I shall take that as a no then.' She chewed thoughtfully on the tip of her pencil, wrote something else in her book and then ripped out the page. 'Will this suffice?'

She held out the paper and, still insulted and incredulous in equal measure, Adam snatched it from her hand. Then almost choked on his own tongue at what was written on it.

'Twenty thousand upon the signing of the marriage register, all the household accounts paid while we reside under the same roof and an annual stipend of ten thousand a year and a house should the marriage break down!' Was she mad? Serious? Joking?

'Obviously all that is dependent on you signing a premarital waiver that stipulates you can never make any claims upon my business. Without that, I am afraid I cannot proceed.' She stood then and rifled in her reticule for a calling card which she held out with a superior tilt of her chin. 'I shall give you until tomorrow to think about it. I will be in my office from eight tomorrow and would appreciate your response before I leave at five.' With that ultimatum issued, she sailed to the door at such speed he had to jog to catch up with her.

He caught her arm before she could open it, her bossiness and totally businesslike approach to marriage jarring in the extreme with what he had always hoped that his would be. 'You have asked me a great many impertinent, personal questions, madam, but I have just one for you. If I am *allowed* one that is?'

Her matter-of-fact mask faltered for a minute at his sarcasm, giving him hope that perhaps she wasn't quite the no-nonsense business-above-all-else woman that she seemed. 'You may if it is just the one—as I too have somewhere else to be imminently.'

Clearly, she intended to keep herself at arm's length. As closed as the little notebook she had scribbled goodness knows what in. 'What's in this for you?'

Perhaps it was his imagination, but she coloured a bit but to her credit did not avoid his gaze. She straightened her shoulders before she shrugged one of them. 'I am scandalously soiled goods as far as my supposed betters are concerned, Major Mayhew. I was deemed *persona non grata* and judged to be unmarriageable a long time ago. But, for the sake of my business, I would like to cease being a social pariah and marrying you would allow me to re-enter society as a respectable woman. And for my own selfish reasons, I would also like to have a child before I am too old to bear one. Marrying one of the ton is the only way that I can kill those two birds with one stone with the expediency they both require, and I should very much like to achieve both goals this year.'

Chapter Three

'So let me get this straight.' Ezra was so stunned by Adam's story that he was yet to lay a card. 'You happened upon an incognito heiress while drunk at the ball, blurted out that you were on the market for one and she has subsequently offered you a twenty-thousand-pound lifeline.'

'If he's prepared to parade her around Mayfair on his arm and knock her up,' said Hawk with his customary bluntness.

'Which shouldn't be a problem if she is as attractive as you say she is.' Ash fanned his cards impatiently to remind Ezra that they were supposed to be playing whist and it was his turn. 'Talk about the luck of the devil, Adam.' His friend shook his head as if he couldn't quite believe it.

A sentiment Adam echoed.

Several hours on and he was still baffled by what had happened in his landlady's cluttered parlour. So baffled he hadn't bothered going to see the judge's verdict in the trial he had been avidly following at the Old Bailey. 'It's too much of a coincidence, isn't it? Too good to be true.'

'Maybe. Unless you still have the luck of the devil and she's legitimate.' Ash gave up hinting at the still dumbstruck Ezra and laid his cards face down on their usual table tucked away in the corner of the gaming room at White's. 'If she took it upon herself to investigate you, it stands to reason you should do the same.'

'I wouldn't know where to start.' Although he had thought about it. Thought about it a great deal while he'd stared into space in stunned bemusement all afternoon.

'The huge scandal she alluded to had to have made the gossip columns. I think they keep all the old newspapers at the circulating library in Leadenhall Street. You could start there.' Ezra's suggestion would have been a good one if time wasn't of the essence.

'I'm not sure all of us working together could get through the last decade's worth of papers before I have to give the terrifying minx my answer by five o'clock tomorrow.'

'Oh, for pity's sake!' Hawk rolled his eyes before he crooked a finger at the steward. 'How is it possible that you three survived on the battlefield for six years on your wits alone but are now completely witless here in Mayfair?' The steward rushed over and Hawk lowered his voice as he slid him a shilling. 'Have you ever heard of a Miss Gwendolyn Trym?'

'The furniture heiress?'

The steward's ready answer as he pocketed the coin earned Adam a jab in the ribs from Ash. 'At least we can confirm she's an heiress.'

'Not a great deal, I'm afraid.' The steward automatically topped up their brandy glasses in case one of his superiors was watching. 'Beyond the huge scandal she was involved in several years back, that is. She's been a bit of a ghost since—unsurprisingly.' He pulled a horrified face. 'Disappeared out of society without a trace almost as quickly as she entered it. New money,' he added with a grimace as if somehow earned money was less worthy than inherited. Which, Adam supposed, here in White's it was. 'One can only presume she was quietly sent to the country by her father. That's what usually happens to girls like that when they become an embarrassment to their family.'

'I am guessing a man was involved?' Soiled goods, she had called herself and despite all her confident bravado, her eyes had clouded as she said it. The experience had left enough scars that Miss Trym had lost her smile. And feared the judgement of others so much that she had mentioned it. Never mind that she was selling herself short by marrying a man who didn't love her when she likely deserved so much better than a husband who could be bought. A sad fact that made his skin prickle with shame.

'Of course,' said the steward, replacing the stopper in the decanter. 'She was seduced by a handsome scoundrel and ran away to Gretna with him within weeks of her debut. He likely dragged her there under false pretences as he certainly didn't marry her. I seem to recall she came back alone and in disgrace. It was all over the scandal sheets at the time.'

'Who was the scoundrel?' Because Adam very much had the urge to wipe the floor with him. What sort of man dragged a woman to Gretna Green then left her there?

'A Lord Bentley, if memory serves.'

'Why does that name ring a bell?' Ash asked before Adam could.

'He was a good-looking good-for-nothing two years above us at Oxford who owed money everywhere.' Hawk never forgot a face. 'But could charm the birds from the trees, the insincere wastrel. Conned me out of ten shillings once and never paid me back.'

Adam racked his brains until an image of the fellow appeared, his anger deepening as he did. 'Yes—I remember him. Always on the scrounge and liked to fondle the maids.' What the blazes had the supremely sensible Miss Trym seen in that libertine? 'What happened to him after the scandal?' If he wasn't dead, there was every chance he soon would be. At the very least, his oh-so-handsome features needed some urgent rearranging. Adam's fists clenched beneath the table at the prospect. 'Did he get his comeuppance?'

'Who knows?' The steward shrugged. 'He hasn't dared show his face in Mayfair since either. There are a lot of fathers in the ton and none of them would allow him anywhere near their daughters after what he did to that silly girl.' Silly was not an adjective that could be used to describe Miss Trym now. Her intelligence was usurped only by her formidableness. 'A slip of a thing she was too, by all accounts. Couldn't have been more than seventeen. Not that anyone *here* would give her any leniency for her age, of course, even though we're all idiots at seventeen. Mayfair holds everyone to a higher standard, irrespective of their lack of years.'

'*We* were all idiots at twenty-one.' Adam experienced a wave of sympathy for Miss Trym as he gestured around the table to his friends. 'Joined up to fight Napoleon expecting to be home within months and lived to rue the day.'

'You can say that again.' Ash toasted him with his glass. 'If I could turn back time, I'd try to talk us out of enlisting.'

'If we could turn back time we all would.' Ezra huffed. 'If we knew then what we know now, none of us would have gone.' Which was telling when Ezra had been the one of the four of them most determined to go.

'Hindsight is a wonderful thing.' The steward offered them all a curt bow after that philosophical comment. 'Let me know if you need anything further, gentlemen.'

Adam watched him go, lost in thought.

Hindsight is a wonderful thing but it always comes too late. He knew without a shadow of a doubt that the Miss Trym he had met earlier would never have recklessly run away with a scoundrel. She'd have weighed and measured the wastrel and found him wanting, preempted the outcome and logged it all in her little book. Then probably whacked him around the head with it.

Yet after hearing all that, certain aspects of her now made sense. Her abrupt and bossy manner and need for control which chafed against the rebel in him. Those plain and inconspicuous clothes. That lack of smile that had bothered him as much as the stoic way she tried to cover her discomfort at the mention of being judged. She was a battle-weary survivor—just like him—and irrevocably changed as a result. What had happened to her all those years ago now defined her, but she had put it behind her and thrived regardless. He respected that. Had hoped to do the same until fate had scuppered his futile dreams once again.

'It appears your Miss Trym is exactly who she

claimed to be.' Ezra picked up his cards again and fanned them. 'Both rich and ruined.'

'She was seventeen for pity's sake!' For some inexplicable reason, Adam surged to his feet, furious on her behalf at the injustice of one youthful mistake which had been so catastrophic for her. Then he was moving. At pace towards the door.

'Where are you going?' Hawk tried to call him back.

'To Cheapside!'

Now that he knew who she was and what she had been through, and that she had been to hell and back too, accepting her offer seemed like the right thing to do for both of them. She might well be saving him and his entire family with her money, but at least he now knew how he could save her in return. Marrying this particular heiress, with all their cards laid open on the table, was the quid pro quo that would ease his conscience.

Let anyone dare treat her like a scandal once she was his wife!

Her mother had retired to bed ages ago, but despite the lateness of the hour, Gwen was too unsettled to sleep. She couldn't quite shake the feeling that she might have made an enormous mistake in making Major Mayhew such a generous offer.

In the heat of the moment, she had given him terms

he could not refuse because she had not wanted him to be able to refuse them. But now, a huge part of her hoped that he would. The Major Mayhew who had seemed to perfectly match her criteria for a husband on paper did not quite match them in the flesh. For a start he was too clever. He was also too handsome and, if those two things weren't quite bad enough, he was also too noble. The sort of man who would sacrifice his own future happiness to keep a roof over his dying brother's head wasn't anywhere close to the selfish, self-absorbed wastrel she had hoped to find.

Major Mayhew clearly took his responsibilities very seriously, which did not bode well for him quietly disappearing from her life with a pocket full of money after he had sired her child. What if he stuck around? Wanted to be part of her daughter's life? Refused to gallop off towards the sunset the moment she was done with him? Then what was she supposed to do with him?

Even at her most foolish, Gwen had always trusted her gut and her gut told her that he was going to be a challenge. Ergo, before he turned up at her office tomorrow, the most prudent thing to do was to rescind her offer via an express letter tonight.

He was a mistake!

A potentially catastrophic one because she already liked him. And like might turn to more if he carried on being as good in person as he was on paper.

More flustered than she had been in her life, she immediately stopped pacing the Persian rug in her study and rushed to her desk. She had her quill in her hand and was poised over the inkwell when the night footman tapped on her door.

'You have a visitor, Miss Trym. A Major Mayhew. I've tried repeatedly to tell him to come back tomorrow but he insists he must speak to you now and refuses to leave the doorstep.'

The same flapping seagulls from earlier suddenly took flight in her tummy. 'Tell him to…' She so wanted to take the coward's way out and send him packing without an audience but with a hastily penned letter and the gift of some cash to tide him over with her best wishes, but she had a feeling he wouldn't budge. 'Show him in, please.' She would jolly well have to find the wherewithal to tell him the bad news to his face.

As the flapping gulls turned into stampeding ostriches, she decided it was best to look as nonchalant as possible, so pretended to be in the midst of writing as he was shown in, even though it was impossible to ignore his presence when her flesh positively tingled with awareness.

She laid down her quill and steepled her fingers. 'This is a surprise, Major Mayhew—although I must say, a timely one. I've been thinking about earlier and—'

'So have I. Incessantly. But I'm in. Obviously I am in.' He suddenly smiled and that did worrying things to her insides. However, if his smile made all her nerve endings fizz, what he did next made them melt. 'I would have been here sooner but I had to collect this.' He rummaged in his waistcoat pocket—this one a vivid turquoise peacock embroidered affair that shouldn't have suited anyone but did him—and pulled out a ring. 'This was my mother's. I hope it meets with your satisfaction.'

She stared at it dumbstruck. Shocked that he had thought of it and yet unbelievably touched that he had. 'You brought me a ring...' She had assumed, when her engagement was announced, she would have to buy her own and that it would be a meaningless trinket—not an heirloom. Not something that meant something to someone. Something pretty and elegant, a simply cut oval ruby the size of her little fingernail surrounded by diamonds, that she probably would have chosen for herself before she talked herself out of it for being too bold.

He shrugged awkwardly. 'It seemed the very least I could do after you proposed.' Then to her utter astonishment he reached across the table, grabbed her hand and slipped it on her finger. 'It fits perfectly. Perhaps that's an omen?' He held her hand while he stared at it, twisting it slightly so that the lamplight caught the stones and made them sparkle. Gwen barely noticed the gem, however, as his touch was playing havoc with her senses.

He let go of her finger and, for a fleeting moment, common sense returned, warning her to yank the thing off and hand it back to him. Except…

It felt right on her finger and she couldn't formulate the correct words to tell him that she had changed her mind. That he wasn't at all what she was looking for, but she hoped he found another, more suitable heiress, to marry as soon as possible. Instead, there was another voice in her head overruling that of common sense. One that was rooting for Major Mayhew, no matter how wrong she already knew him to be. And that rendered her temporarily mute while she stared at his ring confused.

'Are we going through all the rigmarole of the banns, or shall I make up some excuse to the bishop to get a special licence?' He winced. 'I didn't mean that to sound dismissive. Obviously I'm happy with either. With whatever you want…' He threw up his palms, his movements jerky and his expression delightfully awkward. 'I'm nervous, that's the problem. All fingers and thumbs and not quite sure how to behave. I've never had a betrothed before. And we are virtual strangers to boot. But I suppose we won't be for long.'

His gaze swept the length of her before he squeezed his eyes closed. 'Sorry. I didn't mean that to come out quite as impertinent as it sounded or to regard you with such...' He shook his head, more for himself than for her benefit. 'It's just you said that you were in a hurry for children and for children to occur we will need to...' He cracked one eye open, looking mortified, and heaven help her but that combined with his honesty only added to his inexplicable appeal. 'Feel free to interrupt and save us both from my panicked verbal vomit at any time, Miss Trym.' Then he smiled. Laughed actually. As if this situation was funny. 'Please don't make me beg you to put me out of my—*our*—misery.'

'I am not altogether sure what to say?' Her own nerves had paralysed her vocal cords and her heart threatened to beat out of her chest.

'Perhaps you could start with your answer to my initial question? The banns or the special licence?'

Gwen took a steadying breath and reached for the ring, intending to slip it off and decisively return it but found herself spinning it in complete indecision instead. 'My solicitor already has the basic contract drawn, so it shouldn't take him long to add in all the particulars we discussed earlier.' *What was she saying?* 'So perhaps a special licence would be preferable?'

He nodded. 'I can sort that out.' He shuffled from foot to foot, looking every which way but at her.

'Should we set the date here and now or should we wait for your solicitor?'

'Let's agree the date.' At least that would give her something to do other than sit here twiddling her new engagement ring and wondering what the hell she was doing. Gwen reached for the heavy diary on the corner of her desk and flicked through the pages. 'What about a week tomorrow? I have no meetings scheduled.'

Rather than agree straight away, he bent slightly to get a better look at the book. 'You *are* a busy woman, aren't you? There appears to be something every single day, on the hour every hour.' He flipped to the next page and the next. 'Do you ever take a day off, Miss Trym?'

'I sit at the helm of this company, Major Mayhew, and that requires almost all of my time.'

'I see you are very busy the day after too.'

Gwen glanced at the page and saw nothing over and above her ordinary workload. 'So?'

'So I am guessing that unless you cancel all those meetings we won't be bothering with a honeymoon— or even a honey-*day*?'

As his tone sounded critical she became instantly defensive despite the blush creeping up her neck at the mere mention of the word *honeymoon* with all its intimate connotations. 'I don't have the time to waste on a honeymoon and, as you rightly pointed out, we are still virtual strangers.' Never mind that a honeymoon was her idea of hell. They involved too much time in the bedchamber and she would only disappoint them both there.

'True,' he said with a half-smile. 'We should get to know each other a bit first and there is no need to rush.' He shook his head smiling. 'Doing the courting after the nuptials is a different way of doing things, isn't it?'

Courting? Surely he did not seriously think that this would develop into more than it was. 'There will be no need for any of that. This is a marriage of convenience after all.'

'Which will still require us to be shackled together for all eternity, so surely we should try and make the best of it?'

Gwen didn't want to answer that because she had no intention of being shackled to him for longer than it took her to achieve a modicum of respectability and a confirmed pregnancy but found her head nodding anyway.

He smiled with relief and that made her feel disingenuous, although why she should was a mystery when a renowned ladies' man like him would likely be unfaithful to her before the year was out. If it even took him that long once he realised how pathetically and unpalatably frigid she was. A state of affairs she accepted and no longer cared about as she excelled in so many other areas of her life. However, a bigger conundrum was why she was continuing with this farce when she had already made up her mind that he wasn't the one? Something she should definitely tell him.

Now.

Before this got more out of hand than it already had!

'Obviously, I shall rent us a house in Mayfair.' One with a very short lease so that she could return to Cheapside as soon as he had served his purpose. 'But until then, we shall live here.' None of that was what she was supposed to say.

'No we shan't.' Not at all what he was supposed to say either. 'My brother and his family need me and, as I will unfortunately become the head of his house-hold at some point, we are going to have to move into his house.' He mistook her astonishment at his lack of compliance for uncertainty. 'Do not panic—it is plenty big enough and my family are lovely. Irritating of course as families are prone to be—but friendly and fun. Despite all their current challenges.'

That wouldn't be happening. 'I had envisioned being mistress of my own household, I am afraid, but...' Thank goodness he had just given her the perfect way out. 'I do understand that you need to be with your brother at this difficult time. Therefore—'

'Thank you for being so understanding.' His mis-placed relief was palpable. 'These are extenuating circumstances but I know we'll all muddle through while Phillip...' His eyes clouded, letting her witness how much he dreaded that. How much he loved his brother. And that humbled her. Made him far too human and... complex when she wanted superficial. 'Abigail, my sister-in-law, is an affable sort and with Phillip's illness, I know she will appreciate having someone to help her run the household. And will probably appreciate a friend too.' Sadness etched into his handsome face, and it got to her. Mined beneath all her defences and touched her heart. 'I cannot imagine how hard all this is for her, but she is determined to put a brave face on it all for the sake of my brother and the girls.'

This was all becoming far too complicated and far too personal. She was supposed to be purchasing a handy sire for her own daughter, not taking on the shared responsibility of somebody else's! She wasn't an unfeeling monster after all, so how was she supposed to remain detached from him emotionally if she was sucked into his world so thoroughly? She hadn't planned on being a friend to his sister-in-law at her greatest time of need. Or a friend to anyone for that matter. Since her scandal, Gwen didn't really have friends any more—female or otherwise. Those had all dropped her like a hot potato in case their reputations were tainted too! And that had cut her to the quick, so she hadn't bothered trying to make any new ones. Why would she be stupid enough to give anyone that sort of power over her any more? Instead of friends, she had employees, business associates and clients. The only family she had to contend with was her mother, so she hadn't planned on being an aunt either. Nor her husband's rock, which she feared she would have to be while he watched his beloved brother die.

All sequestered under one roof with them as if they were all in it together.

United.

No!

That wasn't at all what she had planned. This noble, unsettlingly, uncompliant chatty man and his beautiful and thoughtful ring had to go!

'I shall have my solicitor be in touch tomorrow.' If she couldn't bring herself to tell him that the deal was off, Mr Collins jolly well could! She stood and gestured to the door. 'Thank you for coming, Major Mayhew.'

He tilted his head, more amusement dancing in his mesmerising deep blue eyes. 'Now that we are engaged, shouldn't you call me Adam?'

'I suppose so,' she replied, purposely not using that unnecessary informality as she walked to the door, forcing him to follow. Then, out of habit, she stuck out her hand. 'It has been a pleasure doing business with you.'

He stared at it for several seconds before he took it. But instead of shaking it as he was supposed to, he did something she wasn't the slightest bit prepared for.

He brought her fingers to his lips and kissed them, and heaven help her she felt it everywhere in the most improper way. 'Good night, Gwendolyn.'

'G-g-good night, Adam.'

She left him with the footman and slammed into the sanctuary of her study. His ring still on her finger. His kiss still seared on her flesh like a brand and her mind quite made up.

She was absolutely, unequivocally and categorically never going to see Major Adam Mayhew ever again.

Chapter Four

'You really do not have to go through with this.' As his best man, his brother Phillip had accompanied Adam in the carriage as they headed to Cheapside. 'When I asked you to look after my family after I am gone, I certainly never meant for you to immediately marry a complete stranger.'

'We aren't strangers. I have met her three times. Granted, I have no recollection of the first time.' Nor had he seen hide nor hair of her since the night of their engagement. Today's wedding had been arranged entirely through her solicitor via correspondence as she had apparently been too busy to meet with him again.

He had tried, of course, even going to her place of work to speak to her but had been given short shrift by her very rude secretary who lived and died by what was written in the diary. Miss Trym, he was told in no uncertain terms, sees nobody without a prior appointment. Not even, or perhaps especially, her husband-to-be!

He had decided not to read too much into that. Simply because the more he thought about it, the more it bothered him, but he had to go through with this regardless. Marrying Miss Trym for her money was the only fast way of stopping the bank from foreclosing on Phillip. 'For the record, I know plenty about my future wife. She is attractive, clever and makes marvellous furniture.'

Allegedly—although he was yet to see any.

'I just wanted you to be prepared for the mess I've made.' Adam's brother huffed, his immense guilt etched into his already pale face. 'I probably shouldn't have told you so soon about my stomach problems. Or at all, in fact, as I knew you'd overreact. You always go off half-cocked before you've properly thought things through.'

Adam knew that he did have a tendency to do that as his rash purchase of his cavalry commission was testament after his father had refused to fund his legal pupillage, but this was different. 'Because finding it all out after you've turned up your toes would have been so much simpler.' Now that they had both accepted the fact that Phillip was dying, they found it easier to talk about it in their typical, blunt and always ironic sibling fashion. 'And you didn't make a mess. You did what you had to do under the most impossible circumstances.'

His brother had used up the bulk of his available

money trying to find a cure rather than pay the mortgage on the house. Adam could not criticise him for that as he would have insisted his brother do precisely that if he had known about his illness. Phillip had never been a spendthrift like their father and had always been the single most sensible and reliable member of the family—but desperate times always called for desperate measures. Things didn't get more desperate than this. 'I just wish you'd have told me sooner so I could have helped sooner.' He had enough saved from his army days to sustain him through his legal pupillage. It wasn't enough to keep the wolves from the Mayhews' expensive Mayfair door, but it would have given Phillip the last six months to focus on healing rather than trying to do that while stressing about their feckless father's lingering shroud of debts.

'I thought I could beat it, then fix everything.' Phillip stared out of the carriage window for a moment, a little lost. 'I'm sorry.'

'If you are going to be a martyring misery guts all day, I'm going to rescind your invitation to my wedding and drop you off here. Who always fought my corner? Who helped purchase my wretched commission? Ran interference between me and our parents for all the years that I was a crushing disappointment to them? Who helped me rebel against our father's staidness by purchasing me the odd, bright waistcoat so that I could further irritate him?' He jabbed his finger in his brother's cravat. 'You did and never once did I properly thank you for it all. Now it is my turn to repay you by sending you off to heaven content in the knowledge that you do not have to worry about the financial security of your lovely wife, who could have done better than you, and your annoying daughters, who are too much like you not to be annoying. And let's face it, if nothing else, this all forces me to grow up, which I've put off for far longer than is seemly.'

In less than an hour he would be a husband. Some-time soon he would also likely be a father. Because despite their lack of honeymoon, his bride-to-be's solicitor had informed him of the location of the wedding night. She had managed to find some time in her calendar to spend this evening in a fancy inn with him within a mile of her Cheapside workshop. Where, he presumed, he would be expected to do his utmost to impregnate the stranger he was about to take vows beside.

'I cannot argue with that. I've been nagging you to stop being an insufferable twit for years.' The ghost of a smile played on his brother's expression. Phillip was blissfully unaware that Adam had spent the last six months as a barrister in training. He had considered telling him hundreds of times but hadn't.

To begin with that was because his brother and his family had wintered with Abigail's parents in Bath and Adam wanted to impart the good news face to face, secure in the knowledge that Phillip would be over the moon for him. But when the visit to Bath was extended and the months stretched, he had still been reluctant to share in his weekly letters that he had secured an apprenticeship. Or that he was thoroughly enjoying every single minute of it despite being little more than a lackey who was given all the drudge work. Almost as if he had known, deep down, that passing the bar was always a pipe dream. Perhaps because he had sensed that something wasn't right with his brother but he hadn't wanted to acknowledge that? Even when Phillip returned last month, before he confessed that he had gone to Bath to take the waters because his health was failing, Adam had bitten his tongue for some reason. Now he was glad he had because Phillip carried enough unnecessary guilt already.

As the carriage slowed, Phillip placed a hand on his arm. 'Are you certain you want to do this?'

Of course Adam bloody well wasn't! All he really knew about the woman waiting for him in the vestry with her solicitor was that she had pots of money, no time in her blasted diary for anything but work, that she didn't smile and that she had once fled to Gretna Green with a scoundrel. But his family were in the midst of a crisis, so this wasn't about him. 'I've never been more certain of anything in my life.'

'If you change your mind, cough when the vicar

asks if anyone objects and I'll pretend to have some sort of seizure so bad it forces him to call off the ceremony.'

'I'm tempted to cough just to witness that.'

As arranged with her solicitor, Adam entered the church by the back door to avoid the few guests waiting in the pews. He had invited just five people. His brother, his sister-in-law Abigail and his comrades-in-arms Hawk, Ash and Ezra. Miss Trym, on the other hand—*Gwendolyn*—had only invited her mother. He had no clue if that was because she was ashamed to be marrying the way they were, if she was ashamed to be marrying him or if she genuinely had nobody else to invite. His bride was an enigma. A completely closed book and, from the way she had been avoiding him all week, seemed content to remain so.

Mr Collins the solicitor quickly ushered him to the vestry where his bride didn't look happy to see him. She was as stony-faced as ever—but even that couldn't disguise her obvious nerves. Her arms were folded. Her spine so stiff, there was every possibility that her modiste had sewn a broom handle into the back of it. Despite the serene silk wedding gown, she looked every inch a woman who was ready to bolt at any moment.

Ironically, that chink in her armour reassured him that she possessed all the normal human emotions but merely hid them better than most. She was doubtless going to be a hard nut to crack—but for the sake of the eternity they were both doomed to suffer together he was determined to do it.

'You look lovely,' he said, hoping it would break the ice in this chilly room.

A hint of a blush stained her cheeks as she flapped an awkward hand towards Mr Collins. 'He has all the necessary papers you need to sign.'

'Right.' So much for breaking the ice. The atmosphere was now so frigid it was a wonder that his breath didn't freeze into a cloud. 'Let's get that part over with, then, shall we?'

Adam took a seat opposite the solicitor and pulled out his reading glasses, which seemed to surprise her. Or maybe it was just the fact that he could read that surprised her as she did not appear to have any high expectation of him or this union.

He had barely scanned the first page of the thick document when she spoke again. 'Everything is exactly as has been discussed, Major Mayhew, and there *are* people waiting for us in the church.'

It irritated that she wanted to hurry him. That she seemed to constantly give out orders and expect them to be followed. But he smiled regardless as he glanced at her over the rims of his spectacles. 'As a businesswoman, do you often sign your name to a contract you haven't read?'

That made her colour some more. 'I am not trying to swindle you, Major.'

'I did not think that you were but your impatience to have me sign this without reading it now makes me wonder. But fear not...' He made a point of turning the first page. 'I am a fast reader and will have finished this in no time if I am spared further interruptions.' She could put that in her pipe and smoke it! The sooner she realised he had his own mind and wasn't one for unquestioningly following orders, the quicker they would get along.

She stiffened at his polite reprimand, trying to appear nonchalant and in control, but she could not quite stop her limbs from fidgeting as she bit her tongue for the next three pages. He reached the fourth and shook his head. 'I asked for this to be removed.' He directed that to Mr Collins as he pointed to the offending clause. 'I do not require an annual stipend of ten thousand pounds and a house if the marriage breaks down.'

Mr Collins flicked a perturbed look to his employer. 'Miss Trym wanted it to remain.'

'Then I fear we are at an impasse as I shan't sign this with that clause still present.' He sat back and took off his glasses. 'I am no lawyer—' And was likely never going to be now. 'But I believe you can do that here and now by striking through it and having both parties signing against the change before a witness.'

'Well…um…' Mr Collins glanced at She-Who-Must-Be-Obeyed again, so Adam did too.

'I am uncomfortable enough taking twenty thousand pounds of your money, Gwendolyn, I can assure you that I will not take more when I am quite capable of earning my own. No matter how many people are currently waiting for us at the altar.'

'Strike it through.' Her nervous energy increased tenfold, and she began to pace as Mr Collins did so, then signed against the change with the solicitor's pen without once looking Adam's way despite having to lean over him to do it.

Satisfied, he continued reading and then, when nothing else in the contract offended, picked up the pen himself. He scratched his name. She added hers and then Mr Collins signed as the witness.

'I shall arrange for the transfer of funds today as agreed.' He stood as he folded the contract into his case. 'I wish you my hearty congratulations on your nuptials.'

As the solicitor exited, the vicar entered. 'If you are both ready, shall we begin?'

Adam could not help noticing that his bride hesitated for several seconds after he had confirmed that he was ready before she nodded her agreement too.

Chapter Five

Gwen was a ball of nerves as she changed into her travelling dress. She had no idea what she was doing or why she was doing it, because she had been convinced that she would come to her senses before she took her vows and call today off. Even at the altar, she had expected to come to her senses, as she had all those years ago at Gretna Green when she realised she had been duped, and bolted—just as she had at Gretna Green.

Except she hadn't.

Against all her better judgement and all her mother's demands that she call this travesty of a wedding off, she had stayed. Said every vow. Accepted another ring and then spent the next three hours pretending to eat the wedding breakfast with a bunch of people she didn't know. Barely saying a word while her groom was nothing but perfectly lovely to her. He made introductions, pulled out chairs for her, stood when she did, made the prettiest toast to her and she had just nodded. Barely smiling. Rarely speaking. Not much better than the waspish shrew she had been in the vestry before the wedding. Behaviour which she was thoroughly ashamed of now that part of the day was done.

It was one thing to keep some sensible emotional distance between them, another entirely to turn her new annoyingly patient and kind husband into the enemy when they needed to muddle together for the next couple of months for the sake of Trym's.

Of course, it hadn't helped that he had surprised her again by flatly refusing to accept any sort of financial settlement for when their marriage faltered. And that he had known how to amend a contract as well as how to read one. And that he clearly read enough to wear spectacles to do so, when he was supposed to be too self-absorbed and vain and stupid for such things. All while looking ludicrously handsome in them too! All things she hadn't planned for and all things not on her carefully considered list of husbandly attributes. She had intended to marry a shallow, selfish man and had plighted her troth to an honourable and decent one instead.

Heaven only knew why!

She slumped on her bed, which she supposed wasn't going to be her bed for a while. Tomorrow, she would move into number nine Hereford Street with her bothersome new husband and his thoroughly lovely family and tonight—a night she was dreading—she would lie with him in a strange bed in an inn.

At the time she had booked it, it had seemed the safest way for the pair of them to spend their wedding night. She had felt uncomfortable about the prospect of them consummating the marriage within earshot of either her mother or his brother, sister-in-law or nieces and had figured neutral territory would make things less awkward. But now she knew that nothing could possibly make tonight any less awkward and she only had herself to blame. He had been the one to suggest that they took their time. That they did their courting after their nuptials. But she had seen no point in that when she had been determined to make a baby with all haste in order to dispatch him as quickly as possible.

Soon, she supposed, she would have to bare some of her body to him so they could do that and, no matter how much she tried to convince herself that she was comfortable with it because the end justified the means, she really wasn't. Despite her capacity to feel attraction for a man, and even arousal, she had already learned the hard way that she did not enjoy intercourse. In truth, she hated it. Her first time had been awful and the second and third not much better—and she had been hopelessly in love with the man atop her. It was all well and good convincing herself that she would go to somewhere else in her mind and disassociate herself from the act while she and the major engaged in it, like she had that third time with Bentley; it was another putting it into practice. Especially tonight, when they barely knew one another.

All her own fault because she had been determined to dictate all the terms. Because the absolute last thing she wanted was to let the charming, handsome, honourable and decent man she had foolishly married know that he unsettled her. Or that, against her better judgement, she already liked him.

That was beyond frustrating as that wasn't supposed to be part of her plan at all.

But what so far was? He was proving to be every inch the mistake she had feared he was but she had ignored all common sense and her carefully considered list of criteria and married him anyway. She still had no earthly clue why.

The maid's soft rap on her door was like a death knell. 'The carriage is ready to go, Mrs Mayhew.'

Mrs Mayhew! *Good grief! What had she done!*

'I'll be right there.'

Like a woman on her way to her own execution, Gwen trudged to the hallway where their small group of guests and her new husband were waiting. She attempted to smile as she was wished well and even managed a small one as he helped her into the carriage, but it melted the second they pulled away.

As did his.

'So…' He sighed. 'I thought that went as well as could be expected.'

'Yes,' she answered, her mouth like gravel and her insides dancing a jig that was making her queasy.

'But it was still awkward. So awkward I got cramp in my toes at one point.' When she didn't respond, he sighed again and reached for her hand. 'Things can only improve from here on in. We'll find a way to make this work—I am sure of it.'

She gently tugged her hand away, because his touch wasn't helping in any way with her erratic pulse. 'And if we don't, I am sure we will find a way to deal with it like sensible adults when the time comes.' It wouldn't hurt to prepare the ground straight away that their time together wasn't permanent.

An unfathomable emotion swirled in his eyes and he was silent for a while, obviously digesting her words and hopefully unearthing their hidden meaning. 'Do you know what?' he finally asked and did not wait for her answer. 'If I knew where that useless snake Bentley was right this minute, I would go there and wipe the floor with him. And I would enjoy it.'

As that was not what she had expected him to say in a million years, she blinked at him in shock. She might have realised he was too clever not to have done some digging into her past, but she could not understand why he suddenly seemed so angry about a mistake of her making that she had consigned to it. 'Why would you do that?'

'Because he hurt you. Because he wronged you. Because he abandoned you. Because he's given you such a low opinion of men in general that you now find it inconceivable that you could be happy with one.' His blue eyes were stormy. Almost as if he meant every single word. 'And because he ruined you and then left you all alone to suffer the consequences.'

'Ah…well…' Oddly touched, she decided to be honest—to a degree. 'While I cannot deny that he wronged me, he didn't abandon me. The scandal sheets assumed that and there seemed little point in trying to correct them when I was ruined either way. But it was me who had the change of heart. Me who left him at Gretna and came back alone and thus, had no choice but to suffer the consequences of my reckless actions alone. I could be Lady Bentley now, exactly as he intended and wholly respectable already, but I chose not to be. Despite knowing that the consequences to my reputation would be dire.' But then marrying a man who she had discovered, in the worst possible way, did not love her would have been much worse. Not that this man that she had married needed to know that tragic and humiliating detail. She had kept that secret from everyone for a decade and wasn't inclined to air it now. Or ever for that matter.

It was just too humiliating. 'Therefore, I am the architect of my own ruin. From start to finish during that whole debacle, from the moment I allowed him to turn my head to the second I changed my mind and fled, I sabotaged myself and lived to rue the day.' Better the world thought her headstrong, unyielding and slightly scary than some pathetically wronged and gullible idiot to be pitied.

He appeared impressed, although goodness only knew why. 'You left him at the altar?'

It wasn't as if she had a choice when she had spied him buried to the hilt inside another woman. Or heard him and his lover laughing about "the frigid milksop with all the money" who had no clue they were about to take it all.

Frigid milksop.

A cruel insult that had haunted and taunted her ever since.

'Do you not think me capable?'

He smirked as he shook his head. 'I sincerely doubt you were less indomitable at seventeen than you are now. Why didn't you go through with it?'

'Because I realised—too late—that he wasn't a man to be trusted.'

'And I am?'

'We have a signed and sealed contract that negates the need for trust.' There she went again—being waspish towards him. Asserting her upper hand. Why did he keep bringing out the worst in her?

Because he sent her off-kilter and that terrified her.

'Ouch.' He winced. 'That put me firmly in my place. Where, I suspect, you fully intend to keep me.'

'Well… I…' When she struggled to find the right words to brush that astute truth aside, he laughed and pointed at her.

'I knew it! I saw that in your face when I made your solicitor remove that clause from our marriage contract! You think you married a man who does as he is told—but I am sorry to inform you that I've never been any good at that. I would be a colonel by now if I had always done as I was told.'

Unfortunately, after seeing how many times the army had reprimanded him for insubordination in his records, she did not doubt that for a minute. It was yet another reason why she feared she had just made the second biggest mistake of her life. Perhaps even the first because at least she hadn't married Bentley. 'I can assure you that there is no way that you can break the terms of that contract, Major Mayhew.' Clearly her sudden bout of waspishness was a disease as it just kept coming. 'A lot of money and work went into making it as watertight as possible.'

He snorted and folded his arms. 'And I can assure you that I have no plans to break it, *Mrs Mayhew.*' He clearly found her continued reluctance to use his first name amusing. 'That contract was all about *your* business and the rest of *your* money, which I have no interest in.'

Or so he kept claiming but that awaited to be seen!

'You were born to it and, by all accounts you have built it and continue to build it into something hugely successful, and all power to you. I don't blame you for legally protecting it and so had no problem sign-ing away any claim upon it.' *And there he went being decent again! The man was insufferable!*

He nudged her with a playful elbow. 'There were, however, no clauses in that watertight contract about how I am supposed to behave as a husband, and I have absolutely no intentions of living up to your low ex-pectations on that score. In fact, I fully intend to ex-ceed them. On every front. Starting now.' It wasn't until he opened the carriage door that she realised they had stopped at the inn. Except it wasn't the inn that she had booked for them. It wasn't even in the same part of London. 'Trust me—the food is nicer here.'

He reached for her hand again to help her down, but she stayed put, her heart racing at the unexpected change of plan.

She had booked two rooms at a coaching inn in the shadow of St Paul's. One for them to do their business in and one for her to retire to once that chore was con-cluded. She had no intention of spending the whole night with him. She was braced for the ten minutes or so that it would take him to find his pleasure, had even saved the adding up of this week's wages bill for something to think about while he hammered his thing inside her, but she did not want to sleep beside him! How on earth was she supposed to relax into slumber with him in her bed? Or get dressed for her workday with any privacy?

As if he read her mind he leaned forward and whispered, 'I have no expectations for tonight beyond us sharing a quiet supper and getting to know one another a little bit in private. You have your own room if you want it.'

Her exhale of relief was too loud and he heard it. 'You did not marry a thoughtless brute either, Gwendolyn. We shall take this at your pace. There is no need to hurry. We have a lifetime for you to have your wicked way with me.' He winked before he practically dragged her out onto the pavement with him. 'And vice versa.' A statement that, unexpectedly, tantalised.

He wrapped her hand around his arm and led them inside while she scrambled to mentally regroup. He spent the next ten minutes charming the innkeeper and his wife, who then rushed around making a huge fuss of them. They were shown to their rooms like royalty where, true to his word, there were two separate bedchambers which sat either side of a cosy private dining room. One contained a small bed and the other a huge four-poster affair that, to add to her nerves, had been turned down on both sides. Both their overnight bags were deposited in there by a maid who seemed determined to unpack them before her unpredictable new husband waved her away.

At the same time as the maid left, several steaming dishes were brought in and placed on the table until there was no space left upon it. Then, just as quickly, all the efficient inn staff departed leaving them all alone.

He once again pulled out a chair for her, all easy charm and with a calmness that she envied. Why the devil was she all at sixes and sevens and he was unperturbed? 'I noticed you didn't eat earlier and as I have no idea yet what you like, I ordered us a selection. I hope you don't mind.'

'Why would I mind?' She offered him her best approximation of a smile, determined to be nicer seeing he was being annoyingly lovely, and he grinned in return.

'Because you did not order it yourself, of course and that doubtless galls.' Then he pulled a mock serious face which was spoiled by the way his eyes danced. 'You strike me as a woman who doesn't appreciate surprises of any kind.'

'Or being teased,' she replied with equal mock solemnity. 'Clearly I should have had that stipulated in the contract too.'

'Thank the lord!' He raised both palms heavenward. 'She does have a sense of humour!'

'If I have been—'

He cut her off with a wag of his finger. 'There is no need to apologise. This is a peculiar situation and neither of us quite know how to behave. Some walking on eggshells was always inevitable while we figured things out. As was today's loss of appetite. I always find it impossible to eat when my stomach is tied in knots.'

'Were you nervous too?' Because at no point had he appeared so but it somehow made her feel better that she wasn't the only one.

'An absolute wreck—but now that the wedding is over, I am starving.' He reached for one of the tureens and lifted the lid. 'What about you?'

To her surprise her stomach rumbled the second the aroma of the rich beef stew entered her nostrils. 'Famished.'

'Then let us tuck in.'

While he ladled a generous portion of stew to their plates, Gwen added potatoes and some delicious smelling buttery greens mixed with bacon. 'So,' he said with a casualness she wished she could emulate. 'Something you should absolutely know about me is that I can eat like a horse. My mother always used to say that I had been born with hollow legs because she could never work out where I put it all.' He replaced the lid on the tureen and glanced at his plate with undisguised joy. 'I have a particular penchant for meals like this because, in my humble opinion, everything tastes better when enrobed in an unctuous sauce. Are you a sauce fan? Or do you like your meat dry?' He pulled another face. 'Because I fear we will never get on if you do.'

'I've never really considered it but...' She pondered it, glad that it was an innocuous question rather than something intensely personal. 'Sauce, I suppose.'

'Good,' he said nodding his approval. 'We had this cook once when I was a boy—only for a short while blessedly—but she insisted on cooking everything for so long it resembled shoe leather. It scarred me for life.' As they ate, he went on to tell her several amusing horror stories about meals he had eaten during her tenure that he wished he hadn't. Fried liver that was so overcooked it bounced off the nursery wall. Lamb chops so tough each mouthful took an eternity to chew. Brisket—which he hadn't thought possible to overcook—so dry he'd had to wash it down with a pint of milk. All interspersed with little asides about his fearsome Scottish nanny who believed in waste not want not and who would make him and his elder brother sit at the table until every scrap of food on their plate was gone. Even till midnight, if necessary, before serving the awful food to them again as a punishment at breakfast if they did not comply. Which, unsurprisingly, by his own admission he hadn't even managed to do as a child either.

'Did you have a nanny?' He liked to gesture with his fork if his animated hands were occupied.

'No. Of course not.' She would have laughed but they came from very different worlds and so understood he probably had little concept of how the other half lived. Aristocrats tended not to mix with the hoi polloi outside of business. 'I come from trade, remember.' Something she was intensely proud of and which she would not apologise for. Especially after the snooty ton had shown their true colours and turned their back on her after she had her heart broken. 'My father was still building his business when I was a girl and my mother ran the office for him, so I grew up in the workshop.'

'No doubt learning at his knee.' He dropped his napkin on the table and she realised, with a start, that he had done such a good job of distracting her with his natural charm and his stories that the meal was concluded. 'Did you enjoy it?'

'I *loved* it,' she said without any hesitation.

His dark head tilted, his expression curious. 'Why?'

As nobody had ever asked her that question before she had to think about it for a moment. 'Because I was always part of something, I suppose. Always learning something. Always in the thick of things. I cannot imagine how I would have coped cooped up in the house with a nanny or governess.'

He sat back in his chair to sip his wine. 'From one

who was cooped up with a strict nanny and then an even stricter tutor while longing to be anywhere else, your childhood sounds idyllic. I wish I had had your opportunities.'

She scoffed at that. 'I sincerely doubt that an aristocratic male, like yourself, was spoiled for opportunities. I doubt you ever wanted for anything.'

'Materially, no. But a truly happy and fulfilled life is about so much more than that, isn't it? You got to be part of something. Being the spare, I have always been expected to have no dreams or ambitions of my own and simply wait in the wings dutifully in case I was needed. Take it from me, that is a frustrating place to be.'

Gwen hadn't considered that. 'I take it your father wasn't sympathetic to your ambitions?'

'My father expected unquestioning compliance and, as I have already stated, that is not my forte. I had too many ideas of my own so I was sent away to school at eleven so that he didn't have to listen to them. He expected me to enter the clergy, so every summer when I came home, at his instigation I had to assist the Bishop of Hertford as, I suppose, a sort of apprentice.'

'I cannot imagine you as a vicar.' For a start, she could not envisage him in the dour black outfits when he seemed to have been born to wear bold waistcoats—although today's was cream. Perhaps, seeing as he was irritatingly thoughtful and intuitive, he had decided to tone it down so as not to outshine the bride?

'I could not imagine me as a vicar either.' He chuckled at the thought. 'I would not have been a particularly good one. I lack the seriousness and piety required and was always too argumentative. Thankfully, the Bishop of Hertford agreed and released me from Purgatory when I turned sixteen. Summers became fun then. Until I turned eighteen and my father refused my request to study law and I had to go to Oxford instead to read dreary theology.'

'Why on earth would he do that when being a lawyer is an excellent and lucrative profession?'

'Because he saw going into law as going into trade and thus bringing shame onto our family.' He laughed at her outraged expression. 'It is all right, you can say it, because I always thought he was a pompous idiot too. Dear Papa had archaic ideas about the importance of lineage and tradition. He liked the gravitas of his title and pontificating in the House of Lords too much to ever consider peeking over the parapet to investigate the modern world. He was positively scathing about new money but had archaic and unrealistic expectations about old money too. He assumed, because of his sacred blue blood, it would just keep coming with no effort required from him whatsoever. That is why, when his peers began investing in canals or shipping or stocks and shares to keep their ancient coffers replenished, he continued to spend with impunity.'

'And left your family in debt.'

'Up to our blue-blooded ears.' He toasted the heavens with his glass. 'Debts I might have been able to help clear sooner if the old goat had allowed me to practice law as I had begged him to. But instead, and in keeping with the archaic tradition of the spare, he insisted I study theology because he did not want me to remain the "reckless, rudderless and dandified disgrace" that he considered me to be. An edict that was a complete waste of my time and his borrowed money as the only thing I excelled in during those three years was being wholly disinterested in the subject.'

'Did you join the army to avoid a career in the church?' She was, perhaps unwisely, genuinely interested in what made him tick.

'Yes—and to vex him. I was angry and frustrated and always so ripe for rebellion. With the hubris of youth, I firmly believed that my time in the military would be a jolly and short affair. That I'd return within months to a victory parade and countless accolades that proved my father entirely wrong about me and I would blithely pursue the rest of my life on my terms with or without his blessing.' His expression became momentarily serious before he drained his glass. 'The war, it turned out, had other plans and was not for the faint-hearted. I certainly lived to rue the decision to join it, that is for sure.'

'You must be glad it is over.'

'Delighted. I might have been a good soldier but soldiering did not suit me.'

'Too many rules?'

'Too many rules and too many stupid, reckless, catastrophic decisions made by people who should never have had the power to make them. But they kept making them because they never had to witness all those good men die so senselessly...' His expression changed and he seemed lost until he caught himself. 'Good grief—that got very maudlin very quickly, didn't it? My apologies.' He shook himself and pasted on a smile. 'Let's change the subject onto something more cheerful. Tell me all about this new planned shop of yours.'

Gwen wanted to hear more about that last cryptic statement because the brief but unmistakably despairing look in his eyes at those *catastrophes* and *senseless* deaths bothered her. However, as common sense told her that the more real and less superficial things she learned about him, the more prone she was to liking him more than she already did, she gave him a rough outline.

'My architect and my builder have assured me that we can open our doors in August next year, so I have just fifteen months to get everything done. A complete redesign and renovation to oversee. Three floors to dress and fill with stock, which all needs to be designed and made. New products to create and to source. Staff to hire. Then there is the advertising in the lead-up. It is a lot to do.'

'I'll say.' She could tell, by his widened eyes, he thought she was being over-ambitious. 'When do you intend to fit having that child you want into your busy calendar? After the shop opens, I presume?'

'Oh, no! I shall be too busy after. That is why I have given myself fifteen months to get everything done. With any luck, the babe will be six months old by the time Trym's opens and will not need the constant attention of a newborn.'

He did a quick calculation on his fingers and his eyes widened some more. 'Assuming that we make a child *straight away.*'

'Well...yes.' Suddenly, the big four-poster behind them loomed larger. 'That *is* the plan. That was always the plan. Hence the need for our hasty marriage and...' She flapped a nervous hand towards the four-poster.

'Right.' He shuffled in his seat awkwardly. 'In that plan of yours, can I clarify if straight away is *straight away*? As in tonight? Or do you define straight away as more *soonish* than immediately so that we can get to know one another a bit more first?'

Oh, good heavens, they were talking about intimacies! A hot blush crept up her neck because they had gone from food to furniture to fornication over the course of just one meal! And with no warning too. Gwen wasn't the least bit prepared for this conversation.

Not the least bit prepared despite her meticulous plan!

'Soonish.' She could feel ugly blotches of red bloom on her face as she panicked. 'Obviously soonish.'

She blamed him for the panic.

Why did he have to be so decent and understanding about it all when, from her experience, a man's urges usually overruled all other considerations? That useless lord she had eloped with hadn't cared one jot whether she had been ready for intimacy. Bentley had hoisted up her skirts at the first inn they had stopped at on the Great North Road, thrust his member inside her repeatedly until he had found his pleasure and hadn't been the least bit bothered about her feelings at all before, during or after the ordeal.

This man opposite her, however, was visibly relieved by her answer. 'Soonish is eminently sensible. After all, there is no need to rush into *it*.'

But there was.

She had a shop to open in fifteen months. One that she had invested huge amounts of money in already. And they were here. Because this was their wedding night. And there was a big bed already turned down and waiting.

And she had braced herself for the ordeal, for goodness' sake!

She had a plan to get through it. Had paid far more than she had planned to make it happen! Wanted this—him—all over and done with so she could get on with her life! And she was nervous enough already that she feared if she put *it* off any longer, then she would never find the courage to do *it* with him at all.

To avoid days, and possibly weeks, of wasted time spent on tenterhooks, she had to be decisive and take back the control that he had, so far, seemed determined to wrest from her. She had to regain the upper hand.

'Although my preference would still be tonight, Adam, if you don't mind.' The sooner he planted his seed in her womb, the quicker she could escape this wholly inconvenient marriage. 'Unless that causes a problem for you?'

Chapter Six

'No…no problem at all.'

Bloody hell!

After their pleasant meal and after working so hard to relax and reassure his obviously tense bride that he had no expectations beyond them getting to know one another better over the coming weeks, Adam hadn't expected to have to perform tonight.

'Good.' She was blushing so much she couldn't look at him, so hopefully she hadn't noticed that he was now as red as a beetroot too. 'The time frame I am up against is tight, after all.' Clearly, her blasted diary was more set in stone than the Ten Commandments! 'Shall I go and get ready?'

'If that is what you want.' Had his smile ever felt so fake? So tight? So blasted painful? 'I shall join you shortly.'

'I would prefer to call you in.' She attempted a smile. 'As you quite rightly guessed, I am not a fan of surprises.'

Neither was he after this one! 'Then summon me once you are ready.' Like a performing monkey. 'There is no rush. No rush at all.' He stood politely as she rose and hurried out of the tiny dining room, then collapsed back in the chair to rest his head in his hands as soon as the bedchamber door closed.

Bloody hell!

He had never had to make love to a woman on demand before. Nor had he ever been tasked with impregnating one for that matter. He had always been careful on that score and done everything possible to prevent a pregnancy because that was the gentlemanly thing to do when one was dallying with a lover. Up until now, all his relationships with women had been undertaken with no expectations attached. They had been affairs where both parties understood that it was just for fun. That was the way of things on the campaign trail. Such things were transient but marvellous while they lasted and there was no deep emotional connection to muddy the waters.

This wasn't that.

The woman currently stripping her clothes off in the bedchamber behind him was his wife. A woman he had taken vows to both love and worship her body with his. Except they did not yet have any emotional connection. He hoped they would because he was a romantic at heart, but such a feeling could not be immediately conjured. He had fancied himself in love twice when he was younger, and both times those relationships had been frustratingly chaste. Nothing had happened physically beyond some passionate kisses and some fevered touching, mostly over clothes.

So this wasn't that either.

This was uniquely different.

He had, openly and honestly, married a woman for her money. They both knew it and so feigning feelings for her that he did not have would not be necessary—but could he feign desire? Because therein lay the rub! Especially as presently all he felt was panic and there was absolutely nothing going on in his nethers.

'I'm ready.'

The same cold sweat that he always experienced before a battle instantly suffused his skin and the urge to run as far away as possible was overwhelming. But he sucked in a calming breath and stood. His greatest talents had always been thinking on his feet and rising to a challenge and he sincerely hoped neither would let him down tonight.

Hopefully something would come up and it would stay up!

Even though she had said that she was ready, Adam still knocked on the bedchamber door while silently praying that she had donned such an outrageously seductive garment to sprawl across the bed in that his uncompliant appendage would suddenly spring to attention.

'Come in.' His bride's tone was as full of anxious foreboding as he was.

He turned the door handle, pushed it open and almost sighed his disappointment aloud. There was no frothy, lacy, translucent seductive garment. At least not that he could discern. Nor was his bride sprawled on the bed in an alluring come-hither pose to tempt him. Instead, she was lying flat on her back on the mattress with the blankets pulled up to her neck and covering every inch of her bar her head and the tightly wound, no-nonsense plait her thick hair was woven in. Worse, she had snuffed out all the candles and drawn the thick curtains so that the moment he closed the door behind him they were plunged into pitch-black darkness.

Trying to remember exactly where the unfamiliar bed was, he took several steps forward. 'Ouch!' The corner of an ottoman caught him in the shin and as he bent to rub the spot he hit his head hard on one of the sturdy oak columns that formed the bedposts. 'Bloody—' He bit back the rest of that expletive while he rubbed his forehead.

'Is everything all right?' That question came disjointed from somewhere close by.

'I cannot see a thing!' Good grief but his head hurt.

'Perhaps following the sound of my voice would help.' Was she serious? 'I am over here.'

Apparently, she was serious and was determined to

make no concessions as far as any illumination was concerned, so he did his best.

'Right here.' She patted the mattress this time as if he were some pet she wanted to encourage to jump upon it. 'You sound very close to me now.' Which he was because he crowned himself again as his head hit the equally solid oak frame of the canopy.

He yelped, groped for the mattress and sat on it while he rubbed his poor cranium again. Already a bump was forming beneath his fingers. 'Would it kill you to light a candle, Gwendolyn, before I bloody kill myself?'

'Why on earth do you need a candle now that you have found the bed?'

It was the snippy, authoritative tone that did it. 'Because if you expect me to simply climb in, climb on and then climax to order, you have another bloody thing coming, woman!'

He shouted sightless into the void as his temper snapped and his inner rebel surfaced with a vengeance. 'I have never engaged in perfunctory, soulless sex in my life and I am not about to start now! If we are having a bloody wedding night, we are having a *wedding night*! Or I shall take my poor, bruised carcass into the other room right this minute and lock my bloody door!'

That outright insubordination, of course, was met with stony silence by She-Who-Must-Be-Obeyed. But frankly, Adam was prepared to let it hang. She might well have bought herself an eternally grateful groom, but he was not a servant to command.

When she said nothing, he huffed. 'Then good night, Gwendolyn, sleep tight.'

He was halfway to the door when she finally spoke. 'I thought darkness would make this aspect of our marriage less awkward.' She sounded miserable and lost, and God help him but that plucked at his heart-strings. 'And instead, I have only made the awkward-ness worse. I am sorry.'

'So am I.' He reached for the door and flung it open to let the light from the dining room flood in but, from her ragged inhale, she clearly thought he was off to his own bed. 'I shouldn't have lost my temper.' He turned to find her sitting up. Her arms hugging her raised knees and her lovely face the very picture of wretchedness and that made him feel wretched too. This wasn't how things were supposed to be and yet, clearly, she believed that they were. No doubt thanks to that ne'er-do-well she had eloped with. 'I did warn you that I have never been good at following orders.'

'I did not mean to sound like I was issuing orders. It is just that I have never been any good at…this sort of thing.' Her eyes lifted to his so uncertain and unsure of herself that it made him wonder what other scars that bloody libertine Bentley had left on her. What he could see of her high-necked and thick nightgown above the bunched covers was more like a suit of armour than a weapon of seduction. 'Something that I had hoped you would not notice in the dark.'

'You do me a great disservice, Gwendolyn, as I can assure you that I would have.' He gestured to her defensive posture on the bed. 'Martyrdom is not much of an aphrodisiac.' He flicked his hand downwards towards his groin apologetically and winced, because honestly, this was one of the most cringing conversations he had ever had in his life. Although they clearly had to have it. There would be no moving forward in this marriage otherwise. 'It certainly doesn't inspire me, if you know what I mean.'

He hadn't meant to hurt her feelings but could tell that he had. 'I will try harder to inspire you if you tell me what you need.'

What *he* needed—not what she needed. Or they needed. Her low aspirations for the physical side of their marriage broke his heart. It was obvious she assumed that she would get no enjoyment from it at all. *What, exactly, had Bentley done to her to make her feel that way?*

Sensing a lightening of mood was urgently required he sniffed the air. 'And now I smell burning martyr—and that, my dear stoic Gwendolyn, is not the perfect scent for romance either.'

'I prefer Gwen, actually.' The corners of her mouth

lifted a tad. 'And I do not expect romance. If I did, I would have stipulated that on our contract.'

'Well—Gwen—' He liked the way her shortened name sounded. It was much less stuffy. Much more… intimate. 'You jolly well should expect it. Especially on your wedding night.'

She brushed that away. 'This isn't my first time.'

'What does that have to do with it?'

She was so uncomfortable she could barely look at him. 'Merely that there is no need for you to go to any trouble on my behalf when there will be no pain involved.'

'Trouble is an interesting choice of word.' Filled with sympathy for her, Adam sat on the mattress. 'Frankly, it upsets me that you assume that I would find making love to you an inconvenience.'

She still could not look at him and shrugged. 'You already said that I do not inspire you.'

'I absolutely did not so do not misquote me. I said that climbing aboard a veritable corpse did not inspire me—because that is what you resembled when I entered the room. It was quite apparent you intended to lie back and think of England while I did my business, and I am simply not made that way.' He reached for her hand and laced his fingers in her freshly stiffened ones. 'I'm a romantic at heart, Gwen, and very much would like to make my wife swoon.'

'I am afraid that I am not the swooning type.' He

could tell by the despondent acceptance in her eyes that she believed that and it annoyed him.

'Oh, for goodness' sake! It is beyond me why such a forthright and formidable woman is prepared for anything less than being left sublimely all-a-quiver in the bedchamber—yet you seem prepared to settle for whatever scraps I deign to send your way. Thanks to the feckless and self-centred Bentley, no doubt, who obviously did such an awful job of things that he's put you off bedsport for life!' He folded his arms and shook his head. 'I'm sorry, sweetheart, but I did not sign up for that. If I am going to be inspired, I have to insist on swooning, sighing and some good old-fashioned passion. It's all-a-quiver or nothing, I am afraid. Tonight, if you still want a wedding night, and all subsequent nights thereafter. Or mornings. Or afternoons.' He wiggled his brows suggestively to coax another smile out of her and it worked.

A little at least.

'I suppose we could try it your way.'

'She says in a tone that suggests she does not hold out much hope. But to me, that sounds like a challenge, Gwen, and the only thing that I excel at more than disobeying orders is rising to a challenge.' And erasing some of the damage that bastard Bentley had done to her in the bedchamber—and out of it—was now his sworn mission. Unfortunate and unforgivable misconceptions about the joining of two bodies which would be his absolute pleasure, as her new husband and lover, to correct with all haste.

Chapter Seven

He grinned wickedly before his eyes swept the length of Gwen's hunched body and slowly—achingly slowly—wandered back up again, and his smug smile turned into one of pure sin.

'You might want to brace yourself.' An apt turn of phrase when she had been braced for precisely this since he had arrived at the church earlier. 'Because I am going to kiss you now, my lovely wife…' He used his finger to tilt her chin so that her lips were level with his while he stared deep into her eyes. 'And I must warn you that I am exceptionally good at it.'

It was on the tip of her tongue to warn him that she was as frigid as a Shetland breeze but didn't. He would realise that soon enough as she had never been a particularly good actress.

Instead, she braced herself as Adam took his time closing the distance between them, allowing his warm breath to caress her mouth before his lips brushed over hers. It was more a whisper than a kiss, over before it had begun, but somehow more potent as a result.

He traced her lips with the pad of his index finger. Again, barely touching but awakening every nerve ending her mouth possessed as he smiled a lazy but totally disarming smile. 'Now it's your turn to kiss me back.'

Gwen swallowed to steel herself but did as he asked. He remained entirely passive as she replicated his kiss, his eyes closing as if he was savouring it. As she went to pull away, he captured her lips again, smiling against them. This kiss was still gentle but lingered longer and, miraculously, kindled something inside her that made her want to kiss him back. The first embers of desire made her pulse quicken and, unconsciously because he seemed content to keep his mouth soft, she surprised herself to be the one to deepen it.

In response, he wound his arm around her waist and tugged her closer, his fingers idly caressing the base of her spine as their upper bodies began to touch. Because they suddenly weren't close enough, she looped her arm around his shoulders just in time for his teeth to nibble on her bottom lip. Almost as if he were asking permission for her to part them.

Unable to do anything else, Gwen found herself melting against him as his tongue toyed languidly with hers. She hadn't expected to enjoy such an intrusion—

but she did. Neither did she expect her body to want his hands to explore it. And vice versa. But she did.

As if he read her mind, he whispered, 'Touch me—you know you want to.'

'Where?' She wanted to inspire him, after all, as there would be no baby otherwise.

'Wherever you want.' He pulled her to sit on his lap and kissed her with such gentle fervency, that peculiar things happened in places unexpected. 'I know you are a woman who likes to be in control...' His lips moved to her neck and found a spot just beneath her ear that really enjoyed being nuzzled. 'And I am a man quite happy to let you be—so long as we both lose our minds by the end. On that stipulation, I refuse to negotiate.'

Convinced that she was incapable of losing her mind under any circumstances and unsure of what to do, Gwen went with her gut and ran her palms over his shoulders and down his back. He was every bit as solid as she had anticipated. She tested his upper arms next, and because he clearly knew that the heavy fabric of his coat was in the way he shrugged it off before his mouth returned to hers.

His biceps flexed beneath the soft linen of his shirt as she trailed her fingertips over them. She could feel the heat of his skin below the fabric and could not help wondering what it felt like. Rather than burrow her hands under his shirt as she wanted to, they went to his neck instead. It was smooth and silky just under his hairline but roughened where the hint of stubble graced his throat. His jaw was rougher still and she liked that. It intrigued her that he had been so clean-shaven while standing at the altar only a few hours ago and now he wasn't. Because he was so dark, she supposed, which in turn made her contemplate if his chest would be as smooth as a classical statue's or if that too would be dusted with hair.

It proved impossible to tell, thanks to his waistcoat and he chuckled again as if he had read her mind. 'You remove anything you want to, Gwen. I really will not mind at all.'

His teeth found her ear before she started on his waistcoat buttons, and that, bizarrely, made her nipples pucker. Enough to distract her from the task so that her fingers fumbled and it seemed to take forever. His, however, seemed to find no difficulty undoing his cravat with only one hand before he tossed it to one side. Finally, as the last button was undone, she slid it over his shoulders with an impatience that surprised her—but that impatience apparently inspired her new husband. He wrapped his arms tightly around her and moaned into her mouth as he kissed her, and, to her great surprise, she rather liked that too.

She lost all sense of time and reason as he kissed her thoroughly and she kissed him back. Minutes or perhaps hours passed as they explored one another's mouths. All she knew was that he was in no hurry to stop and, exactly as he had promised, he excelled at kissing. In fact, he somehow made it an art form. So sublime that it awakened something in her which had thus far been dormant. Needs she hadn't realised she had rushed to the fore and blotted out all rational thought.

She was breathless by the time he tore his lips from hers, but so was he so that made her less self-conscious for the state she was in as his gaze raked hers. His eyes unmistakably darkened with passion.

'Can I touch you too?'

'If you want.' Gwen barely recognised her own voice, it was so ragged with passion.

'But what do *you* want?' He angled his body back, making her miss the solid heat of it. One dark brow quirked as he regarded her with amusement. 'I have to *inspire* you too, remember.'

'I would like to be touched,' she replied, assuming that was what he wanted to hear but recognising that she meant it. Her body wanted his hands on it.

'Where?' he asked not moving an inch.

'Wherever you want. Wasn't that the instruction you gave to me?' She hoped she said that with enough bravado that he would not realise she was suddenly very keen for him to touch her breasts. Her nipples had hardened to such points thanks to his ministrations they were actually beginning to ache.

'Hmmmm…' He eyed her thoughtfully. 'Where to start?' To her complete chagrin, he began with the end of her hair where she had absolutely no feeling whatsoever.

Yet, somehow, as he unknotted the ribbon that secured her bed plait, he managed to unravel it in a way that made her feel as though he were undressing her—and against everything that she had thought possible, she liked that too.

He loosened the strands, then combed his fingers through the tresses with splayed hands before sitting back again to admire his handiwork. 'I knew your hair would be beautiful.' He wound his index finger in a long tendril beside her face and then used it to gently tug her mouth back to his, whispering words that managed to excite her further. 'I cannot wait to see it fanned out on my pillow.'

As he kissed her, his other hand circled her waist again, then smoothed up her back. On its return journey it found the swell of her hip and rested there for an eternity as he thoroughly plundered her mouth once more. But his kiss wasn't the only thing that was distracting her. Beneath her bottom, things were definitely stirring in his lap. Unthinking, she undulated against the bulge in his breeches to check that it was indeed what she suspected and he groaned against her cheek. 'All your fault,' he murmured and she could hear his smile. 'Too much inspiration.' Words that somehow made her feel…seductive. Miraculously so. He wanted her and, to her astonishment, that made her want him. 'Would you like me to take off my shirt?'

'Yes.'

He shifted position and yanked it over his head, then remained still so that she could take it all in. He was not the least bit embarrassed as he watched her eyes devour him with a cocky half-smile. His skin was golden in the soft light coming from the dining room. It sat taut over the male muscles in his shoulders and arms. Crisp, dark hair dusted his pectorals then narrowed and arrowed over his flat abdomen. She went to touch, then hesitated.

'It's all right. I want you to touch me, Gwen.' He reached for her hand and placed it flat over his heart, which beat faster at the prolonged contact when he kissed her again. 'I *really* want you to touch me.'

He made no secret that he enjoyed her tentative exploration of his unclothed upper half; sighing as she traced each rib and shuddering as her palms grazed his nipples. All the while the bulge beneath her bottom was getting harder and more insistent.

'Can I relieve you of this uninspiring nightgown?' Because of course the wretch would want her naked too. Except he was still fully clothed below the waist and she wore nothing whatsoever beneath her nightgown to preserve her modesty.

'Can I close the door first?'

'Of course.'

She jumped off his lap to do just that, but no sooner had she plunged them back into the safety of total darkness than she was bathed in the half moonlight because he had also jumped up to open the curtains.

'I still need to see you.' He sauntered towards her, the weak silver light from the outside casting him in intriguing shadows that emphasised and embellished his masculinity. He looked dangerous—but in a good way. Like he knew exactly what to do and exactly what he wanted and what he wanted was her. 'And you still need to see me. How else will we know how thoroughly we have already seduced one another unless I can witness it in your eyes?'

Was she thoroughly seduced?

Maybe.

Probably. Miraculously, she was at least halfway there. Perhaps three-quarters. Without the intriguing throb of his body beneath her bottom, there was no denying that unfamiliar and uncharacteristic heat and longing had pooled between her legs.

He reached her at the door and then gently pushed her against it while he kissed her again so that she could feel the entire length of his shackled erection against her pelvis. She hadn't expected to enjoy that at all, had expected to hate such impassioned closeness, yet did. He ran the backs of his knuckles up her sides from her hips level to her breasts and, heaven help her, Gwen arched her back until her needy bosoms jutted against the wall of his chest in blatant invitation. He slipped one hand between them so that he could circle her nipple over the fabric with his thumb. 'Can I remove your nightgown?'

'Yes.' She almost added please, she was so aroused, but bit her lip instead as cooler air swirled around first her ankles and then her legs as he tugged the only barrier between them higher.

No doubt to torture her he bunched the fabric taut so that it teased her breasts on its journey upward, making sure he put enough distance between them as he did so in order to watch the reveal. Then all at once, her nightgown was gone and she was stood in all her glory and he was looking at her.

Staring at her in what appeared to be awe.

Positively devouring her with his eyes.

'Oh... Gwen...' Was she imagining the catch in his voice? The reverence in his tone. The appreciation in his eyes. 'You are utter, utter...perfection. More than I deserve.' He watched her some more, his gaze raking her slower this time and lingering on her breasts and then the triangle of dark curls between her legs, before he retraced the path of his eyes with his hands. He ran his fingers down her bare arms from her shoulders to her elbow as his gaze returned to her breasts again. His irises darkened in a way that left her in no doubt that he liked them. 'I am a very lucky man.'

To her surprise, he did not lunge for them. Instead, he kissed her softly again, cupping her breasts and carefully testing their weight. He circled her nipples with his thumbs and smiled as they puckered to points before lowering his head to kiss one.

Gwen made an odd, mewling sound that she had never made before when his tongue swirled around that sensitised tip and, while still doing it, he smiled up at her like the cat who had the cream. 'Do you like that?'

Gracious but he was irritating! 'You know I do.'

'I do.' He chuckled, irritating her all the more. 'How about this?' Without warning, he dipped a finger between her legs, where, to her horror, she was wet with need, and caressed the tight bud of nerves that were causing her the most aggravation.

She moaned.

She couldn't help it because his impertinent and wholly unexpected touch felt sublime.

'Do you like that too, Gwen?'

'Yes.' It stunned her to admit it, but she did. A lot. Enough that her hips had begun to undulate of their own accord to increase the pleasure and he responded in kind, doing something so inexplicably wonderful with only his fingertip, that she practically shouted. 'Good grief, yes!'

'Then you will adore this.' As he teased her nipple with his teeth and tongue, he increased the pressure slightly between her legs, drawing a tight, lazy circle over her slick, intimate flesh. All at once, time, space—the fact that she was standing completely naked in front of a man she had only met three times—all became irrelevant. Because all that mattered were the glorious new sensations he was building in her body that she could not get enough of. Each stroke brought her closer and closer to the edge—of what she did not know—but she was suddenly desperate to experience it all.

Was this what she had read about? The mystical sexual gratification that other women had apparently experienced with no trouble at all but that had, so far, eluded her?

Gwen hadn't thought she was capable of ever feeling it. Had certainly not believed it possible that she could ever enjoy this sort of intrusion from a man after her awful experiences with Bentley. But here she was. Mindless. Boneless. Witless. Completely at the mercy of her own needs. Of his touch. Headed to destination unknown and in a great hurry to get there! All she knew with any certainty was that he seemed to know how to get her there, so all she could do was trust that he did and cling on for the ride until she arrived.

Then it hit her like a battering ram.

A myriad of sensations exploded all at once that began in her pulsing core and then ricocheted throughout her body in clenching waves that made her giddy.

She may, or may not, have called out his name but she certainly collapsed against him. Her breath sawing in and out and all the strength in her gone when the sublime but alien new sensations finally began to fade.

'Bloody hell, woman. Where did that come from so fast? Are you trying to kill me?' He choked that against her ear, struggling to breathe exactly like she was, as if he were undone too. Simply because she was. 'God, I want you so much...' His fingers went to his falls where the bulge pressed against her pelvis was now so hard and insistent it had to be painful. 'I don't think I've ever wanted a woman more.'

His voice was so fervent, his urge to get out of his breeches so frantic, she believed him. And that did odd things to her body too. Made her feel attractive and bold and empowered in a way she never had before. And she wanted him too, despite the potent aftermath of her first ever release. Her body needed something more. Needed to be filled by this vexingly uncompliant man, who was kissing her now as if his very life depended on it.

Suddenly, his erection sprung free and hit her skin. Hot and rigid and, miraculously, she was ready for it—in whatever way he wanted to give it to her. She reached between them to touch it, tracing him with her fingers before wrapping her hand around him to let him know. But he tore his mouth away and spread his palms above her head on the door-frame, his breathing so laboured he could barely speak as he stared deep into her soul.

'Obviously we don't have to do this… Like I said, we'll take this at your pace so there really is no hurry tonight to…' That she had wantonly allowed him all those liberties, had come apart in his arms and he still asked her permission to take the final step both humbled and touched her. Those thoughtful, noble words mined under all her defences and pierced the wall she had built around her heart.

He kept doing that and, ordinarily that would terrify her, but tonight he had turned her into a needy temptress who existed only in the realm of pleasure, so she did not care. Her heart was a problem for another time. Right now, all she wanted was him inside her. Because she wasn't frigid! And, oh, how joyous and freeing a revelation that was!

'Yes, we do.' She rammed her hands against his chest and pushed him towards the mattress. 'Because I've never wanted a man like I want you now.'

And that was the truth. In this moment, she needed him inside her more than she needed air. 'It would kill me if you stopped, Adam.' With another push he toppled backwards onto the bed and dragged her with him.

'Thank goodness.' A sinful grin split his face, and with her help, he shimmied out of his boots and breeches. Then he kissed her. Long, deep and decadent. He rolled on top of her and she welcomed him with shamelessly parted legs. But being the uncompliant sort, as her hips arched towards his, he then went on to insist on kissing almost every bit of her as he teased that sensitive bud again with just his talented fingertip until she could stand it no more.

She was almost there again when he slid into her. She could feel the tension in his back as he waited for her to get used to the shape and size of him. See the veins on his throat and arms bulge and realise that he was on the cusp too but holding back for her.

Waiting for her.

Decent to the absolute last, the wretch, and that pierced her heart too. She undulated beneath him, squeezing the walls of her body tight around him and felt triumphant as his eyes closed and he groaned as if in agony. 'Don't hold back, Adam.'

'I couldn't if I tried.' He plunged deep and a guttural moan of pleasure escaped her mouth.

'More!' *Surely this wasn't her?* She did not recognise the carnal creature she had become. But she loved her. 'Don't stop!'

He didn't reply, he just increased his pace, long smooth thrusts that left her writhing beneath him and clawing at his buttocks.

Almost there.

Almost there...

He grabbed her thighs and tilted them back and

wider, sending him deeper still and it felt divine. So outrageously magnificent that she practically shouted her delight. 'We both have to lose our minds, Mrs Mayhew,' he ground out against her ear as his pelvis gave that sensitive bud of nerves exactly what she now knew it needed. 'That really is non-negotiable.' Of course, the wretch already knew that any reply was unnecessary because all rational thought had left her and a split second later she came apart again.

Only this time he followed.

Calling out her name as his body pulsed inside hers and hers pulsed around his and nothing else but them seemed to matter.

Gwen melted into the mattress as she floated back to earth, enjoying his heavy weight atop her and marvelling at what had just occurred. Who knew it could be like that? That her body could react like that? That it would all feel so uninhibited and alive and...joyous?

'Bloody hell.' His deep, low chuckle warmed her neck before he lifted himself up onto his elbows to stare down at her. An expression of delighted bewilderment on his face too as he rolled off her onto his back. 'That was not at all how I predicted tonight would go. I expected to pick my way along the rutted road of panicked small talk and excruciating embarrassment at a snail's pace, not taking a sudden right turn into mind-blowing ecstasy. You?'

She wasn't yet compos mentis enough to think about

an appropriate answer, so said exactly what popped into her mind. 'I expected to add up the wages bill while you did your business—because all the employees in my business need to be paid tomorrow and I saved it to do while you did me.'

He stared at her incredulously for several seconds and then threw his head back and laughed.

And laughed some more until she joined him. Until tears ran down both of their faces. And that felt absolutely, uninhibitedly joyous too.

Chapter Eight

The bang woke him up.

He squinted into the first rays of dawn leaking through the open curtains and saw a sheet-swaddled Gwen clutching her overnight bag and frozen like a wincing statue.

'I'm sorry.' She bent to pick up the shoe she had dropped. 'I was trying not to wake you.'

'And trying to sneak out too, I'll wager.' He sat up, rubbing the sleep from his eyes. 'Where are you off to at the crack of dawn? Or have you had second thoughts about the wedding and are just running away from me?' He said it as a joke but couldn't deny he wasn't a wee bit concerned that might be the truth. She hadn't looked the most eager bride yesterday, after all, despite the passion they had shared last night and she did have form when it came to fleeing from her groom.

'I have to be at the office early.' She was backing out of the room. 'I have urgent things to do. And I have meetings.' Because of course she did. He had never seen a diary as full as hers was. 'Go back to sleep.' With that, she escaped to the tiny dining room, shutting the door behind her.

Adam flopped back onto his pillow frowning.

Surely this wasn't the way the morning after the splendiferous night before should go? His new wife sneaking out like a thief and him left all alone on his first day of married life, twiddling his thumbs because he had nothing better to do. Were they not even going to eat breakfast together, for pity's sake?

He huffed and sat up again, throwing his legs over the side of the bed and shaking his head. Did the headstrong minx intentionally want to create more awkwardness between them after they had broken down some barriers? Or was she running away because she felt awkward about last night and didn't know how to cope with that?

He padded to the door and flung it open. 'Before you dash off to tot up the payroll, why don't I—' She squeaked at the interruption, clutching the chemise she had been about to pull on against her front as she spun around. But not before she had inadvertently given him the most splendid view of her delicious bare bottom. He grinned at her missish behaviour. He couldn't help it because she hadn't been quite so shy last night. Hadn't been shy at all, for that matter, once she had warmed up. In fact, she had been most demanding and those sort of orders hadn't bothered him in the slightest. 'Why don't I call down for breakfast to be brought up?'

He watched her gaze slowly rake him while she simultaneously blinked and blushed. 'You're naked!'

He glanced down and grinned some more. 'Am I?' To fluster her further, he folded his arms and leaned against the door-frame as he positively smouldered at her. 'Somebody libidinous, brazen and shamelessly wanton must have stripped me of all my clothes last night.'

That comment had the most marvellous effect on her because her lush mouth hung slack and she gaped for several moments while she positively combusted with embarrassment. 'I…um…' Her gaze flicked to his manhood, which was libidinously and brazenly waking up too, and her lovely eyes widened. 'Cover yourself! What if somebody sees you!'

Adam glanced over his shoulder and around the room, then back. 'But only you are here, and you've already seen me like this. And I have already seen what you are currently hiding away beneath your underthings.' He flicked a finger towards her body and wiggled his brows. 'I'll confess, here and now, that I thoroughly enjoyed all that I saw—and explored. And kissed, *Mrs Mayhew*. Or are we somehow now supposed to pretend that we weren't gloriously intimate and uninhibited with each other last night?'

'I… Well… Er…' She chewed on her bottom lip, trying and failing not to notice his growing cock.

'If you come back to bed, Gwen, I would be delighted to give you a repeat performance. In fact, it will doubtless be a better performance all around as I've always been a morning person.' He gestured to the evidence now standing to attention between his legs and enjoyed the way her breath caught as her gaze followed. Then followed some more as he sauntered towards her. 'I guarantee what I have in mind will be more fun than totting up your payroll—which I will be more than happy to help you with once we're done.'

He was less than a foot away when she spun her bare backside towards him again, bent to grab her bag and bolted for the spare room that neither of them had slept in to hide most of herself behind the door. 'I am not used to…' Her voice trailed off and she shrugged. 'This.' She flapped her hand between them. 'I am sorry.'

Perhaps he shouldn't have teased her? Or invited her back to bed straight away in quite the overt manner that he had. '*This* will all get easier, Gwen.'

As he had tortured her enough, Adam smiled and, for her sake, grabbed a chair to hide his modesty behind. 'Why don't you get yourself dressed while I order us some breakfast and then we can talk some more?'

'I can't. I genuinely do have to be at the office early.'

Her expression was now less embarrassed but more pained before the door swung closed and her voice came through it muffled. 'I am already late. I told my coachman to be outside waiting for me at six, it is already a quarter past and my first meeting is at seven.'

That really was a no, he supposed. But still—this was their first morning together and he wasn't keen to let her go. 'You do remember that my brother and sister-in-law are expecting us to move into Hereford Street today?'

'My belongings should arrive there sometime this morning. I arranged for my maid to accompany them and unpack for me to avoid inconveniencing anyone and I shall follow later.'

'Then why don't I come and collect you in Cheapside later this afternoon? Offer some moral support on your inaugural visit to your new home?'

'I won't be at the workshop, I'm afraid.' Her voice was now both muffled and breathless, as if she were dressing in some great hurry. 'I have meetings with suppliers this afternoon and they are dotted everywhere throughout the city.' Was she fobbing him off? 'My coachman will drop me at your brother's at six in plenty of time to settle in before dinner. Abigail informed me yesterday that the family always eat at seven.' Clearly she had organised everything without any need for him to be a part of the proceedings at all.

'Right.' He snapped that because he was a little

peeved that she hadn't thought to mention any of this to him yesterday and was only mentioning it now because he had caught her escape red-handed. 'Then I suppose I shall see you then.' Unless he did the gentlemanly thing and escorted her to her office? But he wouldn't offer because she would only find some excuse to prevent him. Despite their first foray into passion last night, his independent bride seemed determined to keep him at arm's length this morning.

Something he was determined she would not! They were married now, for pity's sake, for better or for worse, and he, at least, intended to begin their first day together as he intended to continue! He might not deserve a happy marriage in the grand scheme of things but he was damned if he wasn't going to give it his best shot!

Adam darted back into the bedchamber and grabbed the fresh set of clothes from his overnight bag, fully intending to be at the door before she attempted to leave through it. But he had barely buttoned up his breeches when she emerged from the other bedchamber fully dressed. That she had flung rather than put her skew-whiff garments on and that her hair was still a bird's nest did not seem to matter. Such was her haste to be rid of him, she strode towards the exit without so much as a backwards glance. 'Have a good day, Adam!'

'But I *want* to escort you to Cheapside. I want to spend some more time with you.'

'That is very sweet of you. Really it is but I have no time whatsoever to spare today. I have to sort out the wages in the carriage so I shall be lousy company.' She was backing out the door, so he grabbed it. 'Besides, I haven't even told my workers yet that I am married.' There was panic in her eyes now. 'Trym's currently has so much on that I cannot abandon them to it. And this is all so new, Adam. I will need some time and space to get used to it all.'

'Gwen, wait—' The door slammed shut behind her before he could argue, and he heard her feet scurry down the stairs before he could even shrug on his shirt. 'I suppose a wifely goodbye kiss is out of the question?' She was too far gone to hear his sarcasm.

He tossed the shirt back on the bed in anger and stalked to the window in time to watch her disappear inside her carriage, annoyed that was apparently that. A day of nothingness now loomed ahead of him while she still seemed to have all the purpose in the world.

What the bloody hell was he supposed to do with himself now?

Abigail had put Gwen into an adjoining bedchamber with Adam, separated by only a shared dressing room rather than the thick castle battlements she would have preferred. Yet there was no denying that there was plenty of room for all the clothes and belongings she had to bring with her to avoid her mother getting suspicious that this wasn't the real sort of marriage Gwen had claimed it would be.

Her bedchamber was a lovely, airy, spacious room facing the garden, with an enormous comfortable-looking bed. The linens were crisp, the décor pleasant. There was absolutely nothing she could complain about—beyond the fact that she apparently had no lock on the connecting door. And she had no clue how to ask for one without causing either offence, embarrassment or both to her hostess.

'I hope everything is to your liking.' Her new sister-in-law smiled expectantly. 'We want, more than anything, for you to feel at home here.'

'It is all lovely.' Gwen pasted a smile on her face. 'Thank you.'

'I am glad you arrived so much earlier than planned. It gives us some time to get to know one another without the boys around.' Abigail brushed a friendly hand down Gwen's arm. 'That is if you would like to take some tea with me downstairs. If you would rather settle in, I will understand—'

'Tea would be lovely. Thank you.' She would actually prefer to sit on her own and lament all of her reckless recent choices, but Gwen's mistakes weren't Abigail's fault. This woman had welcomed Gwen into her house with open arms and all while dealing with the declining health of her husband. However, there was every chance her sister-in-law really did need a friend, as Adam had claimed, and that made Gwen feel just as ill at ease as having her vexatious new husband right next door. Not only did she not want to make any lasting attachments to his family, but being a friend to anyone was a skill she was grossly out of practice at.

She had last had friends at seventeen, before she had been rendered too ruinous to the reputation to remain one, but not a single friend since. She liked to blame her scandal for that but knew that wasn't entirely the case. She had, one way or another, actively avoided making any. Perhaps that was self-preservation because she did not want to suffer the pain of losing any again? Or give people the power to retract their friendship? Or give them any power over her at all for that matter. But how could she avoid it in this case? Apart from actual avoidance of course. Hopefully, all the time Gwen spent at Trym's combined with all the time Abigail would have to spend with her husband, and the short duration of her marriage to Adam would ensure that any friendship between them would not go too deep. 'Just give me a few minutes to freshen up.'

Abigail left Gwen to her new bedchamber with a smile. No sooner did the door close than Gwen flung open the connecting door to their shared dressing room to stare at all her husband's things dotted alongside her own. His comb and cologne on the opposite side of the dressing table to her brushes and perfume. His razor and shaving cup next to her favourite French milled soap on the washstand. Matching wardrobes sat on opposite sides of the single, ornate enamelled and unscreened bathtub which, if he wandered in while she happened to be using it, left her totally exposed to his gaze. And vice versa, she supposed. She could watch him bathe. A prospect that made the sensitive bud of freshly shameless nerves between her legs tingle in anticipation yet that did not make her feel any more comfortable in her new surroundings.

Not that she suspected anything would make her feel particularly comfortable around him after they had been intimate. Adam had unsettled her enough before their wedding night. Now she was a veritable bag of…she would say nerves but that wasn't at all the right term for the upheaval currently happening inside her. How was it possible to want to run far away from a man as fast as her legs could carry her while still wanting to jump back into his arms and part them as soon as was humanly possible?

She was trying to blame the inaugural arrival of lust into her life, although wasn't wholly convinced that was the cause. She had been in a heightened state of *ripeness* ever since he had first touched her last night and that had distracted her all day. It seemed unfathomable that this time yesterday, she had been convinced that she couldn't envisage a way to ever enjoy the marital act and yet today, after he had worked his magic on her much too willing body, she was counting the minutes till he made her witless again. Gwen had almost cancelled all her meetings this morning on the back of him asking her to come back to bed—and that was not her at all! Her work ethic was, or so she had thought up until today, unshakeable. Her business was more important to her than anything else. And yet just the twinkle in his eye and the splendid sight of him in the altogether was apparently all it took to make her forget that she even had a business to run!

And why did he make her second-guess herself quite so much too? She had always planned to go back to work the morning after their nuptials. Thanks to her efforts and stewardship, the order books were stuffed. Trym's had never been so busy and somebody had to oversee all that. Add the new shop into the mix and it was a wonder she had any hours left in the day to spare. But after witnessing first the flirtation and then the disappointment in his hypnotic blue eyes this morning when she had made her excuses to leave, here she was. In his brother's house in Mayfair. Three hours earlier than she said she would be and all because she felt guilty at abandoning him.

Yet where was he? Nowhere to be seen, that's where! Probably out buying himself some new waistcoats to celebrate his twenty thousand!

A thought that only exacerbated her guilt because, somehow and with absolutely no tangible evidence to warrant it, she knew he wouldn't do that.

Drat him!

All proof, if proof was indeed needed, that it was essential to keep some distance between her and the mistake that was her new husband until the need for him to be in her life was null and void. She certainly did not want to have to wake up with him so close by every single morning! Honestly—the sooner she got pregnant the better as then she wouldn't have to lie with him every single night either.

Adam Mayhew was just too dangerous!

Even so, the door to his bedchamber beckoned and, against her will, her feet wandered to it. She nudged it open, irritated by how curious she was to know him properly. His room was a mirror to hers in everything bar the more masculine linens and upholstery. The only sign that he had been in it was the enormous pile of books on his nightstand. They were all too weighty a tome to be novels and that only served to pique her heightened interest in him further. What the devil was the devil reading? She was about to investigate when her maid's approaching voice made Gwen jump guiltily before she darted back into the dressing room.

'Here's your hot water, Miss Trym... I mean *Mrs Mayhew*. I am sorry—but I am still getting used to that.' As Lizzie had been her maid for the last three years, Gwen understood. She hadn't told anyone of her plans to marry until the marriage was practically a fait accompli. Which meant that her maid had even less time to get used to the change in her circumstances than she had.

'I am still getting used to it too.' Although she sincerely doubted she ever would. Being a Trym was so much of who she was. Being a Mayhew made her feel like his and she wasn't sure what she felt about that. Especially when she should be appalled and wasn't.

'This is such a grand house, I hardly know how to behave in it. Or at least I would if everyone wasn't so nice. Her ladyship is lovely and so is her husband, and your husband is…' Lizzie sighed like a woman smitten as she poured some water into the washbowl. 'Really lovely too.'

'You've met him then?' At least the wretch had been here to greet one of today's new additions to the Mayhew household.

'Yes, miss. He was here all morning. Supervising the unpacking. He even did some of it himself, so we had a lovely chat.'

'About what?'

'Why, you of course! He is so taken with you he wants to know all about you. Your favourite colour, your favourite books. What you like to do when you are not working. How you like your tea. You name it, he wanted to know about it.'

Gwen wasn't sure what she felt about that either. 'And you told him, I suppose?'

'Of course I did. They are hardly state secrets after all. But—' Lizzie lowered her tone, as she was prone to when imparting gossip to her mistress. 'I was vague on the subject of your recent suitors as I wasn't sure what you had already told him.'

'He asked about my recent suitors?' Should she interpret that as prying or jealousy? Be outraged or flattered?

'Subtly—but too subtly, if you know what I mean. But obviously I told him that it wasn't my place to gossip about my mistress.' Her maid smiled conspiratorially. 'I think it's good for a man to keep on his toes. We don't want to make him complacent and it's none of his business that there haven't been any.'

'Precisely how vague were you?' Because if Lizzie had lied then Gwen needed to know.

'I merely stated that you are a pretty woman and that it was hardly your fault that you turned heads.'

Gwen liked that. As pathetic as it was, she did not want Adam to know that not a single suitor had approached her in years. 'And how did he respond?'

'He agreed. Then commented on how lucky he was to have married such a beauty.'

'He called me a beauty?' As much as she wished she were above such shallow, romantic nonsense, she really liked that.

'He did. And looked mighty proud as he did so.' Her maid opened the door to the wardrobe which Gwen presumed was hers. 'I assume you would like to change out of your work clothes, Miss T… I mean Mrs Mayhew?' Except it wasn't all hers at all as half of the rail was taken up with his clothing, which was again another stark reminder that Adam had invaded her world.

'Did my dandy of a husband run out of space in his own closet?'

'No miss. This one holds all the garments that need to hang and this—' The maid marched over to the other one and flung it open. 'Has shelves for all the folded.' Neat piles of Gwen's chemises, stays and petticoats sat intimately next to his shirts and what she presumed were his drawers. His stockings next to hers. Even their boots and shoes stood side by side. All much too close for comfort.

Lizzie grabbed a fresh chemise for Gwen and returned to the first wardrobe where the stark contrast in their hanging apparel was depressing, to say the least. Where Adam possessed an array of different coloured coats and waistcoats in so many shades they would put the rainbow to shame, she apparently owned nothing that wasn't a boring dove-grey or beige. Which she supposed made her a pigeon to his peacock. And while she had expressly sought a man who was all show and no substance and so should be delighted he complied with one of her specifications at least, the visual comparison laid out before her still rankled. Exactly when had she become as dull as dishwater?

'What about this pretty grey gown?' asked Lizzie, reaching for one and unaware that she had just thrown insult onto injury. 'Or this taupe? I know you have always had a soft spot for taupe.'

Did she? 'Either or. It makes no difference.' Which was sadly true. Apart from the slight difference in the muted tone, both gowns were interchangeable in their plainness. There wasn't even any lace or embroidery to draw the eye away from the uninspiring blandness. Not even a ribbon to liven up the dull cuts of the bodices.

Good heavens, when had she become so insipid and conservative? Surely she owned some other colours? Some more exciting styles? 'Out of interest, how much of my wardrobe did you leave in Cheapside?'

'Only the forgotten trunks in the attic, Mrs Mayhew. As they've done nothing but gather dust all the years I have worked for you, I assumed you were happy for them to stay where they were. Was there something I should have brought from them that you needed?'

Only if it wasn't grey or beige. 'Not that I can think of, Lizzie. Thank you.'

As her maid laced her into her pigeon's feathers, Gwen's eyes kept wandering to Adam's much more exciting wardrobe with an envy that bothered her. Until she reassured herself that the juxtaposition of their wardrobes was simply a welcome reminder that she and he were not compatible in the long term and so she was likely worrying for nothing. Post-wedding jitters that were brought on by the sudden change in her circumstances and nothing more.

Everyone knew that pigeons and peacocks were never meant to mix!

The sooner the flamboyant wretch made her respectable and impregnated her, the sooner she could remove all the irritating traces of him from her life. A thought that buoyed her as she sailed downstairs to take tea with Abigail, determined to bring up the subject of the urgent need for a lock for some much needed privacy from her vexing new husband right from the outset.

Chapter Nine

'I could teach you all I know about the stock market.' Phillip idly tossed another chunk of bread in the direction of the assorted waterfowl waiting for it on the lapping banks of the Serpentine. 'It's an easy way to make an income once you get the hang of it, so long as you keep an ear to the ground and close eye on the markets.'

'And an easy way to lose your shirt if you don't know what you are doing.' Adam wasn't keen. He had never had his brother's head for numbers, and he wasn't comfortable with effectively gambling with what was left of Gwen's money. It did not matter that that money was part of the agreed marriage settlement or that it was currently sitting in his bank account. In his mind it was still hers. She had made it and she had earned it and so he would not dip into it unless there was a catastrophic emergency. One day, he was adamant in his own mind that he would pay her back every single farthing of that twenty thousand pounds.

It was, undoubtedly, a manly pride thing but he would not be able to look himself in the mirror, or her in the eye, if he remained indebted to her forever. 'I would prefer to earn my living with less risk. Especially as I've had to earn it up to now entirely with risk.'

'Do you have any ideas?'

'Actually...' He tried to appear enthused as he tossed a handful of crumbs at the saddest, weakest looking bird paddling on the periphery, pleased when the poor thing managed to gobble up at least half of them before he was chased off by the aggressive swans who would prefer to see it starve. 'Remember that job offer I received when I first arrived back? From the office of the Secretary of State for War and the colonies. Working for Lord Bathurst and the government. Doing hugely strategic things for the good of the nation from the safety of a nice Whitehall desk?'

'The one you said that you would rather die than do? The one you turned down flat?' Trust his brother to remember that.

'Well... I am rather hoping that the offer still stands, and they will still want to take me on.' Even though he would genuinely rather stick pins in his eyes than sit behind a desk all day and rather flay his skin from his bones than do anything for the blasted military again—but beggars could not be choosers.

'Why on earth would you want that?' Phillip gaped at him like he'd gone mad.

'Because I was an excellent soldier, and upon reflection, it would be nice to use all those skills again.' About as nice as being whacked repeatedly in the ballocks. 'I just wasn't thinking straight when they first offered it to me.'

'Really?' Phillip knew him too well not to be sceptical. 'This from the man who was so done with the military that he couldn't wait to get out of that dratted uniform. Didn't you burn it the same day you resigned your commission?'

Adam winced because his brother had him there too. 'Only because it had seen so much action it wasn't in any fit state to keep.'

'You said, and I quote, that you told them to shove that thankless job because the King and the country and the bloody army had had their pound of flesh out of you.'

'And they had—as a soldier. But this is entirely different as this role requires none of my flesh because it is a well-paid civilian one.'

'I remember how you came back, Adam. How demoralised, damaged and defeated you were by war. How tired of it all you were. How angry you were at the top brass for their constant ineptness. At all the senseless, avoidable slaughter and suffering that you often blamed them for. I saw how relieved you were to be done with it all. It has taken this whole year for you to become…well…more like you again. You cannot go back to that. It will kill you.'

His brother was right but he could not admit that because he now had no choice. 'I will be behind a desk and not in the firing line.'

'As one of the inept top brass you constantly lamented!'

'As a civilian with so much experience of the impact of their ineptness that I can make a real difference to change things for all the future soldiers subject to their will!' Adam hoped that if he repeated that lie often enough to himself he would start to believe it. Perhaps he could save some soldiers' lives? Perhaps that was what the universe had saved him for? 'I can prevent some of that senseless avoidable slaughter when the next war inevitably happens.'

'Maybe some of it,' said Phillip shaking his head as if his little brother had taken leave of all his senses. 'But not all of it. And that will eat away at you. Just like the death of every single one of your fallen comrades still eats away at you!'

'It won't,' he said rising and beckoning his nieces ready to head home, keen not to discuss it any more because he knew that his brother had his measure. He dragged around the guilt of all those deaths like a chain. A year on and each and every one of those deaths he had had no choice but to witness still plagued him. Still made him question why he had survived and why they hadn't. Haunting his dreams and invading his waking thoughts if he didn't keep himself busy. 'The beauty of being behind a desk in Whitehall is that it will all be strategic, from a great distance, and none of this will be personal.' Despite knowing that he would take every single reported death or defeat personally because he had seen too much slaughter and suffering on the battlefield to do otherwise. More links would be added to that chain. More guilt he would have to carry around. And perhaps he should. Perhaps that was the price the universe expected him to pay for keeping him safe? 'Besides, we aren't currently at war so it will all be hypothetical strategizing to begin with, and long may that continue. Perhaps peace will actually prevail with some sensible, battle-weary soldiers running things in Whitehall?' A forlorn hope that he had no faith in when Britain seemed determined to expand its already enormous empire to every continent and used its soldiers to do that.

'What does your wife think of you putting your head back into the lion's mouth?' At Adam's perplexed look his brother rolled his eyes. 'A good husband is supposed to discuss important things with his wife before he makes any decision.'

He could not help scoffing at that. 'Gwen and I are not at the discussing stage. Nor do I ever expect us to be as she seems determined to do her own thing regardless of my thoughts on the matter.' He was still peeved about this morning and the way he had been fobbed off so thoroughly before she had abandoned him for her more important blasted work.

'That will change as she settles into marriage. You are both new to it and still have to learn the dark art of the marital compromise.'

Adam huffed, unconvinced. 'Trust me, she is not the compromising sort.'

'She compromised on the marriage contract by letting you remove that clause you loathed.'

'Only because it saved some of her precious money in the long run.' Adam was being churlish and knew it. His pride was dented, and his feelings were hurt. He and Gwen were only twenty-four hours into their marriage, and he was already floundering. He had no purpose once more and he was never good nowadays when left alone with his thoughts, no say in her affairs, clearly wasn't welcome anywhere near the professional side of her life and wasn't convinced that she wanted any more from him than the fruit of his loins and the benefit of his family's name—yet at least. And he had given up the law for this marriage while she had given up nothing that mattered to her and that grated too. All things, bar the law part, which he had, in frustration, shared with his brother at length this morning when he had turned up to Hereford Street alone.

'She also agreed to move in with us when you said that she had had her heart set on being mistress of her own household.' An unwelcome reminder that jarred with his aggrieved emotions. 'So she plainly can compromise. Talk to her about this.'

'She barely knows me, so I am not sure Gwen is the right one to give me counsel on anything yet. Besides, she has requested I give her time and space, and I cannot give her that if I immediately bombard her with my woes.'

'She is your *wife*, Adam. The more you open up to her, the more she will open up to you. Women like to feel respected and needed and what better way of earning her trust than showing her that you trust her? Seek her opinion before you condemn yourself to a career that you and I both know you will hate.' His brother spread his palms. 'Please, Adam—'

He didn't want to have this conversation with Gwen, any more than he wanted it with Phillip. 'This is entirely my decision to make and my mind is made up. Besides, I've already requested an appointment to test the waters with one of Bathurst's underlings.' With nothing better to do on his first morning as a husband, he had paid a call on an old army comrade who now worked in Whitehall before he had gone to Hereford Street. Where, he had been reassured that the Secretary of State for War was still desperate for good men of exactly his calibre to help shape the future of the army. 'With any luck, I will be one of them too by the end of this week. The pay is apparently excellent.' Which meant, if he achieved nothing else of any value in his life, at least he would be able to take over the responsibility for the household now that his wife had paid for the roof over their heads.

The tea with Abigail was proving to be every bit as awkward as Gwen had feared it would be. Neither of them quite knew what to say and so had resorted to a full fifteen minutes of banal small talk and there seemed to be no end in sight until either of their husbands or the girls returned.

'Your cook has a wonderfully light touch with pastry,' she said reaching for her third jam tart in quick succession to make the protracted silences less protracted.

'She does indeed,' said Abigail reaching for another with a slightly panicked smile. 'And cakes and biscuits. Savoury dishes too. She has a light but magical touch with everything. She is an excellent cook. One that we are very lucky to still have as several shameless guests have tried to pilfer her from under my nose with the promise of higher wages. But Mrs Phipps is fortunately very loyal to us and has always politely turned down all offers. We are blessed with wonderful staff here in Mayhew House. All so fiercely loyal and so...'

Abigail paused for a moment and stared down at the tart in her hand. 'Oh, for goodness' sake... What is the matter with me? Here I am babbling about biscuits and staff when what I really wanted to do this afternoon was…' Tears pooled in her new sister-in-law's eyes as she reached across the dainty tea table to squeeze Gwen's hand. 'What I really wanted to do was thank you! From the bottom of my heart. Your timely generosity has made a dreadful situation so much more bearable for us.'

Gwen waved that away. Deciding there and then that, when faced with tears and fraught emotions, the small talk and protracted silences were actually a blessing. 'It was nothing.'

'It was not nothing.' Abigail had too tight a hold on her hand to be able to tug it from her grasp. 'It was everything, Gwen. To me at least. I do not know how I can even begin to properly thank you for the huge sacrifices you and Adam have made on my family's behalf.'

'I can assure you that I haven't made any sacrifices.'

'Of course you have!' Abigail finally let go of her hand but clearly had no intentions of dropping the subject. 'You married a man you barely know, for a start.'

'Because it suited me to.' For the sake of Trym's. To make a child. 'I knew nothing about you or your situation when I decided to marry Adam.'

'Perhaps…but you left the comforts of your home and postponed the chance to set up your own household to live in the chaos of mine, just so that your husband can be with mine when he needs him most. That is a sacrifice that cannot be overestimated.'

Gwen's toes began to curl inside her slippers at all the undeserved gratitude. 'Moving to this lovely house in Mayfair was hardly a chore and—'

An impassioned hand cut her off. 'You could have bought your own house in Mayfair, but instead have used your money to clear our debts. You have given my husband and I the gift of not having to worry about money for the first time in our married life. And at the most important time too. All the stress about the finances has taken its toll on him. Weighed him down and, thanks to yours and Adam's selflessness, that crushing burden is gone now. We get to spend all the time we have left just enjoying being together and that means the world.'

All the talk of sacrifice and selflessness was making Gwen supremely uncomfortable when her motives had been—and still were—anything but. 'I simply reached an age where I needed a husband and he reached a point in his life where he was in need of a wife.'

She had no clue how much Adam had told his family about her reasons for marrying him. She sincerely hoped he hadn't confided everything about her situation but hadn't specified that he couldn't, which she now regretted as she did not want Abigail's pity or her judgement. Better to keep things vague and bring this awkward topic to a close. 'Therefore, it made perfect sense for us to marry so please do not feel beholden to me on the back of it in any way. Not when this is...' She wiggled her ring finger which now sported a plain gold band below his mother's ruby. '...in essence, a rational and sensible business transaction and most definitely not a sacrifice. One we both entered into with no illusions or unrealistic expectations.'

'Which breaks my heart when I want you both to experience nothing less than the deepest love and most contented happiness that you deserve. The all-encompassing sort I have always enjoyed with my darling Phillip.' Abigail dabbed at her eyes with her handkerchief and forced a smile, even though her heart must have been breaking inside that the love of her life was coming to the end of his. 'Besides, now that fate has decided that we must be sisters, I feel duty-bound as the elder to tell you that a good marriage should be many things, dearest Gwen, but rational, sensible and businesslike it should not.'

'Not everyone marries for love like you so obviously did. In fact, I would say that you and Phillip are more the exception than the rule. Especially here in Mayfair where marriages are founded more on status and security than anything else.'

'Do you seriously expect me to believe that you—an attractive and vibrant woman in her prime—has no desire for love in her life? Or fulfilment or passion?'

After last night's epiphany and her body's subsequent neediness, passion was unlikely to be absent from her life while Adam was in it. But she shrugged. 'I can assure you that I am quite fulfilled enough already. I am, after all, a rational, sensible and business-like woman at heart.'

'Who clearly no longer believes in love after it made a fool of you once.' Abigail's smile was kind this time, but it did make Gwen concerned about precisely how much her new husband had shared with his family about her situation. 'I also, as your new big sister and best friend and ally for life, wanted you to know that I knew all about what happened to you and do not judge you in the slightest for it. Love makes fools of us all at some point.'

'I did not love Lord Bentley.' Because that needed clarifying, no matter what her blabbermouth husband might have said. Having her heart broken was bad enough without anyone else knowing about it. 'I briefly got caught up in the romantic notion that I was but soon saw sense and left the scoundrel in Gretna Green.'

'Did you?' Abigail looked surprised by that before she nodded her approval. 'I am relieved to hear it, for I knew that scoundrel before he caused your scandal and wasn't at all surprised when he did. And I was not alone in that. Half of Mayfair expected nothing but the very worst from him and he lived up to all our low expectations when he convinced you to elope with him. What were you? Barely sixteen? Seventeen?'

'Seventeen,' answered Gwen, giving Adam the benefit of the doubt by assuming that Abigail must have read about it all in the newspapers at the time. 'Just.'

'Practically a child then.' Her self-appointed older sister and best friend shook her head in disgust. 'Bentley always did have the morals of an alley cat, the swine, and most definitely was not worthy of your love.'

'Thank you.' Such heartfelt support and forgiveness from a stranger touched her.

'But Adam is.' Abigail wiggled her brows over her teacup. 'So there is no need to guard your heart against him. Not that any sane woman could when he is thoroughly charming, devastatingly handsome and totally irresistible. You are doomed to be head over heels in love with him in no time.' When Gwen struggled to find a response to that beyond blinking in panic her new sister-in-law giggled. 'You should also know, if you have not already worked it out, Gwen, that I am a hopeless, unashamed romantic.'

'And you should know, if you have not already worked it out, Abigail, that I am not.'

'*Yet.*' The older woman gave her an assessing smile. 'But I have high hopes for the pair of you, even if you do not. You already have too much in common not to get on like a house on fire. As I can personally attest from experience, a stray spark is all it takes to turn that into more.'

Gwen was spared trying to formulate a polite response to that load of old rot by the commotion in the hallway that signalled the return of the rest of the family.

'Girls!' Abigail shouted. 'Come and meet your new aunt!'

'Gwen is here already?' Just Adam's voice made the tiny hairs on the back of Gwen's neck dance in anticipation, but his delighted smile when he dashed through the door made her practically melt. When he immediately came over and kissed her cheek, it was a miracle she did not end up a puddle on the floor. Especially as she suddenly remembered that the last time she had seen him this morning he had been naked. And aroused. And consequently, so had she been for most of the intervening hours since. 'I thought you had important meetings all afternoon that you couldn't get out of?'

'I managed to end it early.'

'Thank you.' He said that as if he meant it and for a moment she found herself smiling back at him, powerless to do anything else.

Right up until she noticed that Abigail, the self-confessed hopeless but obviously hopeful romantic, was smiling knowingly at them as she watched for any sign of those dratted sparks.

Chapter Ten

'It is always easier to seek forgiveness rather than ask permission.' Adam rested his elbows on the dining table where, to Gwen's continued unease, now that the desserts were cleared the conversation had turned to the best way for the Mayhews—collectively—to re-introduce her to society. It also quickly became apparent that her new husband had previously shared every single bit of her reasoning for wanting to do so with his brother and Abigail. 'Therefore, I don't think that we try to re-introduce Gwen gradually. I think we do it with a bang. At one event that everyone is bound to attend. Give them all an evening of unexpected titillation, let them whisper behind their fans until they are blue in their faces and then simply go about our business the very next day as if we have no earthly idea what all the fuss is about.'

'If it is a bang you want, then there is no better place to do it than at the Renshaw Ball at the end of the month.' Phillip threw his hands wide. '*Everyone* is going to that.'

'Then that is perfect!' Adam grinned at his brother. 'I presume we have an invitation?'

'Of course we have. I am a respected viscount who is invited to everything.'

'The Renshaw Ball is in just twenty days,' added Abigail, inadvertently fuelling Gwen's anxiety. 'That does not give us much time to prepare but if the good Lord managed to create the earth in just a week, I daresay we can orchestrate a big splash in thrice that.'

'I really do not think a big bang or splash is the right way to go.' Just the thought of being the object of scrutiny at a crowded society ball was giving Gwen palpitations. And in just three measly weeks too when she wasn't anywhere near braced for the ordeal so soon after her wedding. Surely such stress wasn't conducive to making a baby? 'Especially if they all give me the cut direct—as I can assure you that they will.'

'They can only do that if we give them the opportunity.' Adam reached for her hand on the table and gave it a reassuring squeeze. That only made her palpitations worse—but for entirely different reasons. 'So we don't. We stick to you like glue and manage the entire evening in a way that doesn't allow for any such opportunities.'

'That will still not prevent them from eviscerating my character and dredging up my past in the scandal sheets the following day.' She knew it was inevitable. Had known that before she had even selected her bridegroom, realised that it was a necessary evil to get over with, much like lancing a festering boil, but still dreaded it.

'You should spend the entire evening on the dance floor.' That came from Abigail, who was staring at their joined hands with interest. Then she grinned. 'Play the hopelessly head over heels couple all night. If you do that well enough, all the speculation the next day will be less about eviscerating your character and more about how the pair of you came to be so in love that you got married and how they all managed to miss it. The ton adores nothing more than romantic gossip, after all. Out-of-the-blue romantic gossip most of all. I can see the headlines already...' She painted an arc in the air with her hand. 'The Woman Who Finally Stole the Fickle Hero's Heart.'

Adam's hand stiffened over Gwen's before he retracted it to flick that away. 'I am neither fickle nor a hero. The men that died in the war were the true heroes.' His tense expression suddenly relaxed. Almost as if he forced it to. 'But I think you might have a point about the romance aspect. If we provide them with plenty of fresh, more exciting fodder to gossip about, then the old gossip about Gwen will soon lose momentum. We'd have to sustain the ruse for longer than one ball, of course, to keep the speculation buzzing, but that is easy enough to do with the Season still in full swing.'

'Phillip and I can also do our part by dropping the odd, juicy titbit here and there.' Abigail had an excited gleam in her eye. 'We'd all have to get our story straight beforehand, of course, to ensure we titillate with the right titbit at the right time, but we must also be annoyingly tight-lipped too. Just a nudge or a wink in the right direction will serve the cause better than over-sharing too soon. We must exploit the addictive air of mystery I shall create to the maximum.'

'*I?*' queried Adam. 'Surely that should be *we*?'

Phillip slanted his brother a glance. 'Do you know anyone with a more vivid and fanciful imagination than my wife? Or more interfering? Or anyone more *in* with all the worst gossip-mongers in Mayfair?'

'He makes a fair point.' Abigail's smile was smug. 'I was born for such an assignment.' Then she turned to Gwen. 'While it goes without saying that we must keep your presence here an absolute state secret until we are ready to unveil you, and you must wear something spectacular to the Renshaw Ball. Look so stunning that jaws will drop.'

'I'd much rather blend into the wallpaper.'

'For our cunning plan to work you have to stand out.' Abigail dismissed her reluctance with a grin. 'And to stand out you must be draped in the most mouth-watering gown imaginable. Do you have something in your wardrobe that would work?'

Not unless it was grey or beige. But admitting that aloud with her peacock of a husband sat beside her, resplendent in a deep maroon damask waistcoat, would be mortifying. 'I haven't been invited to a ball in a decade.'

'My wife will have something you can borrow,' offered Phillip kindly.

'Ordinarily, yes I would but this situation requires something special, and we only have three weeks to procure it...' Abigail tapped her lip, frowning but then beamed as if she had had a sudden epiphany. 'I bet I can convince Madame Devy to make you one.'

'Madame Devy!' Gwen might not be a follower of fashion, but even she had heard of the most sought-after modiste in London. 'That would be impossible, even for thrice the price at such short notice!'

'Nonsense.' Abigail dismissed that. 'Once I tell her that absolutely everyone will be talking about you the next morning, she'll happily do it. No amount of money can purchase that sort of advertisement. Dressing the latest *talk of the ton* will be a feather in her cap, especially if her creation is exemplary, so leave it with me. But clear all your appointments tomorrow afternoon so that she can take your measurements and take stock of your colouring and figure. Madame Devy would never make a gown for a lady she hasn't seen, Gwen, and time *is* of the essence here. Now…' Abigail went back to tapping her lip, a determined glint in her eyes while her husband huffed out a sigh.

'Brace yourself, Gwen, and my most sincere apologies for all that my wife is about to subject us to in the coming weeks.'

That earned him a brief, curt look from Abigail before she pointedly ignored him to focus solely on the newlyweds. 'In what hopelessly romantic way can we start your epic love story? For it must be epic if we are going to convince the ton to fall head over heels in love with the pair of you too…'

Poor Gwen looked a bit startled as they made their way upstairs an hour later. He sympathised. He had known Abigail for over a decade and knew how tenacious and unyielding she could be when she got a bee in her bonnet. For someone like Gwen, who was used to being in charge, having someone else snatch command in a veritable *coup d'etat* must be unsettling.

'Abigail is…' He struggled to find the right words to justify the way his sister-in-law had taken such despotic control while still reassuring Gwen that it was for the best. 'A force of nature. But a reliable, well-connected and useful one. There is no one better to help you rise from the ashes of your scandal like a phoenix. We also have three weeks to plan and knowing my sister-in-law, she will have thought of everything by then. She has your best interests at heart. We all do.'

'Have you seen all the soirées and parties she expects us to attend next month?' She turned to him with stunned but anxious eyes. 'And she wants me to sit in a box at the opera on the evening after the Renshaw Ball. Out on full display. Being scrutinised and stared at. Like an insect under a magnifying glass.' She swallowed, hard, genuine fear replacing the anxiety. 'I do not think that I can do it. Not when absolutely everyone will be whispering about me after my sudden and unexpected materialisation out of ten years of exile.'

'They will be whispering about *us* and I will be beside you through all of it. And so will Abigail and Phillip. This is a united Mayhew front and not just you being hung out to dry.'

'Easy for you to say when it isn't you that they will be judging.' By the time they reached the landing, her agitation was increasing. He could sense her rising panic in the stiffened set of her spine and her busy fingers that were doing their best to twist the fringing on her shawl into knots. 'Or Abigail. Or Phillip for that matter either.' She increased her pace, almost as if running away from it all like a frightened deer was the answer. 'The Mayhews might unite behind me but your reputations are intact. It is the scandalous carcass of Miss Gwendolyn Trym they will all want to tear apart. I would prefer a slower reintroduction, thank you very much and so—'

Her fingers had grasped her doorknob by the time he caught her arm, and gently tugged her to face him. 'Firstly, you are a Mayhew now too and, as much as I care little for such nonsense, that name carries a certain gravitas here in the ton. Secondly, if anyone dares attempt to tear apart my wife's character they will have to go through me first. That is if they can get past Abigail, who if you haven't noticed, is now your sworn champion and defender. And thirdly...' The way she was chewing her bottom lip to avoid bursting into tears brought out the protector in him, so he could not stop himself from brushing a reassuring hand over her cheek despite having to be the bearer of unavoidable bad news.

'Whether we introduce you with a splash or a trickle, Gwen, it will not do anything to prevent the gossips from regurgitating your scandal and picking over its carcass like starving vultures. That ship has sailed. The second they realise that the new Mrs Adam Mayhew was the former furniture heiress who eloped with a scoundrel, every bit of that sorry tale will be dredged up from the murky depths and there is nothing we can do about that. Beyond letting it happen while treating the gossip with the disdain it deserves, brazening it out and rising above it.'

Her dark eyes were limpid pools of misery as she

finally nodded. 'I know. Of course I know that. Knew that long before I started this. It's just...' The rest of her fears came out in a tortured sigh that made him cup her cheek again.

'It is perfectly acceptable to be petrified before going into battle, Gwen, even one that you have instigated. To have doubts and to want to run away is a natural response—but we both know you are made of sterner stuff than that. You want to do this for you—and for your business—but you are also not alone any more. For better or for worse, you have me beside you now.' Unthinking, he brought her wedding ring to his lips, then grinned as he kissed it. 'Better still, while I have few skills to recommend me, your potential naysayers, critics, vile gossip-mongers and disparagers all know that your husband is trained to kill.'

The giggle that escaped her mouth was a delicious sound. The tender softening of her features as they melted into a smile of gratitude just for him was better. 'Thank you. I needed that. The levity, I mean, and not the offer to murder my enemies.'

'You are welcome.'

'As you quite rightly said, I did instigate this and it is a bit late to shy away from that now. I need to remember that this is for the greater good of Trym's.' She leaned against her bedchamber door. 'It is funny, isn't it, how wanting something and doing it aren't quite the same thing?'

'They never are.'

'Do you think Abigail's plan is the best one?'

It touched him that she asked. 'I can't think of a better one, can you?'

'Sadly, I cannot.' She worried her bottom lip with her teeth. 'So apparently, for better or for worse, the Renshaw Ball it is.' Then she huffed. 'Now I wish it were over and done with already as the next three weeks of waiting for the axe to fall will be pure, unmitigated torture.'

'Try to distract yourself until then, that is my advice.' He couldn't help himself. He reached for her waist and tugged her into a comforting embrace. 'But it is all going to be all right, Gwen.'

'And if it isn't?'

Seeing as she had snuggled against him, he kissed her forehead. 'We cross that bridge when we come to it.'

'*We.*' She sighed that, as if it were an alien concept.

'Yes—*we.*' He kissed her nose before he rested his against it. 'For better or worse, remember?'

'I do.' Her smile was shy as her gaze slowly lifted to his, hesitating over whatever she was about to say as a blush bloomed on her cheeks. 'Would you distract me from it all tonight?'

All the blood Adam possessed instantly flooded to his groin at that unexpected invitation. 'It would be my absolute pleasure.'

And it was.

Especially as tonight felt like a turning point. Like she was letting down her guard.

Letting him in.

Trying her very best to trust him and that gave him hope and warmed his heart.

Chapter Eleven

'So how goes married life?' Ash's question was accompanied by an eye wiggle as he dealt the first hand of cards.

The four friends had taken to meeting at White's every Wednesday evening since their return from Waterloo, but this was the first one Adam had attended since his hasty wedding three weeks ago. He hadn't attended, not because he had been too busy to come before tonight, but because he had dreaded that precise question.

'My wife is hopelessly in lust with me.' Which was the only truthful positive he could say about the situation.

'Well, that can't be bad!' Ezra slapped him on the back. 'Congratulations!'

'We always knew she'd quickly succumb to your charm despite your inauspicious start.' Ash was grinning now in that man-to-man way that men did when they assumed another was the luckiest bastard alive.

'You've always had a knack with the fairer sex. What's your secret, eh? How do you get women to shed their clothes and warm your sheets so readily.'

'It's a gift.' Adam brushed that comment aside, hoping that if he took their teasing in a good way, they would quickly move on to a less touchy topic. 'Something I was born with and cannot possibly teach you.' He schooled his features into a smug smile as he sorted his cards, made it smugger still when his hand didn't look half bad and decided to use them to briskly change the subject. 'Five shillings says that I am as lucky at cards tonight as I undoubtedly always have been with the ladies.'

As all of them were competitive, that comment earned him all the groans and counterclaims he expected while they all tossed coins into the centre of the table.

'Can we assume from your prolonged absence from this table that the old ball and chain doesn't like you going out and leaving her?' Hawk laid down his first card with a snap.

'Well, of course she doesn't!' Ash answered for him. 'Didn't you hear Adam tell you that she's hopelessly in lust with him? What sane man would willingly leave a *willing* woman at home to come and stare at your miserable face over a table?' He winked at Adam for good measure to drive home his point. 'They might not have gone on an actual honeymoon, but Mr and

Mrs Mayhew are obviously still in their honeymoon period.'

'Clearly at it like rabbits,' added Ezra nudging Adam in the ribs. 'And good luck to them. If passion soon fades like we're all warned it does when you get shackled to a woman for all eternity, then you've got to grab it—and her—while you can!'

Adam made a token effort of joining in the masculine laughter, wondering if he could use his "ball and chain" wanting him home early as an excuse to leave after this first game, smarting that things couldn't be further from the truth.

Yes—his wife was in lust with him and he supposed that was a good thing. Every night without fail she came to his bedchamber and, so far, every single night of their three-week old marriage was thoroughly consummated in every which way possible. The woman who had come to the marital bed with such low expectations now could not seem to get enough of it.

Part of that, he knew, was because she was keen to have a child within the ridiculously tight schedule she had noted in her diary and so they needed to make one with all haste. The other part was because she needed the distraction of his lovemaking to take her mind off the Renshaw Ball tomorrow evening. Because she was dreading it and had taken his advice literally by doing whatever she could to distract herself from that looming prospect at every available opportunity. Unfortunately, that also meant that she spent practically every waking hour at her blasted workplace. And, maybe he was being cynical, but since the second night after their wedding when she had allowed him to glimpse some of her vulnerability before she invited him into her bed, she also seemed to have redoubled her efforts to keep him at arm's length as soon as she was out of it.

He had certainly never been invited to her bed since. And while she came to his for nightly, mind-blowing sex, she made sure never to still be in it by morning. While he slept—which he could not help doing when his body was so thoroughly sated—she sneaked out to sleep in her own and had usually left for Cheapside long before he awoke.

In truth, apart from the odd family dinner that she managed to make it home for, he rarely saw her. When he did, they seldom talked about anything meaning-ful. Or of anything at all for that matter beyond the heated nonsense they both mumbled during coitus. It was disconcerting knowing that your wife liked to be penetrated deep and fast in the moments before she came but having no earthly idea how she had spent her day. Hell, Adam didn't even know how she pre-ferred her breakfast eggs to be cooked, because to know that they would actually have to have a blasted breakfast together!

To make him feel worse, if indeed he could feel

worse than the racing stud he seemed to have been relegated to, Gwen always seemed to find some time in her busy schedule for Abigail! They had been to the modiste's several times together and his sister-in-law had even taken tea with the standoffish minx in her office in Cheapside. Twice! And been shown around her workshop when he had been politely reminded that she was still adjusting to married life and needed a bit more time and blasted space when he had suggested he would like to escort her home from it. But what really galled was that he knew all this only because Abigail had told him. In such a chatty and co-conspiratorial manner, that his brother's wife had no idea that she already knew his wife far better than he did. And that hurt.

'What I find fascinating is that there hasn't been a peep about your change of status from bachelor-about-town to husband in the gossip columns. Is the rampant lust the reason why the rest of the world is yet to be apprised of your nuptials?' Trust Hawk to realise that the news of their marriage had been sealed up tighter than a drum. 'Or has your wife had second thoughts about re-entering the vipers' nest that is society. She'd go up several notches in my estimation if she has as this shallow place isn't worth anyone's blasted effort.'

'We make our society debut as a couple tomorrow at the Renshaw Ball. We're going for one big splash followed by a determined campaign to convince them all that we are a match made in heaven which the ton will just have to accept.'

'You're lying then.' Hawk said that as a statement and not a question, so Adam nodded.

'My sister-in-law is stage-managing the whole affair and is convinced that everyone loves the romance of a pair of hopelessly devoted lovers. We even have a whole fabricated back story all worked out, followed by a very public charm offensive designed to overshadow any dredging up of Gwen's old scandal. And by we, I obviously mean Abigail. But I trust her judgement. It's not as if I can think of a better way to reinstate my wife's damaged reputation here in Mayfair.'

'As your friends, we should probably know that story then, shouldn't we? One of us is bound to be asked about it once you've made your splash.' Ezra made a valid point. 'Especially here. White's is a hive of gossip.'

'It's all very flowery. Romantic love-at-first-sight tosh designed to appeal to the ladies, who my sister-in-law believes are the key to this.'

Enjoying Adam's sudden and obvious discomfort, Ezra leaned forward grinning. 'So...how did you and your beloved Gwendolyn meet in this new version of events?'

'We apparently collided, quite literally, in the street. She was coming out of the Minerva lending library and was distracted by the book in her hand and I was dashing into it, distracted by my pocket watch. I almost knocked her over but managed to grab her at the last minute. Took one look into her lovely eyes as she dangled in my strong, manly arms and was immediately speared by Cupid's arrow.' Saying that aloud to his friends made him cringe because he knew they would laugh.

And they did. 'Was she similarly struck?'

'Sadly no. Apparently, the ladies of the ton would prefer that she took an instant dislike to me. Therefore, my new wife decided she did not appreciate the cut of my jib after I said something much too flirtatious.'

'That makes perfect sense,' said Ezra chuckling. 'You've always been a shameless flirt.'

'Please tell me she rebuffed you repeatedly.' Even the moody Hawk was grinning at Adam's discomfort. 'She will definitely go up several notches in my estimation if she did.'

'Of course she did.' Adam rolled his eyes. 'She refused to accept the bouquet I hand delivered to her house the next day. And the day after and the day after. But I am a tenacious sort, and I eventually wore her down with my persistence.'

'You have always been dogged, you old dog.' Ash chuckled as he laid a card. 'What finally convinced the fictitious version of Gwen that you were the one?'

'I climbed a tree to save her grumpy old cat. According to Abigail, women especially love a man who is kind to animals, and so none can resist one who is.'

'So you now have a grumpy old cat as well as a lusty wife?' asked Ezra.

'It was the family cat, thankfully, so being too decrepit to accept change, it has stayed at her mother's in Cheapside. But obviously, after my heroics on its behalf, the grumpy old cat now adores me.'

'Is that part the truth or part of the fiction?' Hawk was back to frowning. Adam could not tell whether it was at the hand of cards he was staring at so intently before he selected one, or at the concocted story.

'Fiction. He's perennially grumpy—just like you.' Adam did not add that he had never been introduced to the damn cat. Nor invited to accompany Gwen on her frequent visits to her mother either.

In fact, he hadn't seen his mother-in-law since the wedding because his new wife seemed to prefer keeping her life quite separate from his. Time and blasted space again but he could not help wondering if that was just an excuse. Almost as if she did not want them to have any sort of marriage other than one of convenience. Or perhaps he was being cynical and needed to learn some patience?

Or perhaps he should simply expect that this was the best he could hope for and be grateful for it? Fate had spared him, after all, and given him a lusty wife to banish away his nightmares, so things could be worse.

He could be pushing up daisies on some foreign battlefield like half of his platoon, so he was in no position to feel so selfishly aggrieved—even though he did and loathed himself for it. 'Are we playing cards or not?' He tapped the table, hoping that would bring the focus back on the game and away from the conundrum that was his wife but it didn't.

'So what's the plan for tomorrow? I am assuming that you'll want us there for moral support and to embellish your lie.' Ash's frown now matched Hawk's. 'Only, while I applaud the idea of a big splash followed by a charm offensive, I also know that erasing your wife's prior scandal isn't going to be smooth sailing and tomorrow night could be vicious.'

'Not as vicious as the morning after will be when the scandal sheets will have a field day.' Always a veritable ray of sunshine, Hawk told it like it was. 'I assume you are both prepared for that because I guarantee it won't be pretty.'

Adam nodded, distracted by the arrival of his contact at the War Office. 'I fold,' he said rising. 'I'll be back momentarily.' Just as soon as he had reminded the fellow that he was keen to pursue last year's job offer because he was sick and tired of being left in limbo. It had been two weeks since his meeting in Whitehall and since then silence had been deafening. Meanwhile, he was still technically living off Gwen, despite leaving the remainder of her money still untouched in his bank, and that was mortifying. Heading to the inns of court every day kept his mind and his conscience occupied—which was a good thing—but it was little more than a self-indulgence now and that did not sit right either. 'Play without me.'

His friends groaned but he ignored it to get to his target.

'Huntley! How the devil are you?' Adam managed to intercept him before he reached the party of men he was headed towards.

'Mayhew!' Huntley returned the friendly smile, which seemed like a good sign. 'How are you?'

'Good.' He swallowed past the sudden blockage in his throat. 'Eager to get started at the ministry. You?'

They exchanged a few pleasantries before he asked the pertinent question.

'Any news?' They had left it with Huntley assuring him that a cursory appointment with Lord Bathurst would be arranged as soon as he returned from his country estate.

'Sorry about the delay, old chap. The Secretary of State has been rusticating in Gloucestershire all month—but he knows you are finally ready to join our ranks and he's back tomorrow, so we should be able to finalise things. You'll definitely have an appointment next week.'

'Excellent.' Adam forced an enthusiastic smile, reminding himself that his experience on the front line might help the army to save lives and that that was ultimately a good thing. 'I can't wait to get stuck in.'

'I can't wait for you to get stuck in too, old chap. I cannot tell you how useful your experience and skills will be in Whitehall.' Huntley said that like he meant it. 'Actually, it might expedite matters if you're headed to the Renshaw Ball tomorrow. You could catch him there and iron out the formalities. He loathes balls and usually avoids them, so would thank you for any excuse to disappear into a quiet room for an hour. Unfortunately for him, Lady Bathurst is great friends with Lady Renshaw, so he cannot get out of it.'

'I *am* headed to the Renshaw Ball.' As much as the job at the ministry depressed him, Adam was relieved to know that it was still very much on the table. With any luck, he'd soon be earning the decent salary he desperately needed so that he would not feel so hideously beholden to his wife or so guilty for wasting his time on a selfish childhood dream that he could not, in all good conscience, indulge in any longer.

'Then the stars are aligned.' Huntley slapped him on the back. 'I'll see you there!'

Adam watched him leave, in two minds about whether he was happy with the exchange or not, so he did not hear Hawk approach.

'What was that about?'

'A job,' he answered honestly. 'I might have had to marry for money, but I refuse to be a kept man.'

'At the blasted War Office? Have you gone mad? What about your pupillage at the law firm?'

'I have responsibilities now, so those have to take priority. I cannot justify earning nothing for the next two and a half years and I *will not* contribute nothing to the upkeep of my own family.'

'Damn...' He knew Hawk would understand that because he took family responsibilities seriously. His friend digested the words for half a minute and then sighed. His pity for Adam's predicament evident. 'But you scrimped and saved to do this. The law has always been your dream.'

'A pipe dream that I jolly well have to get over.' He shrugged that off, yet it still hurt to say it aloud let alone let the dream go. Something he hadn't done fully because he still turned up at the inns of court every day. His excuse was he had nothing better to do—but soon he would. And it would pay him, which his pupillage didn't. 'My savings were only enough to sustain me through the apprenticeship. Have you any idea how expensive food alone is for six people? Let alone how much fuel costs. And the servants' wages. The upkeep of the house is huge even with the mortgage all paid. My paltry savings won't last a year, I can assure you.'

'But the War Office, Adam...' Hawk huffed his sympathy because he had been to hell and back for King and country too and was equally as scarred. 'If one glosses over the irrefutable fact that you are incapable of taking nonsensical orders and you would have to as one of Bathurst's minions, you loathed the military. Enough that on more than one occasion you lamented your hasty decision to not go into the church.' Why did those that knew him too well keep reminding him of things he had said and done. First Phillip with his reminder that "the bloody army have had their pound of flesh" and "didn't you burn your uniform" and now his best friend was reminding him how bitterly he had regretted the mistake of joining up. 'There must be something else.'

'If there is, I'd rather investigate it once I am getting paid. Hopefully it won't be forever.' Adam hoped that with every fibre of his being. But at the same time acknowledged that if this was the price the universe wanted him to pay, he would pay it and he would try to be thankful while he did so. 'Obviously, I haven't told Huntley that else there would be no way he would waste his time and his recommendation to get me an appointment with Lord Bathurst.'

'It is not a firm offer of employment then?'

'Not yet—but it will be. Huntley is certain that the ministry needs a man like me. He's so convinced, he's even told me that Bathurst will be at the Renshaw Ball tomorrow so that we can finalise all the details there rather than wait for an appointment. He believes Bathurst is keen to have me.'

Hawk was silent but his sudden frown was not. 'But will he still be keen after tomorrow? That's your immediate problem.'

'Why would he not be?'

'Because you are about to cause the mother of all scandals at the Renshaw Ball and the government like to avoid scandals.'

A cold splash of reality that Adam hadn't even considered.

Abigail squeezed her hand. 'Stop panicking, Gwen. I am sure that Madame Devy has made you the prettiest gown anyone has ever seen.'

Gwen was standing on a block in the fitting room of the shop, staring at herself in an enormous mirror while she waited and trying not to cringe as the modiste circled her, assessing.

'Pretty is for silly girls at their first ball. What I have created is a statement. A bold and stunning gown for a confident, bold and stunning woman who knows her worth and does not care one jot if others don't.'

If only that were true!

Gwen was dreading tomorrow night. Her stomach was in knots and her nerves were frayed just thinking about all the disdainful judgement she was going to be subjected to. All the disapproving stares and whispers behind fans. No gown was going to save her from that.

'I'd much rather blend into the wallpaper, if you don't mind.'

'Nonsense.' Madame Devy smiled at Gwen's reflection kindly. 'If one is doomed to set tongues wagging, one should do it without apology.' The modiste tugged at the sleeve of her grey dress with a disapproving frown, exactly as she had with the beige one Gwen had worn for her original consultation. 'Your time in the shadows is done, Mrs Mayhew. Now is your time to shine. Besides, I make the most beautiful and sought-after gowns in London and not wallpaper. If blending in and fading away is your intention, then you'll need to find someone else to clothe you for the Renshaw Ball because what I have made you is a triumph, even if I do say so myself.' She pulled one final face at Gwen's plain day dress and shook her head while simultaneously ushering a hovering assistant closer. 'Let us release you from this abomination to fashion so that we can arrange your hair to display your new gown to its best advantage.'

'You want to do my hair? *Now?*' Gwen could not disguise her incredulity. Thanks to Abigail's insistence on her remaining hidden until tomorrow, she had been smuggled into the back entrance of Madame Devy's shop under the cloak of darkness. 'It is already past ten and this is supposed to be just a final fitting! I have important things to do tomorrow...'

'Oh, shut up and do as you are told.' Abigail was

in the middle of pouring herself a cup of tea and was clearly content to be here for the duration. 'You are about to be transformed from an ugly duckling into a swan, Gwen, so stop complaining and enjoy the process.' Then, as if that was all that needed to be said on the matter, she turned to the modiste. 'I am dying to see your creation. What colour did you go for in the end? Deep green? Turquoise? The gold?'

Gwen instinctively winced at each one as none of the fabrics they had spent hours and hours poring over weeks ago would have been her choice—if she'd actually had a choice. They were all too vibrant. All too daring and obvious. Peacock colours when she was now quite convinced that she was content to remain a pigeon. Abigail, however, would have none of it and the modiste was worse, so all of Gwen's objections were ignored. She was resigned to wearing one of her vexing husband's colours and was dreading it regardless of whether it was the turquoise or the gold. Silently, she prayed that it was the deep green as that was the least exuberant of the lot.

'In the end, I went with none of those,' said Madame Devy with a dismissive flick of her wrist. 'They did not fit my vision and certainly did not suit the design. They were all too insipid.'

That set instant alarm bells ringing. 'Then what colour is it?'

'From the moment I first saw you there was only

one.' A cryptic answer she left at that because she turned to Abigail then. 'As you rightly pointed out, my lady, your sister-in-law has a good figure. A decent bosom. Attractive curves. A nice, long neck. With her black hair I knew instantly that she could carry off something bold.' She finally stopped circling to tug at the hems of the conservative day dress Gwen had donned this morning to go to her workshop in Cheapside. 'In both colour and design. I knew what I created for her would have to be absolutely nothing like this.'

Abigail wandered over to join them, frowning at the dull, grey gown as if she, like Madame Devy, could not quite believe anyone would willingly purchase such a garment, let alone wear it. 'That's precisely what I have always thought. Something bold is definitely in order. Please do not keep us in further suspense! What colour did you choose?'

'I used Mrs Mayhew's engagement ring as my inspiration.'

'You went with red!' Abigail clapped her hands with glee when the modiste nodded despite the fact that the news frankly horrified Gwen.

'Few can truly do it justice but I knew Mrs Mayhew could carry off red with panache.'

'Was the plan to emphasise my unseemly status as a scarlet woman by putting me in a scarlet dress!' *Over her dead body would she wear that!* 'I absolutely will not don a scarlet gown!'

Madame Devy dismissed that protest with another flick of her wrist. 'The silk I used is crimson, not scarlet, Mrs Mayhew, and there is nothing unseemly about the gown I have created. You have to trust me because I can assure you that you will be the belle of the Renshaw Ball as you inspired one of the most stunning gowns I have ever made.' She snapped her fingers at a hovering assistant who immediately dashed off. 'You will love it. I guarantee it.'

'I guarantee I will not.' Gwen gave an emphatic shake of her head. 'Not red. I am afraid I will have to put my foot down and…' Her words died in her throat as the assistant returned carrying a deep blood-red and gold bundle.

Abigail sighed as the assistant unfurled the gown and held it up for them to see. 'Oh, my goodness, that is sublime.'

As much as Gwen wanted to argue, her sister-in-law was right. The gown was utter perfection, although perhaps not for her. The soft drape of the silk was beautiful. The cut elegant and unfussy. The hue of the red more warm than garish. The gossamer gold net that had been used as an overskirt shimmered in the lamplight.

As if she read her mind, Madame Devy smiled. 'This will come fully alive under the ballroom's chandeliers. Because you prefer simplicity, I went for a plain bodice with a square neckline, cut high enough for modesty but low enough to showcase your fine décolleté. It will sit much lower on the back. When a lady has skin as perfect as yours, Mrs Mayhew, it is a crime not to show it off. I've used this gold lace overskirt to soften the crimson and slashed it open at the front so that hints of the silk below are revealed as you move.'

She then turned back to Abigail who was staring at the gown with delight. 'In keeping with the elegant simplicity of the gown, the hair should be neat. Jewellery kept to a minimum. Nothing more beyond a simple gold chain and earrings. She must be the epitome of style and sophistication—just like the furniture her company makes.'

'I agree.' Abigail beamed at Gwen. 'You will turn every single head in that ballroom.'

'But red is—'

Abigail cut her off with a beaming smile. 'Perfect, Gwen. Trust us in that decision and take the risk. Let Madame Devy's ladies do your hair in the manner they think is best and then at least try the gown on so that we all get the full effect before you dismiss it.'

She wanted to shake her head and counter. Point out that she barely knew either of them, let alone trusted them. And as the one taking all the risk, she should be the one who jolly well made all the decisions, but she bit her tongue. She knew enough about reputational damage to know that both these women were taking a risk on her behalf too. Abigail could lose all her standing in society on the back of Gwen's reception at the Renshaw Ball and Madame Devy could lose customers if her gown erred more on the scarlet woman side of things than the style and sophistication she was famous for.

'I shall try it on.'

'Excellent.' The modiste gestured for her to sit in a chair and no sooner than she did, two of her assistants sprang into action on Gwen's head.

Her hair was quickly unpinned and then brushed while she forced herself to calmly sip the tea Abigail handed her as they worked their magic in the hope that it would make her feel less queasy.

She had felt unwell all day worrying about her grand unveiling at the Renshaw Ball tomorrow. In truth, she hadn't felt well all day yesterday either. She had been alternatively queasy and light-headed. The light-headedness no doubt caused by the lack of appetite brought on by the queasiness and the lack of sleep caused by all her worrying.

Although she had slept last night.

Like a baby after Adam had turned her into a wanton, writhing puddle while they had their wicked way with one another. She had awoken with a start, still in his arms at dawn and that had unsettled her further because she kept doing that.

Kept promising herself that their nightly passion

was a temporary means to an end that would not touch her heart, and then she drifted off to sleep in his arms with it full to bursting and had woken on numerous occasions beside him delighted that he was hers.

Right up until that early morning fog in her brain cleared in the cold light of day and she realised how reckless it would be to form any sort of attachment to him when she had a clearly defined plan for her future and he wasn't in it. She wouldn't risk her heart again. Not for anyone.

Thank goodness her temporary husband was a heavy sleeper or he would know how pathetically she snuggled against him every morning before the fear and common sense returned and she fled his bed. She would have no clue how to face him if he did. Or how she would react if he smiled his lazy smile at her and kissed her. Especially when his kisses seemed to be her undoing. Intimacies at night were one thing, but now there seemed to be something so much more intimate about the mornings. Or at the least the promise of them and that wouldn't do. She did not want that spousal cosiness with him when she already liked him far more than she wanted to.

More than liked him, actually, and that was another worry.

Honestly, the sooner he got her pregnant, the better. Because then she wouldn't have to go to his bed ever again and her unwelcome but growing need for him would wane. Which obviously it would—because a fire needed feeding to burn and their nightly passion, although necessary at the moment, only fed those flames. What she was feeling for him was simply lust and not the beginnings of love. And passion faded. There would hopefully soon be no further need of it anyway once they made the child she craved.

Reassured, she took a sip of her tea and then froze as she realised that with all her worries about tomorrow she had quite forgotten about her courses, which should have arrived by now. Courses that she could normally set the clock by every twenty-eight days they were so regular and predictable. Even down to the timing because they always arrived first thing in the morning.

Off-kilter she quickly did the maths in her head twice and both times came to the conclusion that she was four days late. When she had never been late before. Not once since the dratted things had started when she was twelve.

And she was definitely queasy too.

Queasy and tired and not quite herself...

Did that mean...?

Oh, good heavens above! She was pregnant!

'Now it is time for the gown.' Madame Devy's voice came disjointed through Gwen's whirling thoughts. Relief. Disbelief. Apprehension. Excitement.

An uncharacteristic tinge of panic despite this being precisely what she wanted.

Stunned, she allowed herself to be stripped to her chemise and then laced into the bespoke stays the modiste had made to go with her new gown, all the while wondering if she was happy or disappointed at the speed of her pregnancy. Or whether she was excited about it or terrified. It had all happened so soon and at such a fraught time, after all, so she wasn't anywhere near ready for it.

But at least the timing was perfect! And she could tick another item off her plan.

Although why she wanted to rush to Adam and tell him the news when his role in that part of the proceedings was over was anyone's guess.

But she did.

She wanted to witness his reaction. Wanted him to share in her joy. Wanted him to be as excited as she was that they were starting a family. A worrying state of affairs when she needed to remain detached from the man and not think of him—of them—as family as she had always intended.

The gown was threaded over her head and red silk whispered over her skin like a lover as it draped itself over her body. One of the assistants pushed her arms into long, matching evening gloves as the other closed the back of the dress and only when Madame

Devy gave her nod of approval was she led to a covered mirror.

It was a grinning Abigail who did the honours and yanked the blanket from the glass so that an already shocked Gwen could finally see her reflection.

Her gasp was one of surprised pleasure.

'Didn't we tell you that you would look like a princess?'

Dumbfounded, she nodded then grinned herself as joy began to bubble inside her. 'I certainly do not look like a pigeon any more.'

Instead, she was a peacock.

A gloriously pregnant peacock who never had to feel all alone in the world ever again.

One who, more worryingly, couldn't wait to witness Adam's reaction to her transformation too.

Chapter Twelve

Thanks to the six other evening gowns, in varying states of completion that Abigail had also insisted upon for her relaunch, it was past midnight when Gwen finally got home. The house was silent. According to the butler, Adam had retired over an hour ago and the lack of light bleeding beneath his bedchamber door suggested that he had gone to sleep.

She hovered in their connecting dressing room for a full minute while she deliberated waking him to tell him about the baby, then decided that it was too soon to tell anyone, including the child's father. It was still early days, and it was better to be certain. The most prudent thing to do would be to visit her physician before she raised any expectations—including her own. It was always best to work with facts and not feelings. Always.

But even so, she laid her palm over her belly and smiled. She hoped it was a girl but, to her surprise, realised that she would be equally as delighted if it were a boy. A miniature Adam was a charming thought. Although that would complicate things in the long run as he would be the heir to both Trym's and a viscountcy, but she would cross that bridge when she came to it. Tonight, she would simply revel in her timely good fortune in the privacy of her own bedchamber while doing her darndest to be grateful that she never had to share a bed with the oddly compelling man sleeping in the next room ever again.

She undressed and donned her nightgown as quietly as she could so as not to wake him, not trusting herself not to blurt out her secret the second she saw him because the need to do so was so strong. Instead, she slipped under her covers and, conscious of her very early start in the morning, settled into the most comfortable position for sleep.

Except it eluded her and an hour later Gwen found herself still staring at the ceiling. She was on the cusp of rising and going to fetch some warm milk from the kitchen, when she heard him cry out.

An anguished, plaintive sound that suggested something was wrong.

When he cried out again, clearly in some pain, she jumped up from the bed like a shot and dashed through their connecting dressing room to help. However, instead of finding him in an injured heap on the floor or bent double with food poisoning, Adam was still in bed. Tangled in his covers and thrashing about, undoubtedly in the midst of some nightmare.

'Run!' His fists clenched around his sheets as he shouted. Then his breath sawed in and out. 'No! NO!'

'Adam.' She gently touched his arm as she whispered. It was clammy with perspiration. 'Adam—wake up.' He sat bolt upright on a gasp, his eyes snapping open and then blinking as they tried to focus on her in the darkness. 'Everything is all right...it was just a bad dream.'

'Bloody hell.' He leant his forehead against her middle with a ragged sigh, seeking comfort. It would have been churlish not to offer it, especially when she needed to, so she wrapped her arm around his shoulder and used the other hand to smooth his hair. 'I'd hoped I was done with those. Sorry...'

'There is nothing to apologise for.'

'But I woke you up.'

'To do that I'd have to have been asleep and I couldn't.' She hadn't meant to tell him that but it slipped out unbidden.

He lifted his head until their gazes locked. 'Are you worried about tomorrow night?' He reached for her hand as he asked that, his expression sympathetic despite his own recent trauma.

'Actually...' She stopped herself before more of the truth leaked out. 'Yes and no. Just a busy mind in general.' Which was busier still now that she was sitting on his mattress and, heaven help her, she was more worried about him now than she was about tomorrow. Even in the darkness she could see that his face was ashen. His eyes more troubled than she had ever witnessed. 'What did you mean when you said that you thought you were done with those? Do you have nightmares often?'

He shrugged, embarrassed, resting his weight on his hands as he severed the contact between them. 'Not so much of late. But they came thick and fast when I first got home.'

'From the war?'

He nodded. 'Odd really, that it happened after I'd escaped that hell—but I suppose in the midst of it you don't have time to regurgitate and second-guess what occurred in past battles. You are too busy dealing with the present one.'

'Not odd.' Unthinking, she sat beside him on the mattress and laced her fingers in his. Needing to give him comfort as much as she needed to touch him. 'It is human nature to dwell long after an event. I certainly did a great deal of that after my aborted elopement. Wondering what I could and should have done differently or pondering how I could possibly have been so stupid to act so rashly in the first place when it is completely out of character.' The darkness, the man and his child in her belly were clearly scrambling her wits because she wanted to talk to him. Wanted that honesty and connection.

'It is human nature to act rashly. We all do it sometimes. Trust me—I am the master of going off half-cocked. Just ask my brother. Even perennially pragmatic people like you slip up sometimes.' He smiled but she already knew enough of his smiles to spot a strained one when she saw it. 'You need to forgive yourself, Gwen. You were seventeen and we are all idiots at that age.'

Although the sensible, jaded, wary part of her was screaming at her not to probe deeper, knowing that more knowledge about this confusing man would only suck her deeper into his life, she had to know. 'Was it really bad? The war?'

'When is senseless slaughter ever good?' He stared at their connected fingers, his shoulders slumped at the weight of his memories. 'But you become desensitised to it after a while. You have to—to get through it. All things considered, I came out of it largely unscathed. Yet sometimes bits come back to haunt me. Nowadays only when I am tired or sick or...' He sighed. 'Or overburdened.'

An explanation which bothered her some more because the thought of him hurting somehow made her hurt too. 'Which caused tonight's nightmare? Are you ailing or is something particular on your mind?'

He went to speak then his eyes instantly shuttered. 'Nothing that you can help with.'

'That sounds like a mind-your-own-business answer Adam.' And that annoyed her, disproportionately. 'I am your wife.'

'When it suits you to be—although most of the time I suspect you would rather that you weren't bothered by the inconvenience of a husband.' He offered her a half-smile to soften that barb but she could tell he meant every intuitive word of it. 'Am I right?'

It was her turn to look down at their joined hands. 'I've never made any secret of my reasons for marrying you.'

'But you prefer to keep everything else a secret, don't you? We've been married three weeks and I still know practically nothing about you. If I did, then perhaps I would be more inclined to confide in you and vice versa.' His thumb traced a lazy circle on her palm. 'Talk to me. Tell me what is going on in your head. Let me in, Gwen. Please.'

She wanted to.

So much it scared her. Tentacles of panic began to wrap themselves around her innards at the thought of risking her heart again. Or worse, of having it shattered again. She suspected if she did let him in—and allowed herself to love him like her heart seemed to want to—and he disappointed her, the pain of it might kill her this time. 'I am not ready to.' She tugged her fingers from his grasp and stood. 'I am sorry.'

His expression was more resigned than disappointed. 'Do you think you will ever be?'

'I don't know.' That was perhaps too close to the bone. 'Perhaps with some more time and space...' Frankly, the more space the better as he was scrambling her resolve as well as her wits.

'Time and space, eh?' His shoulders slumped, suggesting that he knew she was only fobbing him off and was keen to get away. 'Very well. Take all that you need.'

His demoralised but patient acceptance made her feel wretched. Like a hideous, cowardly, self-centred liar and she knew he deserved better. But she could hardly tell him the truth about her intentions any more than she could allow herself to fall under his alluring spell. She knew she wasn't ready to risk that.

Yet.

Against her better judgement she was definitely wavering. 'Good night, Adam. Try not to have any more nightmares.'

She had turned back towards the door when he responded—but as usual, not at all how she would have expected.

'We were at Albuera. Had been fighting for days and appeared to be winning. Command were convinced that Napoleon's troops would continue to fight our advance from the front once they regrouped and were replenished with reinforcements. But while we were waiting for them to arrive, they sneaked around the side. Four French cavalry regiments suddenly burst out of an olive grove, completely catching us by surprise. In a split second I lost five men.' Gwen turned, her jaded, hardened, terrified heart breaking for him. 'Watched them get cut to ribbons right before my eyes and could do nothing to stop it. I get to relive that every single time I have a nightmare.' The horror and grief were etched deep on his handsome face but he shrugged as if giving her the honour of a window into his soul was of no matter. 'I figure one of us has to start knocking down this enormous wall which exists between us...'

'Adam, I...' Emotion choked her. Both at what he had suffered and because he had suddenly entrusted her with it. She was humbled. Touched. Petrified by how those walls around her heart were crumbling fast despite her resolve—her visceral need—to shore them back up. She wanted to run to him and hug him close but knew that if she did the battle would be lost and her heart would follow. So, once again, out of self-preservation she took the coward's way out and hated herself for it. 'I'm so sorry you had to go through that.'

'So am I but what can you do?' He offered her the ghost of a smile. As if he knew that she was now at war with herself and was fighting the overwhelming urge to dash back to him and envelop him in another comforting hug rather than beat a hasty retreat to her bedchamber. 'There were other battles of course. Other horrors. But for some reason that one hit me harder than the others. Perhaps because it was the first time I genuinely feared for my own life. I was this close to a French sabre.' He held his thumb and index finger an inch apart. 'But by some miracle I survived, when so many didn't that day, and that comes with its own guilt.'

'You feel guilty for living?'

'No… Yes.' He shrugged as he looked anywhere but at her. 'It is complicated.'

'Why do you feel guilty?' She could see that he did. See it in the suddenly stormy depths of his eyes and in the weight on his shoulders.

'I understand—rationally—that in war, whether you live or die is the luck of the draw but I cannot help wondering why the mystical powers of the universe choose to keep me over other, braver, cleverer and more useful men? What is special about me? Why did it choose to spare me?'

'Do you think it had to be for a higher purpose or does your guilt for surviving need it to be?'

His gaze snapped back, his expression perplexed. 'I suppose I want it to be the former because I feel indebted…' He looked so lost for a moment before he pushed that away, then pushed her away too. For the very first time. 'Anyway…talking about it is likely pointless when, as you say, with time and space I am sure I will find the answer on my own eventually.' No sooner had he quoted her than his eyes shuttered again while he waited for her to contradict him.

She so wanted to. It was on the tip of her tongue to tell him that he wasn't alone and that she wanted to help. To ask him to let her in like the world's biggest hypocrite but she couldn't. Once that door opened between them, she knew it would be impossible to close. No matter how much she was wavering, no matter how confounding her feelings for him were, she wasn't brave enough to give up herself fully to him.

Yet.

He watched her indecision and seemed to know instinctively that her caution had won because he could not fully disguise his disappointment. Even so, he smiled. It was resigned and reserved and painful to witness. 'Good night, Gwen. Thanks for waking me from my nightmare. It is much appreciated.'

Breakfast was an awkward affair.

It was the first time Gwen had deigned to join them and only because Abigail had insisted that she take the entire day off from Trym's to prepare for tonight's ball.

He hoped that to everyone else around the table, the tense silence that no amount of his family's inane chatter could properly fill, they would assume was caused by all the nerves for tonight. But only Gwen and he knew that a great deal of the tension came from what had happened between them last night. Because he had asked her to let him in and she had flatly refused. Even after he had confided in her about the cause of his nightmare, spilled some of his guts in the name of conciliation—and pathetic hope—she still could not bring herself to budge an inch. She still apparently needed more time and blasted space and, as a result, had somehow widened the gulf between them. Which meant that not only was this their first ever breakfast together, it was also the first time they had not shared a bed. Even after his confession, even after he had allowed himself to be vulnerable before her and even after his subsequent challenge, she had left him to sleep alone. All the things they needed to say left unsaid and the chasm between them somehow wider as a result.

This morning, she could barely look at him and that suited Adam just fine because looking at her hurt too much. After a sleepless night, he had come to the conclusion that he had been doing his best to lower the barricades between them to attempt to turn their union into a proper marriage and she wasn't even willing to try. Who she really was and what she really thought was, as far as she was concerned, none of his damn business still and that, he supposed, told him all he needed to know. A stark reminder that he should simply be grateful for his lot and not make any further attempts to improve it.

'We should get started.' Abigail rose from the table, holding out her hand to Gwen. 'Or we'll never be ready for tonight.'

'You have eleven hours.' His brother was as baffled by the supposed length of time it would take one woman to get ready for a ball. 'Assuming it somehow takes ten minutes to put a frock on, what the devil are the pair of you going to do with the remaining ten hours and fifty minutes?'

His wife shot him a withering glance. 'Gwen has to look stunning.'

'In case it has escaped your notice, she is already quite stunning enough.' Phillip winked at Gwen as he issued that compliment, and she smiled back at him shyly. 'Isn't she, Adam?'

He nodded with little enthusiasm as he helped himself to more toast, still wounded from her most recent rejection, and her smile melted before she was dragged out of the door.

Churlishly, he was pleased he had hurt her feelings because she didn't give a fig for his.

Phillip waited until the ladies could be heard going up the stairs before he folded his arms and glared. 'What the blazes is going on?'

'Nothing.' Which was the absolute truth. His wife

was as much of a stranger to him this morning as she was the day they said their vows. 'Other than I married a woman who finds our marriage of convenience grossly inconvenient.'

'You don't know that.'

'I do. Aside from the fact that she has made no effort to make this marriage work beyond the bedchamber, she pretty much admitted it last night.' *I've never made any secret of my reasons for marrying you.* A sentence that had haunted him because it confirmed all his paranoia.

His brother sighed. 'These things take time.'

'Time *and bloody space* apparently!' If Gwen said that one more time, Adam was sure the top of his head would explode. 'How are we ever supposed to get to know one another when she refuses to give me any time and takes so much space that we barely collide?' He tossed the toast aside and huffed. 'There are moments—fleeting and far between—where I see something in her eyes that gives me hope for us. Yet each time I do, she pushes me further away. I don't know what to do about that beyond being respectful of her feelings and giving her the time and blasted space she has requested repeatedly.'

'Maybe you need to be more Abigail in your approach?'

Adam scoffed. 'I am sure my standoffish wife, who does her darndest to avoid me like the plague until bedtime, would just love me making a pest of myself during her exceedingly busy days.'

'You're a charming fellow—at least you are when you are not sulking. So be charming. Woo your wife. Unsettle her. Confuse her. You are naturally contrary, after all.' Adam grinned. 'But also be steadfast. Supportive. Understanding. A pest is a nuisance—what you need to become is indispensable. Anticipate her needs. Be thoughtful. Kill her with kindness. Make it impossible for her to avoid you.'

'This is real life, Phillip, and not Shakespeare's *Taming of the Blasted Shrew*!' Kill her with kindness indeed! When he had been nothing but kind. 'But even if it were, to do all those things I would have to spend some time with her, and Gwen doesn't appear to have any.'

'Tonight, she'll have no option but to spend more time with you.'

'Parading about like a fake pair of besotted lovers at a string of social occasions where we shall be gawped at by hundreds isn't the sort of time we need.'

'Surely that depends on how you use it? Who is to say that you can't use it productively to do some real wooing alongside all the fakery? If I were you, I'd start tonight. Use every dance to mine under her defences. And if she likes you with your clothes off, seduce her in the carriage on the way back...' His brother wiggled his brows. 'Some of my fondest memories involve Abigail in the carriage.'

'Urgh…stop!' He shuddered. 'I shall never ride in your carriage again now that I know that you have been naked within it.'

'Gwen has her own carriage and I guarantee she'll never be able to think of it in the same way again after the pair of you have christened it. Memories like that have a habit of recurring, especially if you do a good job of it.' Phillip was grinning now, enjoying Adam's discomfort. 'You do know how to do a good job of it, don't you? I know we've never had *the big brotherly chat* because I always assumed you were naturally blessed with *the Mayhew flair* in the bedchamber, but if you need some pointers on how to best service—'

'That's it! I am going out.' Adam stood, trying to hold back his laughter as he pointed a stern finger at his brother while still feeling oddly buoyed by the wretch's advice. 'And I'll have you know that I need no instruction from you on that score.'

'I am glad to hear it,' Phillip called to his retreating back. 'And remember—be more Abigail and refuse to be ignored!'

Chapter Thirteen

With nothing better to do with his day than ruminate on his problems, Adam took himself off to the Chambers in Lincoln's Inn where he was still technically an apprentice and tried to make himself useful instead.

Every single time he had come here since his marriage, he had promised himself that he would explain to his mentor that today would be his last day because his circumstances had so drastically changed. Except today, he already knew he wasn't going to. He needed the distraction too much and he hoped doing some more legal drudge work would help with that.

'I thought you weren't coming in today?' His mentor, Sir Thomas Lenthall, KC, caught Adam sorting out some old legal files in the back office because the main job of a first year legal pupil was always tidying up the mess made by the actual working lawyers. In truth he didn't mind it because he read everything before he put it back in its rightful place and so learned a great deal doing this menial task.

'I found myself unexpectedly free.' Gwen certainly didn't need him and that was the only reason he could think of to have remained at home. 'So thought I'd finish this.'

'Fancy doing something more demanding?'

'Obviously!'

'I had a woman come in today, begging me to represent her son in court. She's got no money to pay us but was so distraught, the poor dear, I couldn't bring myself to say no despite my current bulging workload.' One of the main reasons why Adam had chosen to be this eminent lawyer's oldest ever pupil was because Sir Thomas was a man of principles who cared more about the little man than he did his big, crown cases. He gave something back and as giving back had seemed like the best way to repay his debt to the universe, he had wanted to learn how to do that from the best. 'It's an interesting case. They have arrested and charged her son with highway robbery and think that he might be that blighter who's been terrorising the Great Western Road this past year.'

'Really?' It was impossible not to know about *that* Highwayman as he had been on quite the spree in the immediate outskirts of London, always targeting the sort of wealthy aristocrats who insisted on an ostentatious crest on their carriages. 'Is it him?'

Sir Thomas threw up his palms. 'Who is to say at this stage—but if he is, with the amount he has stolen, I would have thought he could afford to hire the best barrister in town and not send his mother cap in hand to me.' That was another reason why Adam admired this man. He was undoubtedly one of the best barristers in the country but was too humble to see it. 'I need you to do the legwork for me. Gather all the witness statements and any other evidence and go through it all with a fine-toothed comb to help me prepare a defence. The first order of business is for you to go to Newgate and thoroughly question the accused. Are you up for that?'

A daft question because Adam had waited his whole life to get his teeth into a proper case and this sort of opportunity so early in a pupillage was unheard of. 'Surely the most important question is whether you think I am up to that? I am not the most experienced pupil you—'

'Oh, poppycock,' said his mentor, cutting him off and thrusting a letter at him. 'I suspect you were born ready, Mayhew and frankly, none of my other pupils have your dogged determination to succeed. Or your ability to learn fast. Fast is the operative word here for the trial is in two weeks.'

'So soon?'

'The prosecution is convinced it is an open-and-shut case because the accused was found trying to pawn one of the victims' earrings and the constable is in a hurry to announce to the worried ton that the infamous *Scourge of the Great Western Road* is a scourge no more. Your job is to find the flaw in that hastily prepared prosecution—if there is one.'

Adam didn't need any more convincing and took a hackney straight to Newgate. Having never had any cause to visit a prisoner before, he was unfamiliar with the protocols but hoped Sir Thomas' letter of introduction was enough to get him through the door. Although currently that reinforced door was still closed and the guard was glaring at him through the bars.

'I am here on behalf of Sir Thomas Lenthall to speak to his client Mr William Briggs.' Adam handed him his credentials and waited patiently for the fellow to read them.

After an eternity the letter was posted back through the hatch to him. 'Come back at one.'

'But that is two hours away!' Was he supposed to hang around outside for the duration. 'Why can't I see our client now?'

'Because we're short on guards and there has to be one posted outside a cell when anyone visits a prisoner in case someone tries to help them escape.'

'For pity's sake, I am here on behalf of Sir Thomas Lenthall—the highly respected King's Council—who is representing Mr Briggs in court. The prisoner is entitled to see his defence.'

'I didn't say you couldn't see him, sir, I said you could see him at one.' The hatch slammed shut.

Wondering if a bribe might garner a more positive response, Adam hammered on the door again. When the hatch opened, he smiled at the guard who was practically snarling now. 'We seem to have got off on the wrong foot.' He slipped a shilling through the bars. 'I am here to see Mr William Briggs.'

The guard took the coin. 'Thank you kindly for the shilling sir. I'll be sure to escort you personally to see Mr Briggs when you come back at one.' The hatch closed again leaving Adam no choice but to give up and come back at the specified time or risk losing even more money.

He gazed around Newgate Street wondering what the hell he was going to do with the next two hours. Being a stone's throw from Cheapside, he couldn't even begin his quest to be more Abigail by turning up at Trym's to pay a surprise visit to Gwen—because his wife wasn't at Trym's today thanks to bloody Abigail. Which meant he really was at a loose end now, doomed to twiddle his thumbs for one hundred and twenty interminable minutes because he didn't know a soul in Cheapside. Apart from his elusive mother-in-law, who he had only met once at their wedding because his wife was disinclined to share her with him.

Why was that?

As if the universe was telling him something, a hackney pulled up right in front of him and as its passenger alighted, he climbed in.

'Queen Street please,' he said, suddenly imbued with fresh purpose.

Gwen might have her reasons for not letting him in. Reasons he did not fully understand, but her mother might.

Chapter Fourteen

With all the primping and preening Abigail had planned, and after a long night of recriminations and her growing quandary after Adam's nightmare Gwen had thought today would drag interminably. Instead, it had whizzed past in such a whoosh that the carriage would arrive to take them all to the Renshaw Ball in less than ten minutes.

But at least she finally had those ten minutes to herself—because she needed every single one of them to calm her raging nerves.

It went without saying that she wasn't anywhere near ready for her relaunch into society. How exactly did one brace oneself for universal condemnation and vilification? For being pointed at and whispered about by two hundred people who all considered themselves her better? For being cut by people she had once foolishly thought of as friends before they had dropped her like a hot coal? For having all your past mistakes regurgitated and splashed all over the scandal sheets again? Made worse by the fact that all of that was avoidable. She had brought this upon herself with her ridiculous, hare-brained scheme to earn her respectability back.

What the hell had she been thinking to invite that sort of criticism and dredge up past mistakes and heartache that were best forgotten? On paper, this plan had seemed simple enough. But in practice, this was undoubtedly the most reckless thing she had ever done.

More reckless than running off to Gretna with a scoundrel.

More reckless than marrying a wholly unsuitable stranger because something about him called to her.

More reckless than her irrational desire to let him in, exactly as he had asked, and risk all of her heart again.

Because this mistake wouldn't just destroy her, it could destroy her business too.

If tonight backfired, as she was coming to realise that it very likely could, she would end up doing more harm to Trym's than good. She could lose customers in their droves then end up having to sell her shop in Piccadilly before it even opened as there was no point in having it if everyone was going to boycott it. She could even end up bankrupt because of this! End up having to sell her beloved business just to save it from her idiotic error of judgement...

As her heart raced and the small slice of toast Abigail had forced her to eat threatened to make a reappearance, she had no choice but to give herself a stern talking to as she paced her room.

All this doom saying and panicking wasn't going to help her one jot. She had to trust her plan, which thus far had worked perfectly. After all, she had already purchased her building, found herself a respectable husband from the ton and was already expecting his child. All good omens that the plan she had worked so hard on would ultimately work. And if it didn't, she would simply return to her life in Cheapside, fix the damage she had done to her business and enjoy bringing up her longed-for daughter. Which right at this minute did not sound all that bad.

Whatever happened tonight, it wasn't the end of the world.

As if fate heard her tempting it, she instantly felt a familiar but unwelcome hot trickle between her thighs and stopped dead.

No!

No! Please God don't let her courses have started!

She lifted her skirt to check and tears immediately pricked her eyes when she realised that she wasn't pregnant after all. That they had decided to come now too, right before she had to leave and face the whole judgemental ton, seemed like a very bad omen indeed.

'Gwen.' Of course, to add to her misery, time had

also run out. 'The carriage is here and everyone is downstairs waiting for you.'

'I'll be down in a minute, Abigail.' Just as soon as she had cleaned herself up and padded herself with rags. All her hopes dashed and her heart so heavy she could barely breathe.

She knew if she gave permission for the tears to fall they likely wouldn't stop, so blinked them away and gave her reflection one last look in the mirror. To all intents and purposes, she did indeed look like a princess on the outside exactly as Madame Devy had promised. But inside was a very different story. She felt empty and alone and more devastated by her empty womb than she could have possibly anticipated.

Her limbs were leaden as she left her bedchamber, but she forced a smile as she sailed down the stairs because an audience was gathered at the bottom of it. Abigail and Phillip were beaming at her. And Adam was gazing at her with such admiration. Admiration she knew she did not deserve after the way she had held back from him last night.

'You look breathtaking, Gwen.' He jogged halfway up the stairs to meet her and help her down. 'Utterly beautiful.' He kissed her hand and his lovely behaviour only made her feel so much worse for her own. He was a good man, drat him, and an annoyingly forgiving one. 'Are you ready to dance all night with the

most handsome man in the ballroom while we dazzle
the ton?'

No! Of course she wasn't. The only thing she
wanted to do now was curl up into a ball of regret
and shame and confusion and weep. 'As ready as I
shall ever be.'

'Then let us get this ordeal over with.' He wrapped
her hand around his arm, unaware of how much she
needed his solid, reassuring presence right at this moment.

He led them out of the door, where to her surprise,
her own carriage was waiting behind the viscount's.
As Abigail and her husband climbed into the first, he
opened the door to the second. 'I thought you might
appreciate a few minutes to calm yourself without
Abigail's incessant and optimistic chatter.' Which was
exactly what she needed. 'She means well, but I know
that I always needed some quiet time to prepare myself before I went into battle, and from what I hear of
your day, you've had none. Having our own convey-
ance also means we can leave whenever you want to.
I've told your coachman to wait for us around the corner in Gilbert Street rather than get caught in the inevitable crush here on Grosvenor Square, so that we
can exit hastily if we need to. Just say the word and I
shall spirit you out faster than the wind.'

'Thank you. That was very thoughtful of you.'

'I have my moments.' He settled in beside her rather

than opposite where she would have preferred, warming her with the heat of his body and tempting her to snuggle against it in her hour of need. Hold on to him like an anchor and never let go. 'Would you prefer me to be silent for the duration of this short journey or would you prefer I attempt to distract you from your obvious disquiet with some conversation? Or—' He rummaged beneath the seat and produced a bottle of brandy. 'Can I tempt you with some Dutch courage? I brought two glasses...'

Could he read her mind? As unnerving as that thought was she was grateful for his astuteness. 'Some Dutch courage sounds marvellous.'

'Good,' he said depositing the bottle between them so that he could reach for the glasses. 'Not only will it help settle your nerves, it might also help put some colour in your cheeks. I've never seen you so pale.' He handed her the glass and then cupped her hand around it. 'Are you all right, Gwen?'

'Just nervous.' And broken.

So very broken.

'Understandable.' But rather than pour the drinks he stared deep into her eyes, concerned. 'We do not have to do this if you don't want to. Honestly, just say the word and we'll call tonight off.'

She gestured to her lovely dress, shaking her head. 'A lot of people have gone to a lot of trouble to prepare me for tonight. As much as I am tempted to run for the hills, I cannot let them down.'

'There will be plenty of other balls in the coming weeks for us to launch you again so none of this effort will be wasted.'

He was being so kind and that really wasn't helping her keep her fraught emotions in check. 'Whichever ball I attend first will ultimately be as much of an ordeal as tonight will and it is never wise to put off until tomorrow something that you can do today. The last three weeks of waiting and worrying have been torturous. Postponing this will only prolong that agony. Especially as the outcome will be the same regardless. The ton love nothing more than a scandal and I am about to hand them one on a plate to feast upon.'

'True.' His half-smile was resigned. 'News of our marriage is bound to leak out at some point and you cannot keep sneaking in and out of Hereford Street via the back gate.'

'We walked out the front door tonight, so someone is bound to have seen us.'

'Also true. We must accept our fate—no matter how much we are both dreading it.'

That brought her up short, reminding her that she had only been selfishly thinking of herself today. 'I know why I am dreading it, but why are you?'

'I don't want to see you hurt, Gwen.' He reached for her hand. 'Or hear you insulted or subjected to unfair and scurrilous gossip, and I fear all those things will happen to begin with and there isn't much I can do about it apart from stand stalwartly by your side and glare.' His gaze dropped to their laced fingers and his shoulders slumped. 'I also cannot deny that selfishly, this could backfire on me.'

'I am dragging your good reputation through the mud, aren't I?' And he didn't deserve that.

His eyes snapped up, affronted. 'I couldn't give two figs about my reputation. I care nothing for the judgement of shallow Mayfair.' His fierce expression gave way to one of sheepishness. 'I chose my words poorly a moment ago and did not mean to make you feel bad. It's just I have a potential job lined up. A good one with an excellent salary. It is with the government—the War Office—and...'

The moment he mentioned the government, she understood the stakes. 'They prefer to shy away from scandals.'

He sighed. 'There is a chance they might rescind their offer if they think I will be an embarrassment to them.'

'I am sorry, Adam. Would it be easier for *you* if we postponed tonight?'

'To what point or purpose when the outcome will ultimately be the same. As you so rightly said, the ton love nothing more than a scandal and we are about to hand them one on a plate. Besides—' He shrugged in resignation. 'Lord Bathurst is expecting to meet with me tonight to hash out all the details. I'll scupper my chances if I don't turn up and potentially scupper them if I do. But such is life. You cannot control everything, no matter how much you plan to and sometimes you simply have to accept what it throws you. There will be other jobs if this one doesn't come off, and I suppose, if the worst comes to the worst I could always earn my living as a clergyman.' He forced out a bitter chuckle. 'My father would love that.'

How to broach the subject of money without denting his pride. 'You do know that you do not have to get a job, don't you?'

His eyes instantly narrowed. 'I made it quite clear when we married that I intended to earn my own living and keep my own family, Gwen. I owe that to Phillip and it is a responsibility that I take seriously. I took from you only what my family needed in the short term out of necessity and I will not take a penny more. I will also pay you back just as soon as I am able.'

'Adam—' She found herself talking to his palm.

'Save your breath for I have made my decision.' The determined glint in his eye remained even after he attempted to make light of it. 'You should have married a wastrel if that is the sort of husband you wanted. In case it has escaped your notice, I am not and never have been one of those.'

'I know.' And she did.

She had known he wasn't the run-of-the-mill money-grabbing fortune-hunter she had been so convinced she wanted before she had married him—and yet had married him regardless. But to her astonishment, now she did not completely rue the day. Probably because she was falling for him against all her better judgement and she wasn't sure what she felt about that. Apart from terrified.

'Just know then that there is no hurry for you to get a job and that you might have to wait until the scandal subsides to do so—and that I will not judge you for the delay, or what that costs, when it is actually all my fault.' It was her turn to smile at him in resignation. 'I selfishly dragged you into my mess, so the very least I can do is help you deal with it.' Except holding the smile proved impossible when her heart felt so heavy.

Typically, he saw it falter straight away, the perceptive devil. 'I get the distinct impression that something else is bothering you, Gwen. Something is not right. What aren't you telling me?'

She meant to brush his question away. To put a brave face on it all. Keep her private business private and not let him in, no matter what. But he had, again, freely just confided something important to her and the concern in his eyes, despite all his own worries, proved her undoing. 'I thought that I was pregnant and literally just found out that I am not.' To her mortification her voice caught on the last word and one of the tears she had been holding back spilled over her bottom lashes.

It was obvious by the way his mouth gaped that that was the last thing he had expected her to say or do. 'Oh… Oh…' Then he did the last thing she expected him to do, because he hauled her into his arms. 'Oh, Gwen, I am so sorry. I know how much you want a child.'

'Not as sorry as I am.' She had no clue why she was admitting that. No clue why she burrowed against him and allowed him to see her so vulnerable. Why she was letting him in despite her adamant resolve not to. She blamed his nightmare last night. His persistence to make more of their marriage than she had thought she wanted.

The way her heart yearned whenever he was near.

'I was so convinced that I was, I almost told you last night. It was on the tip of my tongue to do so and n-now…' Oh, good grief, he offered her one bit of affectionate, husbandly comfort and she was already a gibbering wreck. 'It is a bad omen, isn't it? Tonight is going to be a disaster. I can f-f-feel it. This is a sign that my whole plan is going to crumble about my ears and my business will be ruined and you won't get your job…and…and… I'll never have a baby!'

His finger gently tipped up her chin and he kissed her nose. 'It's just ghastly timing, Gwen, nothing more. It seems like the end of the world right now because what we are doing tonight is huge and we are not daft enough to believe it isn't going to be without a great deal of unpleasantness. It stands to reason that any minor setback that occurs in this heightened emotional state feels like a catastrophe—but it really isn't.' He cuddled her close as if he knew that closeness and reassurance was exactly what she needed. 'We've been married for only three weeks. Three fraught weeks too with tonight always looming on the horizon like a plague of boils. You have put too much pressure on yourself to get everything done all at once when the reality is that a bump in the road doesn't mean the end of the journey. It is just a bump.'

She knew he was right. 'I so wanted there to be a baby. And February would have been such perfect timing.' Even as she said it, she knew she was being ridiculous in her expectations, but to his credit he did not laugh at her.

'I know.' He kissed her nose again. 'But I am not sure the miracle of conception works in tandem with your diary, my darling. No matter how much you insist it complies.' Something about the offhand way he called her darling thrilled her. 'The good news is, if at first you don't succeed then try and try again is my motto, and I am only too happy to keep trying with you. And who knows, if we are both exceedingly thorough and put our shoulders to the task, we might make a March baby. Or an April baby. Or a

May one.' He lifted her chin again but placed a lingering kiss on her lips this time that instantly set all her nerve endings dancing. 'I am prepared to suffer the enormous chore of making mad, passionate love to you thrice daily for as long as it takes if that is what you desire.' His grin was wolfish and again, exactly what she needed at this precise moment. 'Because I am exceedingly thoughtful like that.'

His irreverence coaxed a smile out of her. 'May would be cutting it fine when Trym's opens in August.'

He chuckled at her sarcasm, releasing her a little so that he could uncork the bottle of brandy and pour a generous snifter. 'If you grew up in a workshop and turned out all right, I see no reason why our children can't.'

Children.

Plural.

For some reason, that appealed despite it appearing nowhere in her grand plan.

He handed her the drink and then poured his own. 'And selfishly, it will save me a fortune on nannies. My civil service salary will only stretch so far, you know.'

Then he winked and somehow the world seemed a whole lot brighter despite the ordeal ahead.

Chapter Fifteen

Their Graces, the Duke and Duchess of Aveley...

Her fingers dug tighter into Adam's arm with each step they ventured in the long introduction line into the ballroom. He empathised. Tonight was nerve-racking enough for him so he could only imagine how awful this was for her. Yet he was immensely proud of her that she was even here. It showed tremendous courage, determination and character to willingly venture across enemy lines to do what you believed was right. Such things were always a gamble but if this paid off, and it was fifty-fifty that it could, then she would have pulled off quite the coup.

Lord and Lady Fitzwilliam...

He was pleased with the honesty of their conversation in the carriage, although oddly disappointed by her revelation about her failed pregnancy. But at least she had revealed it and that felt like progress. After his frank discussion with her mother this afternoon, he now fully understood that Gwen was such a closed book because she had had her heart broken twice. Once by the scoundrel who had lured her to Gretna and taken her innocence because he wanted her fortune, and then again by the whole ton who had been so quick to judge and hack her out of their ranks. According to Mrs Trym—his brand-new mama and ally—supposed friends she had known for years growing up, abandoned her. Several stabbed her in the back by spreading even more malicious and untrue gossip and the scandal sheets, who used all that vitriol mercilessly to hound her for months.

The whole affair had hit her hard. So hard she had lost weight, her confidence and all her trust in people. Worried sick, after she had spent two months like a shadow in her bedchamber refusing to talk about it with anyone, her father had dragged her fully into the furniture business to help him. Hoping that the diversion would hasten the healing process and that she would return to her previous, sunny and effervescent self if given the time and space to do so.

Except she hadn't.

She not only withdrew from society, but from socialising with anyone outside of her parents. The business, according to his mother-in-law, then became her life and she had spent the last ten years hiding from any other sort of life behind it.

Her mother had warned Adam that he would need both tenacity and patience to knock down her walls.

Gwen's solitary habits were entrenched so he would need to fight fire with fire as well as continually prove to her that she was safe with him. Each time his stubborn wife tried to climb back into the sanctity of the solitary cocoon she had built to protect herself from being hurt, he either had to drag her back out or sneak in there with her.

And more than anything, he had been advised to continue flummoxing her, which he rather liked the sound of. Especially as her mother had confessed that she had never witnessed her unflappable daughter as flummoxed by anyone as she was by him.

The Viscount and Viscountess of Fobbing...

Gwen's fingers tightened on his arm like a vice as his brother and sister-in-law were introduced, so he placed his hand over hers in reassurance. 'Just gaze at me as if nobody else in this room exists or stare them straight in the eye and dare them to look down their pompous noses at you. You can do this, Gwen and I'm with you all the way.'

She smiled back at him as if her life depended on it in time for their announcement.

Major Adam Mayhew and Mrs Adam Mayhew...

The gasp from the crowd gathered at the bottom of the stairs was audible and immediately the whispers and stares started. This was the first the ton had heard about his nuptials and, as Abigail had predicted, the surprise news spread amongst the Renshaws' crush of revellers like wildfire.

To her credit, his sister-in-law could not have timed their fashionably late arrival more perfectly, because three-quarters of the guests were already here, so the arrival of Mrs Adam Mayhew so out of the blue caused quite the buzz. There were also just too many people for the pair of them to be successfully ambushed.

Those that tried were immediately intercepted by his brother and his wife who had formed a subtle barrier between Gwen and Adam and the rest of the room. Abigail, of course, played her part to perfection, accepting congratulations on their behalf and sprinkling around scintillating pleasantries like confetti that drifted their way in disjointed snippets as they forged their way determinedly to the dance floor where they were supposed to spend the entire night.

'*Of course we are delighted for the happy couple... Such a match made in heaven... Love at first sight... At least for him... Whirlwind courtship... Newlyweds... Only have eyes for each other... Soooo romantic...*'

Gwen's eyes were locked on his, her beaming smile nailed in place as he deftly navigated a path through the throng. The only time they stopped was when the hostess suddenly appeared before them.

Because it would have been very poor form not to, Adam bowed politely. 'Lady Renshaw, how lovely it is to be here. Allow me to introduce my wife, Mrs Gwendolyn Mayhew.'

'The pleasure is all mine.' Lady Renshaw looked his wife up and down with more curiosity than recognition. 'Although I do not believe I have had the pleasure before, Mrs Mayhew. Are you new to town?'

'To this part, yes, I suppose I am.' Then, to his surprise, Gwen smiled at the woman with a mischievous but gloriously confident twinkle in her eye, holding her gaze with all the confidence of a duchess. 'I come from *trade*, Lady Renshaw, I hope you will not hold that against me.'

'I wouldn't dream of it, Mrs Mayhew.' Their hostess smiled, because what else could she do to such a direct challenge when all eyes were upon them. 'We are an egalitarian lot here who care nothing of such distinctions, do we?' Lady Renshaw directed that to everyone in their immediate vicinity who all heartily nodded their agreement. 'What sort of trade are you in?'

'Furniture,' Gwen said without hesitation or apology. Only Adam was permitted to know how nervous she was about that brazen and unexpected confession as her fingers automatically gripped his arm tighter. 'The Trym Furniture Company to be exact. Have you heard of it?'

Lady Renshaw blinked in clear understanding of what that bombshell actually meant but dissembled quickly in the face of his wife's bold challenge. 'I have indeed. I have a delightful pair of Trym end tables in my drawing room. Such excellent quality. And on the subject of delightful, I must compliment you on your gown, it really is quite lovely, Mrs Mayhew. So lovely it has to be a Devy. Am I right?'

'You are indeed, Lady Renshaw.'

'You have clearly inherited your father's eye for style.' Then their hostess turned her focus to Adam. 'I must compliment you on your lovely bride, Major Mayhew and offer my most sincere congratulations to the pair of you. Although I must have missed the announcement of your betrothal in *The Times*. The last I heard, you were a carefree bachelor about town.' The challenge in her gaze for more was unmistakable, so like Gwen he refused to disappoint.

'We married in haste by special licence, Lady Renshaw, at *my* instigation.' Gwen might have veered from Abigail's carefully constructed script, but he wouldn't. 'I had such a job of getting her to agree to marry me, I didn't want to give my darling and discerning bride any time to come to her senses about me and change her mind.' He tugged Gwen's gloved hand to his lips and they smiled at one another as if they were quite besotted, which for him tonight required little acting at all when his wife was undoubtedly the most beautiful woman in the room. 'If you will excuse us, I am afraid that I simply have to dance with her.'

'Of course.'

The crowd parted like the Red Sea to let them through, so silent as they too digested all that unexpected gossip that it was deafening. Then all at once, they buzzed like a hive.

'And so it begins,' Gwen whispered as they reached the dance floor. As the current dance was in its closing stages, they waited arm in arm on the periphery for it to finish.

'Where did all that "I come from trade" come from?' He whispered too in case they were overheard by one of the many people openly staring at them. 'I do not recall that in Abigail's drip-things-in-slowly instructions.'

'All your fault.' She smiled and for the first time since they had arrived here it didn't look fake. 'You did tell me to dare them to look down their noses at me and, in that precise moment, it felt appropriate to get the inevitable over and done with rather than prolong the agony.'

'I am flattered that you took my advice.' And he was. It felt like another step forward.

'I figured they would find out soon enough anyway and whichever way the ton choose to feel about me, the faster I know it, the quicker I know where I stand. Only then can I plan a way around it.'

'That all sounds so much more positive and sensible than all your nonsense about bad omens.'

'All your fault too.' There was an odd emotion in her eyes when she smiled at him this time. One that, if he was not mistaken, dangerously resembled affection. 'A bump in the road doesn't mean the end of the journey and I have decided not to let them beat me.'

'That's my girl.' Leaning in and kissing her felt like the most natural thing to do. And obviously, his lips needed to linger when she kissed him back. It was the opening strains of the waltz and not the weight of so many eyes on them that convinced him to stop. 'Are you ready for our first ever dance?' It felt oddly symbolic that it was a waltz because that was the dance of love. Something overwhelming and intense was certainly happening in the vicinity of his heart and he welcomed it with open arms because it just felt right. Even if he didn't deserve any more good luck.

'As I will ever be.' She was still smiling at him when he led her onto the floor and spun her into his arms. 'I shall apologise in advance if I step on your toes. I haven't done this in ten years and certainly not in front of a gawking audience.'

'Then prepare to be swept off your feet, Mrs Mayhew, for I am almost as good a dancer as I am a lover.' She blushed prettily as he hauled her scandalously close. 'Let's give them a show.'

Exactly as planned, they danced for an hour, and throughout Adam did his best to distract her. It was impossible to ignore all the staring and the whispers, so he did not try to. Instead, he told her snippets of gossip about some of the gawping onlookers and poked fun at the sartorial choices of some of the others. They made a game out of counting headdress feathers and, after he identified certain people, she was able to recall exactly what furniture Trym's had made for them and how tardy they were in settling their accounts. Time both whizzed past and slowed and they managed to enjoy themselves despite being the obvious centre of attention.

Right up until he spotted Lord Bathurst and she felt him stiffen.

'What's wrong?'

'The Secretary of State for War has just arrived—and he is staring at me.'

Adam did not need to add that Lady Bathurst was whispering something in her husband's ear that was doubtless about them, as Gwen's expression became resigned but determined. 'Then let us get that part of this evening over with too and go talk to him.'

'I am not leaving you to the wolves alone, Gwen.'

'I shall glue myself to Abigail and Phillip until your return, I promise. But we both know that your best chance of securing that position at the ministry is for Lord Bathurst to meet the man before his good opinion of you is tainted by the poison of my scandal.'

He hated to hear her speak like that. 'I don't care about your scandal.'

'I know.' She began to drag him from the floor. 'But you care about this job and he is expecting to talk to you—so you are going to talk to him.' Before he could argue, because now that push had come to shove, the absolute last thing he wanted to do was talk to Lord Bathurst about that blasted awful job, she had already beckoned Abigail and his brother over. 'I am afraid it is your turn to nanny me as my husband has urgent business he needs to attend to.' She released him with a small shove. 'Good luck.' Then to his complete delight added two words that were music to his undeserving ears. 'My darling.'

Chapter Sixteen

She awoke to a knock on her door and the solid feel of Adam beneath her cheek.

'I've got all the newspapers as requested, Mrs Mayhew.'

Before Gwen could scream at her maid not to come in, his sleepy rumble beat her to it. 'Bring them in, Lizzie.' He stretched and kissed the top of her head a split second before Lizzie entered, trying to hide her knowing smile and failing miserably while her mistress scrambled from his embrace into a sitting position.

'Good morning to the both of you.' Lizzie deposited a tray at the end of the bed which held a teapot as well as the stack of morning papers. 'I'll just go fetch a second cup for you, Major.'

Completely unembarrassed to be caught in her bed, he smiled. 'You are an angel, Lizzie. And should you also happen to stumble across a few rounds of toast and a large pot of strawberry jam, you will also win the accolade of being my absolute favourite member of staff today.'

'Consider it done, sir.' Lizzie yanked open the curtains before bobbing a curtsey, shooting Gwen one last look that said she heartily approved, and disappeared.

Adam on the other hand was squinting at the very early morning sun now streaming through the windows. 'Why the blazes did you have the newspapers brought in at the crack of dawn, woman? Don't you ever sleep past five?'

'I have an early meeting this morning.' One she would already be out of bed and in a hurry to escape to if she didn't fear that the evidence of her courses might be on her nightgown and sheets. It was bad enough that she had, in a moment of extreme emotional weakness, confessed to him that they had started, but she absolutely would die of embarrassment if he saw them. Which meant that she was stuck with him until he left.

'When don't you have an early meeting?' He was frowning now. 'And today of all days too. When a member of the press is bound to try and ambush you at Trym's.'

'They can try. No one gets past my secretary.'

'Huh,' he grunted, looking peeved, 'maybe so, but it's the journey between your carriage door and the door to the workshop that bothers me, so that is why I am going to escort you there.' Before she instinctively argued against that, he pressed a finger to her lips that immediately set them tingling. 'That is non-negotiable this morning, Gwen, so you are just going to have to suffer me.'

'But—' He silenced her with a kiss. It was fast and firm and, heaven help her, she felt it everywhere.

'I either escort you this morning and drop you safely at your door or I lay siege to your office for the rest of the day to stand guard over you. Your choice.' Then, as if no further discussion were required he changed the subject. 'I don't know about you, but I slept like a log—although I certainly didn't expect to after last night.'

Showing absolutely no signs of moving, he collapsed back against the pillows and idly scratched his chest. Thankfully, most of it was covered by the crumpled linen shirt he still wore, but the rest of his clothing, including his breeches, lay in a heap on the floor. Which all suggested that at some point, he must have stripped and climbed properly in beside her after she had nodded off last night. Although how she had come to be in his arms was still a mystery. Waking so abruptly with her head tucked beneath his chin and her hand resting intimately against his chest had been mortifying, especially as the option of sneaking out without him noticing like she usually did was gone.

The last thing she remembered was him sitting beside her on the mattress while he insisted that she drink the hot milk that he had personally brought into her bedchamber after they had arrived back home. When she had been in such a state of heightened agitation after the prolonged ordeal of being the single most interesting and gossiped-about spectacle at the Renshaws', that she feared she would never be able to relax enough to sleep.

Her mind had been whirring like a top and she honestly had no clue which way the wind would blow. For every person who had deigned to smile at her in that ballroom, another ten had simply stared.

But somewhere between starting the hot beverage while listening to the soothing sound of his voice as he recounted the details of his long and, to her mind, exceedingly dull sounding meeting with Lord Bathurst, she must have miraculously drifted off. She recalled him saying that his new employer thought it best to delay his start at the War Office for at least a month to let the dust settle on the news of their wedding and had some recollection of Adam telling her, in an uncharacteristically unanimated way, of the sorts of things Bathurst wanted him to do. It involved charts and maps and troop numbers and somewhere during that her exhausted mind had shut down. Then, in his typically uncompliant way, Adam must have decided that it was perfectly acceptable to climb into bed beside her despite her being sound asleep and him being uninvited!

She really wasn't sure what she felt about that—beyond unsettled and oddly grateful—but tried to mask that by hauling the bedcovers under her armpits and shuffling a bit further away from the alluring heat of his body. 'Care to explain why you are in here and not in there?' She pointed to the connecting door.

He ignored her slightly snippy tone. 'I was hardly going to abandon you in your hour of need, now was I?' Clearly, he wasn't the least bit contrite about his unsolicited encroachment into her most private space because he just smiled as he rolled onto his side to look at her. The concern in his gaze went some way towards making his unwelcome presence more welcome. 'Especially when you were so obviously upset about some of the nonsense you were subjected to last night.'

'It could have been worse.' Which it very much could have. For the most part, she had suffered more unsubtle stares and whispers than outright hostility. A specimen in a jar rather than a complete social pariah. 'At least only one person dared to give me the cut direct when I had expected there to be more.' Although few ventured to make any effort to include her in further conversation after they had satisfied their curiosity or gleaned some gossip, which was its own sort of cut. Instead, she had been scrutinised like an insect under a microscope while the ton decided how they collectively felt about her. Something she would doubtless learn herself too in the newspapers taunting her at the foot of the bed.

'Try not to take Lady Arbuthnot's silly cut too much to heart. She's always been a rude and sanctimonious fuddy-duddy and very few like her.' That pointed insult had come as Gwen and the rest of the Mayhews were leaving, when the old woman had marched right in front of her at the exit to purposefully glare and then turn her back on her before she stomped off. It had, fortunately, come right at the end of the evening so she didn't have to remain and pretend that it hadn't hurt her, but it had been about as public a slight as it was possible to have been dealt. At least sixty people must have witnessed it, which meant that it would have spread around that ballroom like wildfire as soon as they departed and was bound to be referenced somewhere in her stack of newspapers.

So too must a recollection of her husband's insultingly loud quip of "Can someone help Lady Arbuthnot find her broomstick as is she obviously late for the coven." Although, as inappropriate and ungentlemanly as his comment was, it did make many of the onlookers roar with laughter. It had even managed to make Gwen feel a bit better about the unpleasant encounter as he spirited her away and she had been supremely thankful that he had been there at the time.

As much as she did not want to acknowledge how much it touched her, Adam had been her rock last night. Both before, during and after the ball—the noble, much-too-likeable wretch. She knew she wouldn't have got through it without him. His calm, irreverent and reassuring presence had turned the potentially horrific ordeal into an arduous occasion and his response to the vile woman who had gone out of her way to cut her had been, at the time, perfect. She supposed the court of public opinion would ultimately decide whether it had been appropriate, and she simultaneously feared and was curious about what the press would say. For bitter experience told her that whichever way they went, the ton was sure to follow.

'Let us hope that Lady Arbuthnot doesn't have quite the influence that she thinks she does.' She leaned forward for one of the newspapers to check, only to have him beat her to them and bat them out of her reach.

'Tea first. Everything is always better when one is fortified with tea.'

As if he conjured her, Lizzie reappeared with the extra cup and the toast. 'Would you like me to pour, sir?'

'No need.' Adam waved her away. 'I can do it.'

'When would you like me to come back and help you dress for work, Mrs Mayhew?'

Again, he took it upon himself to answer. 'Give us at least half an hour, Lizzie.'

'Very good, sir.'

No sooner had Lizzie left than he rose from the bed,

seemingly unaware that the tails of his shirt barely covered his backside, and blissfully unaware how much she ogled him as he poured them both tea.

Despite having seen his body in all its fully naked glory many times, there was a big difference between seeing it in the dark and witnessing it now. He seemed larger everywhere somehow in daylight. More present and vital. More... Adam and less ignorable and that was a worry. Especially as his sleep-rumpled hair, morning stubble and distinct lack of breeches suited him.

She only just managed to tear her eyes from his fine rider's legs before he turned back around with a smile that did odd things to her not-so-hardened-as-she-would-like heart. 'Milk and one sugar—exactly how you like it.'

'Thank you.'

He brought his own tea back to the bed and, to her chagrin climbed back in beside her. 'I suppose we'd best begin the post-mortem.' He grabbed a broadsheet. 'Let's ease ourselves in with *The Times* and build up to the gutter press. What say you?'

'It sounds like a plan.'

'I know how much you like one of those.' He grinned and began to flick through the newspaper for the society pages and then groaned as he jumped off the bed, taking *The Times* with him. 'I need my reading spectacles.' He padded through their connecting door and within moments padded back wearing them and the combination of a half-naked, rumpled and scholarly Adam sent her pulse ratcheting.

'"*Lady Renshaw has always had the coup of hosting one of the most anticipated balls of the season...*"' He read aloud as he climbed back into bed beside her. '"*Except none of the two hundred and fifty-six guests present could have possibly anticipated the coup that hostess achieved last night. For who could possibly have imagined that the celebrated war hero Major Adam Mayhew would surprise everyone with his inaugural appearance with his new bride? Or that the mysterious new Mrs Mayhew, who instantly set the room abuzz with fevered speculation, wasn't quite as new to everyone as they had first assumed.*"'

'I suppose this is the part where my scandal gets regurgitated?' she interrupted with an air of resignation.

Adam pulled a face as he continued. '"*For those with longer memories than most who prefer to lie about their age would claim to have, she used to be Miss Gwendolyn Trym. The furniture heiress who eloped to Gretna Green with the disgraced peer Lord Anthony Bentley in the year 1806 but who failed, quite scandalously, to ever take his name. However, if you are assuming that the then Miss Trym faded into the oblivion of exiled ruination after being abandoned at the altar, think again. For it appears that she not only inherited the entire Trym furniture business but*

*she has run it single-handed for the last four years
as well. And has, in that time, tripled the company's
profits too.'*

He paused there to flick the paper down so that he
could slant her a glance. 'Did you really triple them?'

'I did.'

'Impressive.' He went back to the paper. '"*Major
and Mrs Mayhew apparently wed by special licence
after a whirlwind courtship, which would seem quite
a convenient and unbelievable explanation for their
hasty nuptials under all normal circumstances but it
seems, in this case, that the seemingly besotted couple are indeed besotted as more than one witness has
stated that Major Mayhew could not bring himself
to take his famously wandering eyes off his beautiful wife.*"'

Adam dropped the newspaper to his lap. 'Well, that
certainly could have been worse, couldn't it? At least
they got most of their facts straight. We need to quash
the misconception that you were jilted as that makes
you sound like a victim, and you are most definitely
not one of those.' He appeared peeved that they had
the gall to even assume it and that warmed her.

'Is that the only fact they got wrong or could you
really not take your famously wandering eyes off me?'
Gwen had meant that to sound dismissive and slightly
sarcastic, an attempt to lighten the tone, but to her chagrin it came out sounding more flirtatious.

'Guilty as charged.' He raked her with his gaze, making his appreciation of her quite plain. 'But then you were utterly ravishing last night.' If that lovely compliment wasn't enough, he planted another unexpected and too brief kiss on her lips that left her thoroughly off-kilter. 'For the record, you also look utterly ravishing this morning but I suppose mother nature has thwarted any chance of me seducing you today?' He shot her a hopeful but heated wolfish look. 'Unless...'

Thoroughly tempted despite her monthly visitor, she still shook her head. 'Definitely not.' But she was surprised that her being indisposed did not seem to bother him and even more surprised that she wished it did not bother her. There was something oddly seductive about spending a lazy morning in bed with him. Just the two of them, cocooned against the world, unfettered by the usual social restrictions and expectations.

She could, Gwen realised with a start, get used to this.

Sultry nights making their children—plural—and cosy mornings snuggled together while their young family still slept.

'Shame,' he said reaching for the *London Tribune* and tossing her the *London Courier*, unaware of the peculiar effect he was having on both her grand plan and her resolve this morning. 'Do let me know if you change your mind.'

To her continued surprise, they managed to spend the next half hour reading in companionable silence while munching on toast, only speaking when they found something pertinent to read to one another. All the stories about her followed a similar theme. They mentioned the hasty wedding by special licence, alluding to some disbelief about the story of the whirlwind courtship but not dismissing it outright. Several commented upon her dress which, two claimed, was the envy of every woman there. All the publications without fail reminded their readers of her past scandal in varying levels of detail, but the majority begrudgingly gave her some credit for picking herself up after it, dusting herself off and taking Trym's from strength to strength. It wasn't overly positive and it wasn't overly negative, so on balance it could have been worse.

However, in tacit agreement, they had left the most spiteful of the scandal sheets until last and sensing things were about to take a nasty turn, she handed it to Adam to read and braced herself for some proper unpleasantness.

"'*Lady Arbuthnot did what everyone else was too polite to do at the Renshaw Ball last night.*'" He winced at the opening line. "'*For she was the only one brave enough to give that brazen hussy Mrs Gwendolyn Mayhew* nee *Trym the cut she deserved. One cannot fathom why the handsome and eligible Waterloo hero decided to marry such a wholly unsavoury and common bride as he could have had his pick of this season's diamonds. However, there is no accounting for taste and Major Mayhew has repeatedly displayed his woeful lack of it in his consistently garish choice of waistcoats. Last night's gaudy turquoise monstrosity was no exception, although his disgusting waistcoat paled against his shameless new wife's oddly apt choice of gown. One wonders if one of the ton's most notorious scarlet women was purposefully being ironic in choosing scarlet silk for her pathetic attempt to weasel her way back into society? Or if she is, as her previous reckless behaviour suggests, as vacuous as her tasteless spouse?"'*

It took several moments for all that vitriol to fully sink in. 'I knew someone would make a scurrilous comment about the red gown, but I wasn't expecting to be called a brazen hussy. At least not in print. Did they really also call me common too?'

He double-checked the article and nodded. 'Common *and* unsavoury. And vacuous too.'

'I think vacuous is actually the most insulting thing out of all of it.'

'Sticks and stones.' Then he shuffled closer, wrapped an arm around her shoulder and kissed her nose. 'Sticks and stones, my darling.' She wasn't sure what was the most disarming, his embrace, the kiss or the fact that he kept calling her his darling, as all three had the most distracting effect. 'But saying that, I'm absolutely spitting feathers at the worst insult that tawdry publication has printed. Livid enough to head to their office this very minute and demand a retraction. I might even sue for libel.'

'At the scarlet woman reference?' She shrugged, not as upset by the comparison as she had initially thought she would be. 'How is that any worse than calling me a brazen hussy when they both mean the same thing?'

'You thought I would waste my righteous umbrage on something so piffling and paltry?' He glared as if she had gone quite mad.

'Then what has got your dander up?'

'That they called my fine turquoise waistcoat a garish monstrosity, of course.'

His eyes twinkled with mischief as soon as her jaw dropped and when her bark of laughter escaped at his irreverence he silenced it with a kiss. Then hauled her into his lap when she forgot herself and all her resolve to resist him and kissed him back.

Then, because his kisses always had the power to completely scramble her wits, would likely have continued to kiss him in perpetuity if Lizzie hadn't come back and reminded her to get ready for work.

Chapter Seventeen

Adam loved poring over witness statements. There was something so satisfying about finding those seemingly inconsequential details in pages and pages of otherwise more exciting text that could spin a case on its head. Especially if it saved an unfortunate soul from punishment. In this case, the young and terrified man charged with highway robbery.

With his promised job at the ministry postponed for at least a month, he was indulging himself with one last hurrah with the law, supremely grateful for the time and the opportunity to do some real good. It was the first and only case he would ever be entrusted with, after all, and so he was determined to do it and his only client all the justice they deserved.

That was why he had spent the last few days going through the twenty-two witness statements of those who had been robbed by the highwayman with a fine-toothed comb. And why he was more convinced than ever that the accused—William Briggs—was innocent.

Whoever the actual highwayman was, it could not possibly be him. The real *Scourge of the Great Western Road*, as the newspapers had dubbed him, was described as at least six feet tall and broad—muscular like a labourer or a pugilist. Whereas the lad in custody was a good six inches shorter than that and was so skinny a good gust of wind could blow him over. Also, the real scourge had foolishly tugged his mask down to steal a kiss from six of the ladies he had robbed. Although he had been too canny to allow any of those doubly violated women to see his face, they had all mentioned the intense rasp of his whiskers. Whiskers apparently so rough that they had left one of those unfortunate young ladies—a Lady Octavia Talbot—with whisker burns that had lasted for many days afterwards.

However, poor William Briggs wasn't even capable of growing a beard yet, let alone giving a woman whisker burns. But to have that fact proved without a doubt in court, he had personally come to Newgate this afternoon and instructed him to try. Now he hoped the combination of the witness description and the puny accused's patchy, wispy chin at the trial would be enough to secure a not guilty verdict. Especially if he could convince one of the victims who the actual highwayman had kissed so roughly to testify in court so that they could be cross-examined on the stand. Even better, it would be a powerful thing indeed if he could ask the owner of the stolen earring William had found—the young lady with the whisker burns—if she believed the slender, terrified boy in the dock was the same brute who had violated her.

For good measure, he had also paid the prison guard handsomely not to give the lad a razor between now and the trial because he wanted another witness to attest to the fact that the pertinent paltry whiskers on show had not been tampered with in ten days. Assuming his mentor agreed with his discovery and went immediately down that route in court, the trial wouldn't last the day. Because that was certainly the route Adam would go down if he were the barrister for the defence. In fact, he'd be more brazen about it and have the defendant masked up like a highwayman when he was first brought in, read the witness descriptions aloud in his opening arguments and then do a big reveal.

Ta da! I put it to you, m'lud, that my learned friend for the prosecution no longer has a case...

But of course, his planned theatrical brand of lawyering wasn't going to happen any more now that he was going to earn his living at the War Office. A thought that instantly soured his buoyant mood, so he banished it.

Refusing to wallow in pessimism after his produc-

tive day and the distinct improvement in relations between him and his wife, he decided to walk the short
distance to Cheapside despite the gathering rain clouds
above and it being a good hour earlier than his Gwen
would finish her work for the day.

Since the Renshaw Ball, and much to her lessen-
ing chagrin, he had insisted on escorting her to and
from Trym's, using the excuse of protecting her from
the press as justification. However, although there remained a grain of truth in that, because five days on
and the press still weren't done with them, the real
reason he continued to insist was because those half
hour carriage rides across the city with just the two of
them guaranteed him an hour every day conversing
with his lovely bride alone. That added to the show
they had to put on each evening at whatever social occasion Abigail dragged them to and combined with
his frequent forays through the connecting door into
her bedchamber just to chat, ensured that he was really getting to know her and subtly but determinedly
wooing her while he did.

Already, after only five days, his efforts were paying dividends because she wasn't quite so standoffish around him and very definitely smiled more. And
confided more. At least until she remembered that she
wanted to maintain those barriers between them and
did whatever she could to withdraw again. Not that
he gave her much time or space to.

And talking of barriers…

He stared up at the huge gold-leafed Trym Furniture Company sign on the front of the enormous Cheapside workshop-cum-showroom and wondered why she still hadn't invited him inside it. Especially when he had come here every single evening for the last five days to pick her up. Yet she had always been hovering by the door waiting for him whenever he arrived, her carriage already standing by the pavement.

But she wasn't waiting for him this afternoon because he was early, so it seemed daft not to exploit an opportunity to flummox her some more by invading a little bit more of the life she tried to keep him separate from.

'Good afternoon.' He offered his best disarming smile to the same sour-faced secretary who had sent him packing the last time he had dared venture into Gwen's inner sanctum weeks ago. 'I have come to collect my wife.'

The witch glanced at the big clock on the wall. 'I am afraid that she is busy with the master cabinetmaker for at least the next hour and cannot be disturbed, so if you would care to take a seat, she will be out by five as usual when her day ends.' The woman gestured to the bench opposite her huge desk that blocked the outside world and the door to Gwen's. 'I shall let Miss Trym—'

'She is Mrs Mayhew now.' He enjoyed the way the

officious harridan's eyes widened as he skirted around her desk and grabbed the sacred door handle. 'Husbands, I think you will find, can disturb their wives whenever they please.'

He darted in before she could stop him and was met with a waft of a combination of sawdust and polish as he gazed around the wide-open but busy space that was the Trym workshop. At least forty men beavered away at as many benches on different pieces of furniture in varying degrees of completion. Over in one corner, framed by racks filled with heavy bolts of fabric, a team of upholsterers finished them off, hammering tacks in what appeared to be perfect unison.

'Sir—' The blasted secretary grabbed his arm firmly before he could go any further. 'I must insist that you accompany me outside until *Mrs Mayhew* is finished with her meeting.'

'Well,' he said with a slightly bemused glare at where her fingers bit into his bicep. 'You can try and stop me if you want to but I really don't fancy your chances.' The woman blinked at that but still maintained her grip. 'Or you can unhand me and walk beside me if you insist on being my chaperone?' When the woman still did not let go, he shot her his cheekiest grin as he danced on the spot like a boxer to test her mettle and her patience while she continued to hold on to his sleeve for grim death. 'Or we can fight. I've never wrestled with a woman before, but I am certainly game if you are.'

She released him, affronted, and scurried forward in what he assumed was Gwen's direction, so he followed. As he turned into a cavernous side room, there she was. Standing facing away from him in the centre of a circle of chairs with a grey-haired man in a brown leather apron. One hand on her hip, the other tapping her chin as if she was in the middle of pondering something of great importance and looking more lovely in her no-nonsense beige dress and apron than anyone had a right to.

It was fascinating seeing her in her element and he could have surreptitiously watched her for hours because he wanted to know everything about her, but sadly that was not to be today.

'Miss Trym!' shrieked the annoying secretary. 'I told this gentleman he needed to wait outside but—'

As his wife turned her mouth opened in an O of surprise and, rather charmingly, she instantly began to blush. 'Adam!'

'Hello, Gwen.' To irritate the secretary and because he wanted to, he strode into the centre of the circle and planted a kiss upon his delightfully flummoxed wife's cheek.

'What are you doing here so early?'

'I misread my pocket watch.' It was on the tip of his tongue to tell her that he had been in Newgate, because he was dying to share that with her, but he stopped himself in the nick of time. The least said about his soon-to-be aborted dream of practicing law to anyone, the better now that he had found gainful, paid employment. Dreams didn't pay the bills and he was damned if he was going to allow her to—and he had a feeling that she might well offer if she knew his ambitions had always lain elsewhere. 'And I unexpectedly find myself with some time to kill.'

'Oh... Right... Well...' Her gaze wandered to her staring workers who were clearly as intrigued to see him as he was them, and she blushed some more. 'Mr Cobb here and I were just finishing up so I shan't be long.'

'Splendid.' To further irritate the secretary who seemed to think that Gwen had just given him his cue to leave, he jerked his head towards a lone armchair against the wall several yards away. 'I'll wait for you over there. No rush.'

He made himself comfortable, but his presence clearly made his new wife very uncomfortable as she kept glancing back towards him while she continued her meeting with the cabinetmaker. Each time he smiled at her in return, it recharged her blush, so he did his best to look elsewhere after a while to spare her from them. The last thing he wanted to do was anything that made her feel awkward in front of her workers or to give these men anything more to gossip about. He knew how hard it was to earn the respect of your subordinates, and it was clear Gwen had definitely done that. Adam also recognised how hard it was for a woman to succeed in a man's world. In the traditional run of things, what was hers would have automatically become his the second they had married and husbands tended to take over. Everyone here would know that, and he did not want anyone to think that it was his intention to ever undermine or usurp her.

Instead, he amused himself with some recognisance to better understand the lay of the land, noticing first of all that every single employee here wore decent sturdy boots. He had seen enough poverty in his time both here in London and on the campaign trail to appreciate what that meant. Shoes were for a huge swath of the population a nice-to-have and not a need-to-have, which suggested that either Gwen supplied them with suitable footwear or paid them enough that they could afford it. Similarly, although practical and dusty from the work being done, nobody was wearing rags. There were also several apprentices dotted around the place assisting the obvious craftsmen. Boys of no younger than fourteen, he'd estimate, and all looking supremely well fed, which told Adam that his wife did not put profits over people or use child labour to cut down her manufacturing costs. The many tin mugs dotted around the room also told him that these men were regularly watered while they worked. Telling details about her character that warmed his heart.

There was another big clock on the wall and when it struck five, a one-armed man in a brown overall came out and blew a whistle. That was clearly the signal for the end of the working day for the Trym Furniture Company's employees as they began to wind up whatever they were doing and put away their tools while the apprentices ran wide brooms over the floor. Nobody, he noted, rushed out, which suggested these men not only took pride in their work but that they respected their employer enough to do their best by her. When they did leave, they did so cheerily, doffing their caps to him as they passed. Filing out chatting and smiling with a spring in their steps rather than trudging away worn out and worn down—and that spoke volumes too. This was an excellent place to work and Gwen was an exemplary employer. A discovery that made Adam doubly proud of her. She cared about people and gave something back. Just like his mentor Sir Thomas Lenthall.

Just like he always intended to.

Another ten minutes ticked by and finally, her meeting with the master cabinetmaker ended, and she came towards him almost shyly. 'Sorry that took so long.'

'I really didn't mind waiting. Besides, I've been dying to see inside this place you adore so much, so it has given me a good excuse to nose around and see what I think of it.' Which was true.

'Really?' Her dark brows furrowed. 'What is your verdict?'

Buoyed that she had even asked he grinned. 'I am impressed.' Her ready smile told him that she cared about his conclusions and that pleased him immensely. 'You not only make fine furniture, but you obviously treat and pay your staff very well.'

That he had chosen that as the first thing to comment upon clearly surprised her but she brushed her achievement away. 'Trym's deals in quality and so hires only the best craftsmen, so we like to keep them.'

'I know the "we" in that sentence means you.'

Again, she diverted the credit elsewhere. 'My father started off as an apprentice cabinetmaker and the dreadful way he was treated by his master ensured that he was never going to replicate those mistakes when he set up his own shop. In truth, it makes sound business sense to keep our workers happy. They are fiercely loyal and take pride in what they do. And, as a result, will always step up and do more when occasional needs must.'

'How did your foreman lose his arm?'

As he had hoped, his quick pivot resulted in a gloriously honest answer. 'A brewery cart overturned and he got crushed by all the falling barrels.' She flicked her hand unconsciously towards the door. 'Poor Tom broke several ribs too and was in a bad way for quite some time.'

'Recently?'

'Two years ago.' So under her watch. 'It is a shame because he used to be such an excellent carpenter.' And now he was her foreman. Still employed despite his disability and despite his unfortunate accident being nothing to do with Trym's.

'I should imagine it is impossible to be a carpenter with only one arm.'

'It is but he is still an excellent teacher and runs a very tight ship here, so I wouldn't be without him.'

Adam slanted her a knowing glance. 'Your workers are apparently not the only ones who are fiercely loyal.' Then nudged her playfully. 'I always knew you had a soft heart beneath your businesslike exterior.'

That he knew that clearly bothered her, so before she could dismiss that too he pivoted again. 'What are all these chairs for?' He wandered towards the circle she had been discussing so intently with her master cabinetmaker. 'And why do none of them match?'

'Because they are samples of some of the new designs we might carry when the shop in Piccadilly opens its doors.'

'Already? I thought you said it wouldn't be until the end of next summer when your shop opens? The renovations on the building haven't even started yet.'

'True—but it will be a big shop and so will need a

great deal of furniture to fill it. All of which has to be made in tandem with all the orders from the existing business which still need fulfilling. We also need to ensure that we have all the wood and fabric in stock in plenty of time too as it would be foolhardy to try to sell a customer something that would take forever for us to fulfil.' That she constantly referred to Trym's as 'we' suggested she thought of it like a family. A collective rather than a reflection of herself, and yet to him it was obvious that it was both. Gwen's practical, detailed and clever hand was evident in every single part of this workshop. 'Therefore, it makes sense to do all the testing well in advance and if we can compare a bunch of similar designs altogether all the better.' She gestured to the circle. 'Hence this group of mismatched chairs. Now that we've made a sample of each of the prospective new designs, we have spent the last hour separating the wheat from the chaff.'

'Aesthetically, you mean?'

'And practically. A chair is meant to be sat on, after all, and not just looked at. The whole point of opening the shop in the first place is so that people can try before they buy.' She offered him a slightly less awkward smile. 'I'd value your opinion too, if you'd care to try them.'

'Are you sure? I know nothing whatsoever about furniture.'

'But you know what feels comfortable and it might

be useful to know how comfortable these are for...'
She flapped her hand up the length of him. 'A man
of your size.'

'I am an exceptional physical specimen, I know.'
Touched that she had asked him, Adam took his time
trying each chair and then arranging them into groups
while she watched him with bemused folded arms.

When he finally stepped back with his own arms
folded, hers went back to her hips. 'Well?'

'This is the wheat.' He pointed towards his three favourites then frowned at the four he now loathed. 'And
those are the chaff. The other five fall in the middle.'

'The middle being neither underwhelming nor overwhelming?'

'Indeed. They are whelming, if whelming is actually a word.'

'Why did you pick those three as the best?' She
asked that while pulling her little notebook out of
her apron pocket, ready to jot down his response and
that tickled him. It was such a *Gwen* thing to do as
clearly that blasted book went everywhere with her.
He wouldn't have minded taking a peek at it too, as he
knew it would tell him so much more about the way
her brilliant mind worked, but he knew she wouldn't
allow that. At least not yet while some of her walls
were still standing.

'Well, if we are being all official...' He glared at
her book. 'I decided to take your advice literally. A

chair is meant to be sat on, after all, so I put comfort over the aesthetics. I rested most easily in these three but do not necessarily think them the most attractive.'

She ran her fingers over one of them, a pretty straight-backed affair with scrolled and padded arms that he had consigned to his chaff pile. 'I am surprised you did not like this one. It is both elegant and simple and very well-padded—informally formal. The high back and deep armrests were designed with relaxation in mind and I found it tremendously comfortable. Did you not?'

'Perhaps I might have if I were your delectable shape and size.' He wiggled his brows suggestively because he knew his flirting always flummoxed her. 'But I prefer my elbows not to be set at a rigid ninety degrees to my body and my knees to be further away from my chin when I relax. I'd probably adore it if it was around a foot bigger in all directions.'

'Interesting,' she said, jotting that down. 'Perhaps we could offer it in different sizes? Make it thoroughly bespoke in all ways.' As she seemed to be talking more for her notebook than for him, he let her ramble, enjoying watching her be the quality furniture goddess that she was as she scribbled furiously in her increasingly intriguing little book. 'We've never done that before—but it is an interesting concept. Small, medium and freakishly cumbersome...' Her gaze lifted to his, her dark eyes dancing and she grinned. 'Like you.'

He liked playful Gwen and was seeing her more and more. 'We both know that you mean irresistibly handsome.' He winked at her, chuckling at her answering eye roll. 'Are you ready to go? Only Abigail has given us strict instructions to be home by six so that we look resplendent for the soirée later and time is a ticking.' He jerked his head towards the giant clock. 'You know what she's like. If we are late, we'll have to go to the dratted affair without any supper and I am too freakishly cumbersome to survive on canapés alone. This fine physique needs its meat and potatoes or else I shall wither away.'

She giggled before she pulled a face. 'All these parties are so exhausting! Do the ton ever do anything other than socialise? I am struggling to keep up.'

'That is because the ton sleep till noon, and you always get up with the lark.' He waggled his arm and, without thinking, she took it and hugged it close. 'But let us quietly agree between us to leave after an hour because I am sick and tired of socialising too. I could do with an early night.' Preferably cuddled up with her as the soft press of her delectable bosom against his bicep was giving his body ideas. 'As I am sure you could too.' If his rudimentary understanding of the mysteries of a woman's courses were correct, hers should be done now and that meant that they could get back to physical intimacy again. Something he was looking forward to immensely. Especially as he planned to use it to flummox her even more now that flummoxing his lovely wife was his new mission.

'I like that plan.'

'I am glad.' There was already a twitch in his breeches at the prospect of tonight. Only this time, rather than being consumed with the merely physical passion they had always had for one another, he was determined to make proper love to her. Show her, in no uncertain terms with his body, all the feelings that were developing hard and fast in his heart. If these last five days of flummoxing Gwen had taught him anything, it was that he really, really liked his wife. She was clever. She was witty. She was obviously big-hearted. She was special and he wanted not just more of her but all of her. Not just her body but her heart and soul. And her love. It might well be tempting fate a step too far after it had already given him more than enough but he really wanted that. Especially seeing as he was falling more and more in love with her.

She gathered her belongings and they made their way to her waiting carriage. No sooner had it made the short trip onto Holborn than with an ominous rumble of thunder, the heavens opened. In no time, the carriage slowed to a snail's pace as the roads became instantly clogged, as they were always prone to do when bad weather brought out the worst in the city.

All around them, street vendors and pedestrians got in the way of the horses in their hurry to escape the rain which was coming down in sheets that pummelled the carriage's windows so hard they vibrated.

'This isn't good,' said Gwen stating the obvious. 'Our chances of making it back to Hereford Street in the next half an hour to appease Abigail are slim.'

Adam wiped a peephole in the rapidly gathering condensation to survey the carnage in time to witness a bright flash of lightning closely followed by a clap of thunder so loud that the windows of the carriage actually rattled. 'I would say they are non-existent.' He let out a pathetic sigh. 'I am clearly doomed to survive on just canapés alone tonight.'

'I am afraid it looks that way.' She squeezed his hand in sympathy and left it resting atop his. 'I would suggest that it would be quicker to walk but I don't fancy being a drowned rat and I dare say Abigail and my maid would not thank me for turning up like that when it already takes forever to make me look *resplendent*.'

Her unconscious touch wasn't helping with the situation inside his breeches as it was giving his body even more ideas. 'We are just going to have to sit it out and hope this storm passes quickly.' Although...

Phillip had stated that some of his best passionate encounters with his wife had been in a carriage and if they were going to be stuck in this one for a while, some passion might be the perfect way to pass the time. Gwen and he had never been intimate in the daylight before. Their bodies had only ever found oblivion in the ethereal anonymity of the night-time. Closely followed by the all-encompassing oblivion of sleep which gave them—and by them he meant Gwen—some distance between the act and the aftermath to reinstate the barricades by escaping.

Yet now, if they were intimate, they would have to coexist in that aftermath and he would be able to do everything in his power to distract her from shutting him out. Better still, he could prolong it. Eke out the pleasure by reminding her of it in both his words and his deeds each time he had her alone at the soirée. In the bedchamber, when her wits were suitably scrambled with lust, Gwen always liked it when he told her exactly what he was going to do to her just before he did it. So why not use that tonight? Thoroughly seduce her again by finding every quiet opportunity he could to remind her of all the sinful things he had done to bring her to completion in this carriage so that neither of them would be able to wait to reenact it all over again at bedtime. An idea that made him instantly as hard as a rock.

But would she allow him to seduce her now? That was the problem.

As if the universe was on his side for once, the next

clap of thunder rattled the entire carriage which then shuddered to a stop.

'There is fat chance of this storm passing quickly.' She huffed. 'We could be stuck here for an hour. Possibly two.' Which was music to Adam's ears. 'If I'd known that before I left the warehouse, I could have stayed there and done some work. It is not as if I do not have enough of it. This is a complete waste of my time.'

'It doesn't have to be.' When opportunity knocked, he was a firm believer in welcoming it in and an hour or two to make love to his beautiful wife was too good an opportunity to miss. So he leaned closer and nuzzled her ear. 'We could use it productively to make that baby you want by next spring.'

She sat back, shocked and very definitely flummoxed by that suggestion. 'Adam! We are in the middle of the city! In broad daylight!'

'And?'

'And it wouldn't be proper.'

'But it would be fun,' he said leaning back in and nibbling her neck. 'And thrilling and, oh, so naughty.' He allowed his teeth to tug on her earlobe, a place that was particularly sensitive. 'Wouldn't you like to be naughty with me?' As he knew it would, her neck arched, so he pressed his advantage and kissed his way along her jaw, gathering her closer as he did so.

'It seems like forever since I was last inside you and I am *yearning*.'

'No.' It was the most half-hearted no he had ever heard, especially as her neck had arched some more to give him better access to the sensitive spot where her pulse beat beneath his lips. 'Later.'

'Just a little kiss then?' Gwen was a huge fan of kissing and he was a huge fan of kissing her. 'To at least tide me over till later.'

'Just a little one.' Her mouth softened and parted in invitation and she sighed as his lips whispered over hers.

'I adore kissing you.' He deepened it and, as he had hoped her fingers curled around his lapels to pull him closer. 'Have you missed this?'

'Yes.' Her whispered admission spurred him on and he kissed her some more.

It was Gwen's tongue that sought his first and he revelled in that. Revelled more as she moaned into his mouth when his hand cupped her breast and his thumb massaged the already straining tip. God but he adored her breasts. Adored the way she pressed them into his palms as her passions built. Adored more that she was such a passionate and sensual creature and that he had been the one to unlock that side of her.

'I want you so badly.' To prove that he hauled her into his lap so that she could feel the insistent bulge she had put there. 'I want to be inside you. I want to fill you. I want to take us both to heaven right now.'

'We can't,' she mumbled between fevered kisses. 'Someone will see.'

'The windows are so steamed up already nobody will be able to see a thing and they will only get steamier as things progress.' He slipped his hand beneath her petticoats to caress her stockinged thighs. 'Open your legs for me, Gwen. Let me pleasure you.'

'We shouldn't...' But she was already complying with his request, her breath coming in short, choppy puffs as she offered him a guilty and delightfully shy smile.

'But you clearly want me to.' He gently slid his hand higher until it rested by the already damp curls at the apex of her thighs. 'Don't you?'

'*Yes.*'

She whimpered as he dipped his finger between her slick folds, her whole body softening in anticipation and then immediately stiffening as he found the sensitive bud of nerves within that they both needed him to adore. 'Have you missed my touch, Gwen?' He traced lazy circles around it with his index finger and she nodded, biting down on her bottom lip as her eyelids fluttered closed. 'Do you want me to stop?' She shook her head and then sunk back into his arms with a shiver when he slipped his finger inside her, arching her hips against the heel of his hand eagerly in search of her climax.

He brought her close but to torture her, not close enough, taking it in turns to caress her and kiss her and thoroughly enjoying the way all her inhibitions melted as she bucked and writhed in his arms.

'Please, Adam!'

He hooked one of her breasts out of her bodice and sucked the puckered tip into his mouth. 'I want to make proper love to you. I want to be inside you.'

'I want that too.' She undulated against his erection. 'So much.' Then she stared up at him with such longing it took his breath away.

'Then have me,' he said tugging her to sit astride him. 'I am all yours.' Which, he suspected was true in more ways than one. Gwen consumed him and flummoxed him too in equal measure.

Together, they wrestled with the buttons and breeches and shirts, but it was her who hoisted up her skirts when his erection sprang free so that intimate skin touched intimate skin. He kissed her as she guided him inside, moaning as he filled her and making him cry out as she began to move. But when she tried to quicken the pace and bring the madness to the end, he held her hips tight.

'Slowly, love. Torment us both. It's not as if we are in a hurry, are we?'

She glanced at the thoroughly steamy windows as the rain pelted the carriage and smiled. 'I suppose not.'

When she next began to move it was an exercise in the most sublime restraint as she slid her body up and down the length of him. Adam unlaced her bodice and slipped her arms out of it so that he could worship her breasts, and she threw her head back as she rode him so that she could thrust them to and from his mouth. Rotating and lifting her hips until they could both barely stand it.

'Oh, Adam…don't stop.' As her body quickened, she closed her eyes, every inch the temptress as she murmured her pleasure. Watching her like that, in broad daylight, on the cusp of an orgasm and putty in his hands while the rest of the world blurred all around them, was the single most erotic thing he had ever seen.

Then all at once there was no restraint.

No patience.

No pretence.

No shame.

No guilt.

No barriers.

All that mattered was them and this.

'Look at me,' he choked out before it was too late, dragging her head back so that it was level with his. 'I want you to witness what you do to me. I want to see what I do to you.'

He kissed her and when her eyes fluttered closed he tore his mouth away. 'Look at me, Gwen. Let me in.'

On a ragged sigh she nodded and stared into his very soul. All her feelings—all her glorious indecision about him—about them—writ plain. That was all Adam needed for now. It was certainly more than he had ever dared hope for. 'Oh, Gwen...'

When the end came—when they came—it still came as an almighty shock. One that left them both panting and breathless as they collapsed in a heap against one another.

'Oh, my goodness!' She sat back on his knees, her skirts still around her waist along with the bodice of her dress. Oblivious to the fact that she was completely bare-breasted now in the middle of the city in broad daylight. She giggled and they jiggled. 'Oh. My. Goodness.'

'My sentiments exactly.' They smiled soppily at one another, because honestly what else could one do after such a spectacular bout of unabashed and frenzied passion. 'What on earth did I do to deserve such a seductive and passionate wife?'

'You think me seductive *and* passionate?' She seemed both surprised and delighted by that compliment.

'Deliciously so. Why would I not?'

Something odd swirled in her eyes despite her blasé

shrug. 'Because I was convinced that I was quite… frigid—before you.'

No doubt thanks to Bloody Bentley again! But instead of roaring his anger at that fool's clumsy destruction of Gwen's youthful confidence, he decided not to sully this otherwise perfect moment with any mention of the snake and instead gestured to his thoroughly naked chest. 'As a rule, I don't think a frigid woman would rip my clothes off with quite the gusto that you just did.'

'You might have a point there.' She held up her clenched palm to reveal one of the buttons of his waistcoat which she must have torn off in her haste to divest him of it. And she laughed. Properly, joyously, unashamedly laughed. 'You do seem to have lost your shirt.'

He reached over to gently tweak her nipple. 'You also seem to have lost yours, you shameless, beautiful brazen hussy.'

'I am a brazen hussy, aren't I?' She beamed with a combination of pride and wonder before she kissed him. 'With you at least.'

'I adore it.' He almost said that he adored her too but feared that truth might make her panic and withdraw from him. Or dare the universe to snatch her away. 'I adore being naughty and improper with you in broad daylight and right in the middle of the city too.'

That reminder of where they were caused her to

momentarily panic until she saw that the windows were so steamed up that nobody could possibly see through them and flopped back into the seat beside him again like a woman thoroughly sated and happy to be so. 'Do you suppose we are still in Holborn?'

'Hard to tell.' Adam risked rubbing a tiny penny-sized hole in the mist and then panicked himself when he realised that not only had the storm stopped, but the roads had cleared. 'Bloody hell, Gwen! We're in Mayfair!'

'We can't be!' She yanked her bodice up and stuffed her breasts inside it as he grabbed his shirt and did his best to shrug it back on in the confined space. A feat that proved almost impossible thanks to the sweat he had just worked up.

'We're just passing Berkeley Square!' Which meant they had less than two minutes to make themselves look presentable before the coachman pulled up outside the house.

A task they had failed miserably by the time the carriage slowed. Gwen's hair resembled a bird's nest, his cravat was a disaster and there was no disguising the fact that his waistcoat couldn't be done up because she had ripped off more than one button—but at least they were both dressed when a footman opened the door.

Fortunately, the footman was too well trained, or too used to seeing his brother and his wife turn up so similarly dishevelled to do more than raise a momentary eyebrow before he welcomed them both home.

But any hopes they had of sneaking into the house and up the stairs before anyone else noticed were shattered when a harried Abigail greeted them at the door. 'What time do you call this! I said six and it's almost seven!' Then, his sister-in-law's mouth hung slack as she realised why they were so late.

'Sorry.' Poor Gwen kept her head down as she scurried past, her face the exact same shade as a beetroot. 'The roads were awful.'

That was when blasted Phillip joined his wife in the hallway, took one look at the pair of them and grinned. 'You'd best go and help Gwen get ready, dearest, as for some inexplicable reason the poor thing looks like she's been dragged through a hedge backwards.' His brother then skewered Adam with a mischievous glare. 'I wonder why?'

'It was quite some storm,' he said, determined to brazen it out as he tried to follow Abigail up the stairs. 'Didn't you hear all the thunder and the wind?'

His brother grabbed the tails of his coat and yanked him back. 'So…' He flicked one of the remaining waistcoat buttons that was hanging by a damning thread. 'I am glad to see that you took my advice and you are now a full carriage convert.' And then the wretch laughed. 'Let us hope that you did a good enough job of it that she will never be able to sit in the damn thing again without thinking scandalously of you.'

Chapter Eighteen

Gwen almost fell off her chair when her secretary knocked on the door and announced the arrival of her solicitor, disgusted at herself for wool-gathering again when she had so many more important things to do.

Although she supposed she could hardly call what she had been doing wool-gathering, more daydreaming about the vexing man she had married who was occupying more and more of her thoughts with every passing day. Things had shifted in their relationship since the Renshaw Ball and they simultaneously called to her, excited her, baffled her and terrified her in equal measure. She wanted to blame the overwhelming lust she had for him and the way he scrambled her mind when they were intimate—which was a lot—but she knew that was dishonest. Because her undeniable and apparently insatiable passion for Adam aside, there was so much more about the time she spent with him that appealed. So much so, that more often than not she forgot to rebuff him when he invaded her privacy—which was often—and undoubtedly looked forward to their time together.

He was, the unpredictable wretch, too funny, too intuitive, too charming, too inquisitive and too damn irresistible to ignore—not that she wanted to most of the time either. And he was so honest as well, in the most unforgivably disarming way, confiding in her private things about himself that made her feel closer to him and, heaven help her, protective of him. Like the causes of his occasional nightmares or his concerns about his brother's health or just that he found being the constant source of public scrutiny as uncomfortable as she did.

Being thrust together near daily wasn't helping her maintain her distance from him either as he was her rock at all the many social occasions that they were dragged to. And my goodness, did he know exactly how to seduce her and often at the most inconvenient times. In the week since their scandalous behaviour in her carriage, thanks to the persistent rainy weather blighting London, he had had his wicked way with her twice in it since. Twice more when he had found a clandestine spot for them to sneak off to at the evening soirées they had attended since too and, despite her best efforts to leave his bed each night after he had fallen asleep, he had taken to wandering through their connecting door naked and aroused. Almost as if he knew that she only had to see him like that and she became aroused too. Thanks to him, she had been fifteen minutes late to her first meeting this morning and even the memory of the sinfully good things he had done to her body before breakfast made her skin instantly heat.

The wretch!

Worse, it was becoming increasingly obvious that she wasn't just falling for him—she had already fallen. And likely hard. She knew the symptoms and all this wool-gathering was definitely one of them. Which was why she found herself constantly questioning and re-evaluating her initial plan and was seriously considering giving their marriage a proper go.

His fault.

Not only was she thoroughly enjoying being married to him, that casual mention of children—plural—had started her contemplating what she had never thought she ever would again with a man.

Forever.

'Good afternoon, Mrs Mayhew.'

'Good afternoon, Mr Collins.' She gestured for her solicitor to sit in the chair opposite her desk, oddly peeved that he was interrupting her obsessive contemplation of Adam. 'I trust you are well.'

'Indeed I am, although I do not need to ask you how you are as I can see you are positively glowing. Life in Mayfair must suit you.' Thank goodness her solicitor could not read her mind, which was still swimming with carnal images of Adam from this morning!

'It isn't as bad as I thought it would be.' Apart from the awful Lady Arbuthnot, nobody else had cut her. She was more a curiosity than a social pariah but, to her delight, increasingly tolerated which boded well for the business. Even the scandal sheets spoke less of her past scandal and speculated more on her whirlwind romance. 'Society's Sweethearts' had been one of this morning's headlines after their trip to the theatre last night. An article she had already read three times because they kept referring to Adam as 'the madly in love Major' and she had liked that. 'Do you have the finished contracts?'

Mr Collins had been negotiating on her behalf with all the tradesmen who would work on the renovations for Trym's of Piccadilly. Work that was due to start in earnest by the end of June now that the builders had begun to work on the site.

'I do indeed.' He lifted his leather briefcase onto her desk and snapped it open. 'Here are the contracts for the plasterers, the decorators and the glaziers. And some quotes from Hyde's the sign makers. As we suspected, the sheer size of the word Trym that you intend to put on the front in gold leaf is indeed a fortune and might be better done with gold paint instead.'

'No,' she said, shaking her head. 'It must match what we have here, and gold leaf screams the quality and luxury that this company is famous for, so we shall have to swallow the cost for the exterior. I expect the smaller door signs to be in gold leaf too. I will not scrimp on the customer's first view of Trym's. I want that name to dominate Piccadilly.' She smiled at him as she knew he only had her best interests at heart. Mr Collins had known her since she was a child and had been the family's solicitor ever since her father had started this business. 'We shall be competing with Mr Fortnum and Mr Mason's iconic Eau de Nil woodwork, after all.'

'I knew you were going to say that.'

'Will you stay for tea, Mr Collins?' Despite it being almost five and time to leave, tonight she was at a loose end. Adam had another meeting at the War Office today and then always had dinner and played cards with his army comrades at White's on a Wednesday, so wasn't escorting her home. He had, of course, offered to forgo his standing appointment to White's to accompany her to the dreary reading salon that Abigail was dragging her to later at the Duchess of Aveley's, but it didn't seem fair to make him suffer that when few gentlemen attended. Especially as Phillip had flatly refused to go.

'Sadly, I cannot.' He snapped his case closed. 'Mrs Collins and I are off to visit our daughter tonight and I am on strict instructions to be home by six or she will have my guts for garters.' He stood and shook her hand. 'Besides, I am sure your husband is itching to see you to tell you about his *exciting* day. It is not every day that one gets to see inside Newgate.'

'Newgate? Why on earth would he go there?'

'I have no clue but I saw him not an hour ago just as I was leaving the Old Bailey. Perhaps he knows one of the prisoners?'

'What sort of man do you think I married, Mr Collins? Adam doesn't know any criminals.' She was pretty certain he would have mentioned it if he did. He was an open book about most things, after all. 'I know for a fact that he had an important meeting in Whitehall today, where he will soon be going to work, so you must have mistaken somebody else for him.'

The solicitor frowned. 'I suppose I could have done but he is pretty unique. What with his height and his penchant for bold silk waistcoats.' Then he shrugged. 'Or perhaps I need to simply wear my spectacles more as Mrs Collins keeps nagging me to? Old age is a cruel mistress.'

He left, and with nothing else to do but head back to Hereford Street ready to be primped for the deathly dull reading salon, Gwen followed suit shortly after.

But the journey home alone felt odd without Adam beside her and she realised, with a start, that she missed talking to him about her day, and so the half-an-hour trip back to Mayfair dragged interminably. Made so much worse because her lust-addled mind kept remembering all of the wicked things he had done to her in this carriage this past week. She'd probably never be able to ride in it again without thinking of him buried deep inside her, the wretch, while she rode him like a wanton jockey on a horse. Or how he had yesterday, in the absence of any condensation on the windows to hide them, dropped to his knees and kissed her between her legs, which, heaven help her, she was quite in the mood for now.

She was in quite a state by the time she got home and any hopes she had harboured of colliding with Adam before he left for the evening so that he could alleviate some of her tension were dashed as the house was quiet. The only person she could find was Phillip, who was reading *The Times* in the drawing room.

'Has Adam gone to White's already?'

'Not that I know of.' Phillip looked pale as he dropped his newspaper, although she knew better than to mention it. He was a stoic, cheerful sort who preferred not to dwell on his illness and she admired that about him. 'He's not returned from Whitehall yet.'

'Really? His meeting there was supposed to start at ten.'

Phillip grunted. 'Knowing the War Office they've probably already put him to work and will expect him to do it unpaid. They like to have their pound of flesh and clearly haven't had enough of Adam's.'

It was obvious he did not approve of his brother

working there. Or perhaps of him working at all when Adam would, inevitably, inherit Phillip's viscountcy. 'Do you think pursuing a non-aristocratic career is beneath him?'

Phillip scowled, affronted. 'Of course not! But—' He sighed. 'He shouldn't go back to the military, Gwen. Not even from behind the safety of a desk in Whitehall. He loathed it. Loathed the idiocy of the top brass more.'

'He did?' This was news to her.

'When you have seen as much senseless and violent death as Adam has, it is hard to move on. But he has. At least as much as a man can who has been damaged by war. I know he can be irreverent and always tries to make the best of things but I also know how thoroughly he takes things to heart. Strategizing for the War Office will play on his mind as much as the events he endured at the front will. If he has to send other young men into battle and they don't come back, it will destroy him. Please talk him out of that job!'

'But he's looking forward to that job.'

'Did you not know that he previously turned it down flat?'

'He turned it down?' Adam hadn't mentioned that.

'Said he could think of nothing more abhorrent than working for the enemy—because after six years of their incompetence he very much considered the War Office the enemy. I am certain he still does. You never saw him when he first returned, Gwen, so could not possibly have any concept of how haunted his eyes were or how horrendous his nightmares were, or how much every single death he witnessed still plays on his mind.'

'Like he feels guilty for not being in the ground with them.'

'He does! He shouldn't but he does.' Phillip's obvious distress worried her. 'That is why I need you to talk him out of that job, Gwen. There are hundreds of other things he could do to earn a living and still keep his pride intact. He has a brilliant mind. Excelled at university. Even had a pupillage lined up at one of the best legal firms in the country and would doubtless be the very best lawyer in the land at this precise moment if our idiot of a father hadn't sabotaged his chances and pushed him into that uniform. My brother was never meant to be a soldier and he is worth so much more than the War Office!'

'I shall talk to him about it.'

Phillip slumped in relief. 'Thank you. I cannot tell you what a weight off my mind that is. My little brother is as stubborn as he is proud and he refuses to listen to me and believe me, I have begged him to turn that position down again for weeks.'

'This is the first I have heard of that.' But then this was the first she had heard of Adam previously turning down the Whitehall job too, so clearly her vexing husband was keeping secrets from her and that annoyed her.

She left Phillip and climbed the stairs, expecting her bedchamber to be empty, but rather serendipitously, Adam was in it. Staring out the window.

'I am glad you are home.' And she was. Her mind was whirring and, as irritated that she was that her husband hadn't been completely honest with her, she did not want him to take the Whitehall job if Phillip was right. 'We need to talk.'

'I'll say we do,' he said in an uncharacteristically clipped tone as he turned around, and then to her horror, tossed her notebook on the bed between them, his handsome face a mask of hurt and fury. 'For I am intrigued to know the exact day that you plan to leave me and our apparent sham of a marriage behind.'

When Adam had bounded up the stairs, already late for his dinner at White's with his friends, the only thing he had planned to do was change his clothes. The sedate waistcoat he had donned for his meeting at the War Office felt too much like a uniform and he didn't want the reminder of that depressing, soulless place to spoil his evening. But then he had spotted Gwen's little notebook on the floor of their dressing room and hadn't been able to stop himself from taking a peek inside. Although now he wished he hadn't.

By the way his manipulative and lying wife's face paled, she did too.

'Adam... I...'

'At least I now know why you were so insistent on that blasted clause just in case the marriage broke down and why you apparently needed so much bloody time and space!' Bile rose in his throat as he realised what a total fool he had been. That would teach him, he supposed, for wanting more from the universe when it had already granted so blasted much. But to make him fall head over heels in love, to give him false hope to dream, then to snatch it all so cruelly away seemed like the worst sort of punishment. A callous way to remind him that his reservoir of good luck was well and truly empty.

'It's not what you think.' Although even she could not disguise that it actually very much was what he thought. Her expression was pained and she couldn't meet his eyes.

'Then tell me exactly what I should think about this—' He snatched the notebook from the mattress and opened it to the most damning page. '"*Specific Criteria for My Prospective Husband.*"' As he read the title of her lovely little list aloud, she winced.

'That was when—' He cut her off with a raised palm.

'"Number one—He must be of noble birth or have connections impressive enough or useful enough to

Trym's to compensate for his lack of title. Number two—A fortune-hunter."' Adam supposed he fitted that specification perfectly but it still hurt to read it. '"Number three"—and this is *so* very flattering— "All show and no substance (preferably brainless)."'

'I wrote those things before I met you!' She spread her hands placating.

'And then you met me,' he ground out, utterly humiliated and totally defeated. 'And then fortunately I clearly matched number four because you proposed immediately.' He jabbed the pertinent point in the notebook. '"A fine, *fertile* physical specimen with good teeth, preferably under the age of forty."' Adam felt used. Dirty. 'Congratulations on purchasing such a fine and brainless stud for hire.'

'I never once thought you brainless and I told you I wanted a child from the outset.' Clearly, she was keen to defend the indefensible.

'You did indeed. However, you neglected to mention before we took our vows that you never intended to honour them!' Bloody hell but he was an idiot! All this time he had wasted trying to be understanding. Trying to woo her. Falling in love with her and doing his level best to make her fall in love with him too. 'Or did you forget number bloody five?'

'Adam, please...' She touched his arm and he yanked it away.

'"Number five"—and this is my absolute favourite—"A man who preferably has a wandering eye or some other *unsavoury* hobby which would ensure ample excuse to insist upon a quiet separation once he ceases being useful (hopefully within three to four months)."' He jabbed the book again, disgusted at the implication and the short timeline. 'Three to four bloody months!'

He was merely a slot in her busy diary.

A task.

An appointment.

One she was eager to get over and done with so that she could move on with her life without him in it.

'I thought I wanted—'

He cut off her comment with a raised palm, not wanting to hear her lame excuses when his poor heart was bleeding from her calculated betrayal. 'It's such a pity, isn't it, now that the ton seem inclined to forgive you for your trespasses, that I failed to impregnate you in a timely manner, or you could be gone now. *Isn't it?*' He flung the horrid little book on the floor between them. 'But there was one major flaw in your plan, Gwendolyn—you forgot to specify in either your notebook or our watertight marriage contract that you needed a husband who was good at following orders—and I am not!' He strode to the door, too disgusted with her and himself to be able to stand being in the same room with her a moment longer. 'Forget the baby, Gwen. I can no longer bear to so much as look at you, so I can assure you that fornicating is now well and truly out of the question!'

Chapter Nineteen

Adam stayed at Hawk's that night.

Ironically, he had needed some time and some space to work out what to do. The heartbroken, wronged and petulant side of him wanted to tell her to pack her bags and get out of his life now that he had served her purpose. But the pathetic, hopelessly in love part of him wanted to beg her to reconsider. To give him a chance to prove that their marriage could work if she would only allow it. His pride, his principles and that blasted twenty thousand she had paid him to marry her were an albatross around his neck and he had entered into the marriage knowing that she had paid it to get her reputation restored. It wasn't fully yet and the frustrated lawyer in him was obligated to fulfil that part of their verbal agreement despite it not being enshrined in ink.

The child part of that agreement, however, she would have to forgo. Aside from the fact that he refused to make love to a lying witch who had never had any intentions of ever loving him back, he could not consciously bring a son or daughter into the world and not be an intrinsic part of their lives. How could he be the father his offspring deserved if he and his disingenuous wife lived under separate roofs? Unless, of course, they had already made one during their copious fornication sessions in this last week. Sessions he had instigated because he had been too optimistic, too happy and too romantically involved with her that he had been blind to the truth.

Well, the scales had certainly fallen from his eyes now!

Not that the knowledge gave him the power to not feel totally wretched about it all. His poor, battered heart felt like a ball that had been kicked around and he was dreading seeing her again.

'The prodigal brother returns!' Already dressed and waiting for tonight's hideous social obligation, Phillip greeted him in the hallway with a stern expression. 'Where the bloody hell have you been? We are supposed to leave in fifteen minutes! Abigail has been frantic and your poor wife has been worried sick about you!'

He sincerely doubted that. If Gwen was worried about anything, it was having her carefully laid plans thwarted. 'I've had things to do.' Moping mostly. 'But don't worry, I'll still be ready on time.'

Adam headed to the stairs without stopping. He

didn't need a lecture and he certainly didn't need any more marital advice. He was halfway up them when his duplicitous wife appeared on the landing with Abigail.

Her step faltered when she saw him and she swallowed at the intensity of his steely gaze. But thankfully, she said nothing. What was there to say? They were done and that was that. The sooner they both accepted that, the better all round.

'There you are!' Abigail's hands went to her hips. 'How dare you disappear without a trace for twenty-four hours and then turn up like a bad penny! We've all been worried sick!'

'I am not a child,' he muttered barging past. 'And do not require anyone's permission to go out.'

'Out, yes—but out all night! What on earth have you been doing?'

'Can we discuss that later? I need to change.' He slammed into his bedchamber and leaned against the door. He supposed he did owe Abigail and his brother an apology and he would be sure to give them one in private, but his wife could go to hell as far as he was concerned. Just as soon as the hurt subsided and he stopped caring. Or noticing that she looked so pale and tired and…as wretched as he did.

He stalked to the dressing room and tried not to notice all her gowns hanging next to his coats, grabbed the first outfit that came to hand and donned it quickly.

Then, his shoulders steeled, headed downstairs where the three of them waited silently for him.

'Shall we?' He gestured to the door rather than offer his arm, forcing her to leave without him. Her step faltered again when she realised that he had dismissed her carriage because there was not a cat's chance in hell that he was going to suffer being alone with her. But she pretended to take it in her stride as his brother helped the ladies inside, glaring at him as he heaved himself in.

Sensing things weren't right with the newlyweds, his brother and Abigail did their best to fill the tense, awkward silence of the journey but Adam was content to let it hang, so did not engage in any small talk. It was impossible to clear the air anyway. He could cope with living the public lie he had agreed to, but he was damned if he was going to do that in private!

He briefly lent her his arm as they entered the ballroom and extracted it as soon as he could. Then they stood as a tense quartet around the refreshment table. Abigail and Phillip exchanged awkward pleasantries while Gwen and he sipped uncomfortable drinks in stony silence. He knew they all expected him to dance with her, because that was what the supposed sweethearts of society always did, but he couldn't. Holding her in his arms would just be too painful. Especially as the last time he had done it he had been convinced that she was finally letting him in.

Idiot!

'Adam—Gwen... Have you met Lord and Lady Talbot?' Abigail's voice interrupted his self-pity and, for appearances' sake, he pasted on a polite smile.

'It is a pleasure to meet you.'

Refusing to allow him to leave it at that, Abigail decided to drag him kicking and screaming into an unwanted conversation by threading her arm through his to stop any escape. 'How are you both? It has been ages since we've seen you.' For some reason there was sympathy in his sister-in-law's eyes. 'Obviously, we heard the news.'

'We've been at our country estate since it happened,' said Lord Talbot. 'A thing like that puts one right off London.'

As Abigail could tell that Adam's mind was already wandering back to his own problems, she nudged him. 'Lord and Lady Talbot were robbed. At gunpoint. By the *Scourge of the Great Western Road*.'

That snapped him to attention. 'Really?' He searched his mind for the list of victims, trying to match this pair with the reams and reams of witness testimony that he had waded through. 'That must have been dreadful.' *Talbot... Talbot?* Why did that name sound particularly familiar. 'Did he get away with much?'

'My wife's emeralds. Five sovereigns. My signet ring.' Lord Talbot began to recall all the highwayman had taken and that was when Adam had an epiphany. Lady Octavia Talbot was the one who had been kissed so violently by the brute that she had been left bruised and covered in whisker burns that had lasted for days!

He slanted a glance at Lady Talbot and something didn't quite ring true. The Scourge only took advantage of exceedingly pretty young ladies and while the woman before him was reasonably handsome, she had to be pushing sixty.

'He also took my daughter's pearls,' continued Lord Talbot. 'Ripped them clean from her neck while he held his pistol to my temple.'

'You have a daughter?'

'We have five—but only Octavia, our youngest, was with us that fateful night.' Lady Talbot gestured to an exceedingly pretty young lady who was dancing. One Adam suddenly needed to meet.

There were only six women on the planet who could attest to the roughness of the Scourge's thick whiskers and not one of them had yet answered his letters requesting them to testify in court.

Adam, in his determined quest to make her suffer, had abandoned her for the Talbots. Or more particularly, the very pretty Miss Octavia Talbot who he was currently waltzing with in her stead. She knew she had no right to feel aggrieved by that slight given what he had read, and accepted that she probably deserved this awful stint in Purgatory as penance for writing those awful words, but she was still desperate to talk to the wretch and properly apologise.

She even had a speech worked out. One she was dreading because it required her to lay her bludgeoned, wary heart bare to him while she begged his forgiveness and admitted that she had tried her best not to fall in love with him because love scared her so. But—as she had learned quickly the second he'd rejected her last night—that ship had already sailed.

She loved him.

Wholly and completely and she needed him to know that whatever her stupid plan had been, there was no way that she could ever leave him now.

If the last month with him had taught her anything, apart from how to love again and how lovely making love to the right man was, it was that she had built up all her defences to deter another cheating scoundrel like Bentley. In doing so, she had tarred every man with the same brush. Except the man she had married could not be less like that libertine if he tried. Adam wasn't cruel or greedy or selfish. He was kind and thoughtful. Noble and genuine and did not possess any of the hideous character traits that she had believed he would.

That was why, against her character, she was going to eat a large slice of humble pie. Hell, she would even beg if that was what he needed! Because she needed him. Needed him like she needed air and water and did not want to ever have to spend another day without him.

She waited from a quiet corner for the waltz to end, determined to intercept her sulking, wounded husband before he could avoid her again, drag him somewhere private and have it out with him. Watched him kiss Lady Olivia's hand. Watched him then lean close and whisper something in her ear. Watched her nod. And then he was off like a shot, walking with such purpose she could barely keep up.

When he reached the French doors, he shot a surreptitious look around and then slipped through onto the terrace. Knowing that would be the perfect place for Gwen to issue her grovelling apology, she followed. And was barely twenty feet away from that door when Lady Octavia suddenly approached it from the other side. Just like Adam, his much-too-pretty dancing partner gave a quick, furtive look around and then followed him outside.

Surely not for a tryst?

He was too decent. Too kind. Too noble for that sort of revenge. Surely?

As much as Gwen wanted to dismiss her worst fears, the entrenched doubts wrought from bitter experience crept in. Because it wouldn't be the first time she had been hoodwinked by a charmer and one of the reasons she had picked Adam was because of his reputation as a flirt.

Unwanted images flooded her mind. Of Adam buried to the hilt inside the pretty woman he had sneaked outside with. Of them laughing at her while they did the deed.

The frigid milksop with all the money.

But he would not do that, surely? Not Adam. No matter how angry he was.

She was being stupid. Cynical. Allowing her past to taint her present—which was exactly what had caused her rift with Adam in the first place. Determined to trust him even though trust had never come easily to her, Gwen tried to banish those unhelpful suspicions but the fear still curdled in her belly as she followed them outside. But even after three laps of the garden, she never found them and somehow that only made her irrational fears much worse.

When he finally did return to the ballroom an hour later, his eyes kept wandering to Lady Octavia. So many times that her paranoia increased, then ran wild when he failed to return with them in the carriage.

Then failed to come home at all for the second night in a row.

Chapter Twenty

'The Mayhew men are complex creatures, Gwen.' To cheer her up, Abigail had dragged her out for a walk in Hyde Park. 'Whenever I put Phillip in a snit, he likes to go off somewhere to wallow in a vat of self-righteous self-pity. Granted, he usually takes himself no further than his study, but he is just as infuriating and intractable as his brother and flatly refuses to be apologised to. But he will come around.'

'Will he? Adam has made it impossible to apologise to him and as each day passes I am coming to think that he doesn't want me to.' She hadn't seen hide nor hair of him now for five days. 'Perhaps I just need to accept that this is the end and things are unrepairable.'

'Or perhaps, in his own, idiotic way, he is trying to teach you that absence makes the heart grow fonder?' Her friend's smile was weak. 'Or maybe he just needs a bit more time to lick his wounds before he is ready to listen to any reason. It was quite an awful list to be confronted with, wasn't it?'

Gwen nodded. In desperation and at her wits' end, she had confessed almost all to Abigail days ago, which had included divulging the contents of the awful list. The ridiculous, regrettable, unforgivable list that she should have burned straight after her wedding night. 'I just wish he would give me the chance to explain.'

She had not appraised Abigail fully of the rationale behind it. The scars left by Bentley and the "frigid milksop with all the money" moment ran too deep to expose, even to a friend. But she recognised her husband deserved to hear the truth, the whole truth and nothing but the truth if she was ever going to win him back. Yet as necessary a confession as that was, the thought of making herself so vulnerable before him still gave her palpitations.

'He is bound to turn up like a bad penny just before the ball tonight like he did last time and when he does, I'll find some excuse to leave the pair of you alone in the carriage so that you can have a heart-to-heart.'

'I suppose he would have to hear me out then.'

'Indeed—and you get all the fun of making up in it.' Her friend wiggled her brows. 'Wouldn't it be scandalous if the pair of you had to take such a long detour to do that properly that you didn't make it to the ball?' She fanned herself with her hand, making Gwen giggle.

'And how would you explain our absence to the

Marchioness when she is expecting us? Hers was the first personal invitation I have actually received, after all.'

'*Love,*' sighed Abigail. 'Which is surely the very best excuse in the world to do anything reckless.' Then she nudged Gwen with her elbow. 'We both know that you love Adam, despite your silly reluctance to admit it aloud.'

'But what if I've killed any chance of him returning my feelings?' A thought that had plagued her constantly all week. 'What if I have inadvertently pushed him elsewhere?'

'Oh, for goodness' sake! How many times do I have to tell you that he only has eyes for you and that he only waltzed with Lady Octavia to make you jealous?'

'He didn't only waltz with her Abigail, he sneaked out onto the terrace with her too.'

'You are being cynical. You know you are. Because they did not steal away onto the terrace together. They coincidentally and innocently exited the same French doors several minutes apart.'

'Less than two minutes apart.' Perhaps she was cynical but both Adam and the stunning Lady Octavia had looked too furtive before their separate exits for the reason to be as innocent as Abigail believed. 'Isn't not leaving a ballroom together common practice when one is having a tryst?'

'Adam is a charming fellow, but even he could not

charm a woman that fast into having a clandestine tryst on the terrace with him. Or have you forgotten that he had never met the Talbots until ten minutes before he asked their youngest daughter for that dance?'

'Maybe.' Gwen hated herself for her instinctive mistrust and wished she could brush it all away as nonsense like Abigail, but her past experiences kept haunting her. In her lowest moments, usually in the middle of the night while her elusive husband avoided sleeping in his bed, she pictured him intimately entwined with someone else. Seeking solace from his lying, manipulating wife with a woman who would never consider making such an abominable list.

'Definitely.' Abigail threaded her arm through hers and dragged her towards the park gates. 'Why don't we head back and take some extra time to make you look thoroughly ravishing for later so that Adam will have to ravish you when he comes home.'

'*If* he comes home. We don't know where he is, remember?' But in one of those strange and inexplicable twists of fate, no sooner had that comment left her lips than she spied him. Walking with purpose on the street outside the park.

'Talk of the devil and the devil appears.' Abigail grinned. 'Didn't I tell you he would be back today?'

'You did.' But her relief was short-lived as instead of turning onto Hereford Street and his brother's house,

Adam carried along Park Lane, hurried across the Uxbridge Road and disappeared into Portman Street.

Wordless, Gwen and Abigail quickened their pace to follow him, reaching the outer edge of Portman Place just in time to watch him cast an exceedingly furtive glance around before bounding up the stairs of number eighteen. The door instantly opened for him and then closed just as quickly behind him.

'Well...' Abigail was doing a very poor job of disguising her disquiet. 'I am sure there is a perfectly reasonable explanation and that you have absolutely nothing to worry about.'

'Why would I worry about him visiting that house?' But Gwen already was.

Her sister-in-law's attempt at a reassuring smile was brittle. 'Because that just so happens to be the Talbot residence.'

'I am sorry, Major Mayhew, but it is out of the question. I will not allow Octavia to stand in the dock of the Old Bailey!' Lord Talbot's fists were clenched. 'It is bad enough what that scoundrel did to violate my daughter—but she does not need the world to know. She could be ruined on the back of it!'

Adam knew that wasn't the case but he could imagine, if he had a daughter, he would be just as overprotective. 'The world does not need to know that *the Scourge* kissed her. We can skip over that part of her testimony and will not even allude to it during the cross-examination. We will do whatever it takes to ensure that your daughter's honour is not impugned and will have her in and out in a flash, I promise— but I implore you sir. Let her tell the court in person what happened.'

'Octavia's statement should be enough! We were told when she gave it that it was, and now all of a sudden, you want to drag her into court! Why should she be cross-examined when all she has told is the truth?'

'Because a young man's life hangs in the balance—'

'And so it should!' Lord Talbot was pacing the floor of his drawing room while his wife and daughter sat wide-eyed and mute on the sofa. 'He deserves to hang for what he did to her! I'd shoot the blighter myself if they would let me!' Then his finger wagged inches from Adam's face. 'I'm tempted to shoot you too for bringing this to my door! You had no right to approach my daughter with this! None at all!'

Unfortunately, Lord Talbot was partially right.

Although there was no rule that said that a representative of the prosecution could not approach a witness, being six months below the age of majority, they would need her father's written permission for her to take the stand. Despite days of trying via letter, with Lady Octavia's blessing, they still didn't have it. Hence, he was here. Trying to convince the man to give it and doing a very poor job of it.

The finger wagged again. 'I've a good mind to get you disbarred!'

Adam took that threat with the pinch of salt it deserved because to be disbarred, he would have first had to have been called to the bar. Which he hadn't. And never would now but that still did not mean he would not give poor William Briggs' case all the effort it deserved. 'Believe me, Lord Talbot, if the man currently accused of all these heinous crimes is *the Scourge*, he deserves to hang. But what if he isn't? What if they have the wrong man in Newgate? Not only will a gross miscarriage of justice occur when he swings from the Tyburn Tree—but the real crook gets away scot-free and your daughter still does not receive the justice she deserves.'

'Well... I...' Clearly a reasonable man beneath all his protective fatherly bluster, Talbot had no immediate answer to that.

'I would have to carry the guilt of sending the wrong man to the gallows to my grave.' That came from Lady Octavia. 'I do not want that on my conscience, Papa.' Then she smiled at him. 'I should also like the opportunity to look him in the eye if he is the villain. I should like him to know that despite what he did to me, and despite the pistol he held at your head, that he does not frighten us. And I should like to help send the devil to hell—if indeed he is the devil that deserves to go there.'

Adam could not help liking and admiring the Talbots' youngest daughter. She had some steel in her spine and some fire in her belly and, although it pained him to constantly have to make the comparison when he was doing his darndest to forget about the manipulative, lying witch he had married, she reminded him a great deal of Gwen.

'Please, Papa.' Lady Octavia rose and squeezed her father's hand. 'Allow me to do the right thing. It *is* what I want to do.'

The older man's expression softened and he nodded, then turned to Adam again and wagged his finger some more. 'Mark my words, if one mention of that kiss is made in that courtroom, I am coming after you with my gun!'

'Allow me to walk you to the door, Major Mayhew.' Lady Octavia was no fool and knew exactly when a retreat was called for, and Adam was only too glad to follow.

In the privacy of the hallway, he thanked her. 'You are a very brave young lady and I owe you.'

She opened the door and followed him out onto the step. 'I said I would take the stand, Major, because that is the right thing to do. And I shall tell the truth. But I will not attempt to exonerate your Mr Briggs if he is the man who robbed us—and I *will* know immediately if it is him. I saw the whites of his eyes as he held a pistol to my father's head and laughed, so they are seared in here.' She tapped her temple.

'All I ask is that you tell the truth, the whole truth and nothing but the truth, Lady Octavia.' She smiled at that as she opened the front door and he grinned back. 'Thank you.'

He kissed her hand because he was grateful.

Because he was impressed with her gumption. Her principles. Her fearlessness.

Because he was relieved.

And not to make his wife jealous because she was watching them from the bushes. In truth, it never even occurred to him that Gwen might be there.

Chapter Twenty-One

Adam was in the middle of shaving for the blasted ball he felt contractually obligated to attend when Gwen emerged through their connecting door.

'Look what the cat dragged in.'

He had hoped for some contrition. An apology. Something convincing and heartfelt enough that it would give him the opportunity to forgive her—because he so wanted to forgive her. But the icy glare, folded arms and the acid positively dripping from her lips were anything but.

How dare she have the gall to be angry at him when she was the one completely in the wrong! 'I said that I would honour our agreement as far as restoring your reputation was concerned.' He wiped the remaining soap from his face, supremely hurt that she clearly had no plans to make any amends but covered it in matching vitriol. 'Although I would like it noted that I am here under duress and would rather gargle nails than spend the evening pretending to be besotted by you.'

'That is entirely mutual!' It was obvious that She-Who-Must-Be-Obeyed hadn't taken his lack of obeying well this past week because she practically spat that. 'Ironic, though, that you feel obligated to honour our contract but not our wedding vows which should surely take precedence! Although I suppose I shouldn't be the least bit surprised they meant nothing to you!'

Now she had crossed a line. 'Those vows meant more to me than they ever did you! At least I kept them and assumed when we said till death us do part, that we were staying together for eternity.' He balled up the towel and tossed it across the room rather than shake her by the shoulders like he wanted to. 'You are the one who lied before God, Gwen.' He pointed heavenward. 'And neglected to tell both him and me that for you, eternity was three to four blasted months!'

'Do not quote those vows to me in such a sanctimonious manner, you hypocrite!'

It was staggering how blind to her own behaviour she was. How unreasonable she was being. Had bloody been! 'I'm the hypocrite?'

Her hands went immediately to her hips. 'Well, I am certainly not the one who has been unfaithful!'

'Unfaithful?' Now she was making absolutely no sense. 'Do you have evidence to prove that egregious and erroneous accusation or have you just gone stark, staring mad?'

'Do not play the innocent with me, Adam! I saw you with my own eyes! Sneaking off with Lady Octavia at the ball and then sneaking into her house this afternoon! Slobbering all over her hand too with absolutely no shame!'

'Ah…yes. For heaven forbid you would give any worthless and superfluous man the benefit of the doubt after Bentley.' Because of course the unreasonable and jaded harridan would think the worst of him too. Although that she had, had wounded. It was as if she didn't know him at all. So, of course, he shrugged, rather than deny it.

Behaved like a petulant, aggrieved child.

Lashed out in pain and anger and wretched disappointment. 'Or fight for him. For us. Would you? We men are all the same, after all, aren't we? Thank goodness you always have our measure, Gwen, and were always prepared for the worst. Well done you. You wanted a husband with a wandering eye—even stipulated it on your bloody list—so you shouldn't be the least bit surprised that I lowered myself to do precisely what you expected and sought comfort elsewhere?'

Her outraged mouth hung slack for a moment because she had clearly been expecting a denial. Or perhaps she expected him to get down on his knees and beg? As tempted as he was to do exactly that to make this awfulness end and to convince her to stay, begging had never been in his lexicon. Rebellion against blatant unfairness and injustice, however, was second nature.

'We men are all the same, after all. Besides, my *alleged* infidelity, according to your blasted criteria, gives you *ample excuse to insist upon a quiet separation once I have ceased being useful.*' It was easy to quote directly when every single word on her awful list seemed to be carved into his flesh. 'Which I presume I am if you are now receiving invitations of your own from the high and mighty like the Marchioness of Burstead!' He should have stopped there.

Taken a breath.

Realised that neither of them were in any fit state to have the conversation they needed to.

Or hauled her into his arms and told her that he loved her and wanted nothing more than for her to love him back. To trust him. Because he couldn't be unfaithful to her if he tried. Gwen was it for him.

His everything.

But instead, more bile spewed from his lips because he wanted her to hurt as much as he was. 'So yes— you caught me red-handed.' He held his palms up as if in surrender when, in actuality, he was tossing fuel on the fire he desperately wanted to extinguish. '*Mea culpa!* I spend every second that I can in the warm and comforting arms of Lady Octavia!'

Gwen's head snapped back as if she had been slapped but still he could not stop.

'It is a pleasant diversion from my blessedly short and disappointing marriage to a secretive, lying, uncompromising and controlling cold fish!'

Needless to say, he stormed out at that point. Spent another lonely, interminable sleepless night at the inn near the law chambers he had holed himself up in this past week, pondering incessantly how wronged he felt and how wrong he was likely behaving. Despite all his best efforts for them to become closer, Gwen didn't actually know him at all. Worse, she clearly did not want to either as she seemed to be looking for a way out by firing such an outrageous accusation at him. And, of course, the verdict had been guilty because she didn't even want to hear otherwise.

'Adam!' Ash shoved him. 'Are you going to lay a blasted card or do you need more time to stare furiously into space?'

'Er…' He dissembled quickly and tossed one down, regretting his decision to come here tonight too. Two hours ago he had hoped the traditional Wednesday at White's with his friends would distract him from his woes, but now realised that nothing could. He was, for want of a better word, heartbroken. 'Sorry.'

'Care to let us in?' Ezra's request echoed too much what he constantly asked Gwen, and so like Gwen, he shook his head.

'I've just had a long day.' At least that was true.

With William's trial a matter of hours away now, he had spent the entire day making sure that he had dotted every *i* and crossed every *t* in the detailed case for the defence before he had passed it all over to Sir Thomas Lenthall. Being a diligent sort who valued his excellent reputation, Sir Thomas had then quizzed him extensively on it all. His subsequent pat on the back for a job well done and an invitation to assist him in court had been the only bright moment in a week mired in darkness. 'I doubtless need an early night.'

Which would have been the perfect excuse to give his apologies and leave because he felt too wretched for cards, except his brother suddenly stalked towards their card table and his thunderous expression suggested that his evening was about to get much worse.

'I knew I would finally find you here! What the hell do you think you are doing?'

As always, it was Phillip's disappointed, accusatory tone that had Adam setting his jaw. 'Playing whist.'

'Sarcasm! Splendid. It is nice to see that you have fully regressed to the eight-year-old child that you are behaving like.'

'I do not need a lecture, Phillip.'

'Well, you are bloody well going to get one! But whether I deliver it in private or wash all your dirty linen here in full view of White's is up to you.' Like Adam, Phillip had never been quick to temper, but just like him, when it went it went and his big brother could out-stubborn and out-belligerent anyone. 'Do I need to count to five like our nanny used to do when you threw a tantrum?'

'Oh, for pity's sake!' Adam surged from the table and stalked from the card room, the shocked room of patrons as silent as the grave as he disappeared into the hallway and his brother followed. Only when they were ensconced in the privacy of one of the empty rooms did he fold his arms. 'Well?'

'You are behaving like a blasted idiot!' All of Phillip's temper exploded. 'And your poor wife is devastated!'

'Devastated at being found out, no doubt. Gwen likes to be in charge and her performing monkey isn't doing as he is told.'

'She packed her bags yesterday and left.' News that shook him to his core. 'I would have told you that yesterday so you could have stopped her—but of course you were too busy sulking and nobody knew where you were!'

'She was always going to leave anyway so it's likely for the best.' Although the urge to run and fetch her back was so overwhelming he almost sprinted for the door.

Phillip sighed as some of his anger deflated into sympathy. 'That list wasn't nice, I know, but—'

'But she did everything to shut me out. Right from the outset. She was never committed to the marriage.

The best she ever did when I tried my damnedest to win her over was pay me lip service.' His own anger deflated with that truth. 'She made a fool out of me, Phillip.'

'I understand that but…' Anger hovered again on his brother's expression. 'Getting petty revenge with Lady Octavia was beyond the pale. Gwen did not deserve that.'

Did nobody know him! 'Oh, for pity's sake! I was not unfaithful to Gwen!'

'Abigail saw you too, Adam. Clandestinely going into her house and leaving it almost an hour later. You kissed her hand—'

'I was thanking her!'

Phillip threw up his hands, his disbelief apparent. 'You admitted to your wife you spent the afternoon in her bed!'

'I lied!' he shouted, feeling pathetic and churlish. 'She thought me guilty already so…' He raked a hand through his hair. 'So…'

'You mutinied again.' Phillip slumped into a chair. 'Oh, for goodness' sake! Why do you always do this? Why do you always go off half-cocked when someone backs you into a corner? Gwen is your wife—not our blasted father or the army top brass.'

'She used me as a racing stud and always planned to leave me.' Bloody hell, but that was somehow more humiliating when said aloud. 'How else was I supposed to react?'

'By using your blasted brain, Adam!' Phillip jabbed him in the ribs. 'Couldn't you see that she already loved you?'

'She doesn't.'

Phillip regarded him with pity this time. 'A woman doesn't get as angry as Gwen is if she isn't in love, you fool!'

'On the contrary. Gwen...' Had had her heart broken before. Was wary. Probably scared of making the same mistake again—just as he kept doing. Heaven help him but his brother was right. If she had wanted him gone she should have been rejoicing in his supposed infidelity, not spitting feathers. 'Oh...*damnation*!' He let the back of his head bash the wall as he leant against it. 'I've made a massive mistake, haven't I?'

'One undoubtedly as massive as your rash decision to join the army and we all know how that petty rebellion against our infuriating father ended.' Phillip huffed. 'Perhaps you can fix this if you go to her on bended knees and explain why you had such a suspiciously clandestine meeting with the beautiful Lady Octavia.' Then his brother's brows furrowed. 'Which was?'

Chapter Twenty-Two

After a second night of weeping into her pillow in her old bedchamber in Cheapside, Gwen had finally dropped off exhausted sometime around dawn and slept till ten. However, despite the uncharacteristically late morning, all she was capable of doing now that she was in her carriage on her way to Trym's, was holing up in her office so that she could grieve.

Losing Adam certainly felt like a death. Her own stupid fault, she supposed, for trusting and falling for a man again when she had promised herself that that would never happen. His parting shot had destroyed her and had occupied her mind ever since.

A secretive, duplicitous and controlling cold fish.

Coming from Adam that somehow seemed so much worse than the frigid milksop Bentley had accused her of being. Probably because Adam had hit the nail on the head with his insult.

She had been secretive. And cold. She had pushed him away, partly out of self-preservation and partly out of fear. She had also lied to him. Repeatedly. Using the excuse of time and space rather than being honest from the outset and telling him that she had only ever intended theirs to be a temporary marriage.

At least initially, at any rate. When she had begun to question that, she had still kept it a secret that she was daring to dream of forever. She had also been controlling, expecting him to fall into line with her grand plan and not cause her any uncomfortable complications. As if Adam could fall into any line he did not want to be in! And in doing, she supposed she had as good as pushed him into Octavia's arms. That did not justify that he had fallen into them so readily, however, and that he had done something so callous out of pure revenge had hammered the final nail in the coffin of their marriage.

There was no coming back from that. His betrayal had broken her heart and, because her heart had been hardened over the last ten years, instead of a hole being ripped into it like Bentley had done, Adam had cruelly shattered it into a million tiny pieces. Like a glass under the heel of his big and cumbersome boot. A blow that had been doubly hard to take because she loved the wretch and hadn't believed him capable of such callousness.

Running, at the time, had seemed like the safest option but with every fibre of her being aching at the loss of him and a couple of days of distance she wasn't so sure she should have. Despite his "*mea culpa*" confession, doubts about it had crept in almost immediately because she still could not believe he was that cruel and consequently she was at war with herself. The rediscovered hopeless romantic that had emerged from its decade-long hibernation begged her to give him the opportunity to retract his hurtful words and clarify what he had meant when he had said '*Heaven forbid you would give any worthless and superfluous man the benefit of the doubt after Bentley—or fight for him. For us. Would you?*'

Why the blazes would he expect her to fight for him—for them—after what he had done unless he hadn't actually done it? She had witnessed that disappointment in his emotive blue eyes then too, the wretch, followed by the way they dimmed when she remained mute despite that plaintive voice screaming in her head to do just that. Even as he'd gone on to admit the affair, that pathetic, hopeful voice remained unconvinced that the vexing man of principles she had so recklessly married was capable of being so unprincipled, no matter what nonsense he had decided to spew to the contrary at her accusation.

The same voice had been drowned out by the bruised, pessimistic and cynical one that always shouted louder.

As usual.

That overcautious and righteously indignant other

half of her wanted to forget that *they* had ever existed. To chalk their brief liaison up as a partially successful experiment that had helped restore her tarnished reputation enough that her new shop would open without being mired in too much scandal. To remember that her short time with Adam was nothing more than the business transaction that she had first intended it to be. To move on and to seamlessly move back to the life she temporarily left as if nothing seismic had shifted.

Except it had.

She wasn't the same woman she had been a month ago and wanted more. So much more.

As her carriage slowed, she stared mournfully at the solid walls of her workshop. Walls that she had lived for to the exception of all else. Walls that she had ruthlessly married a stranger for. Walls that had been her sanctuary for a decade after she had withdrawn into them after Bentley's betrayal. An irony that was not lost on her now that Adam had done much the same.

Except now those walls felt more like a prison than a cocoon. Her life's work somehow pointless now that decades without Adam loomed before her. What the blazes was she doing all this for when she had nobody to share it all with? No family to pass it on to either when she had so wanted children—*plural*.

His children.

Their children.

A home filled with noise and love.

With all its lazy, intimate mornings and pleasant mealtimes. Sociable evenings. Passionate nights in their bed. Or afternoons wherever the mood struck them. Like here in her carriage, which was now so intrinsically linked to all her memories of him that she knew she would have to replace it as soon as possible. For how else was she supposed to ever forget the love of her life? Or forget what he had done.

If he had actually done it, which, God help her, she doubted more and more with every passing hour. Because this was Adam. Who had always been a conundrum of a man, drat him—right from the outset. As frustratingly uncompliant and unpredictable as he was gallingly noble and understanding. Refusing to accept the original terms of their marriage contract despite how much that offending clause would have benefitted him. Appearing to give her the time and space she asked for while always subtly invading it so thoroughly. Forcing her to be part of a family. Forcing his friendship on her. His unstinting support. Challenging her constantly to let him in as he effortlessly mined under all her defences and sneaked in anyway. Making her fall in love with him against all her better judgement because he—they—just felt right.

Was she really going to throw all that away because the wretch had spat a lie at her in anger after she had accused him of worse nor given him the chance to explain. With hindsight, he had resembled a man thoroughly confused by her initial accusation and he had, to begin with, asserted, most vociferously, that he had honoured all of his vows. Unlike her. And surely *all of them* included the fundamental fidelity part?

This had all the hallmarks of a mistake. Perhaps the most epic one she had ever made.

Before she lost her nerve, Gwen rapped on the ceiling of her carriage. 'Take me to Hereford Street!' It was time that they both told the truth.

Sir Thomas cut an imposing figure as he made mincemeat of the final prosecution witness in Court number three of the Old Bailey. The constable was getting increasingly flustered as he had to keep rifling through his stack of papers to find all the witness descriptions of the highwayman they had been robbed by. As Adam knew already, they were unsurprisingly all the same and they did not match the slight young man in the dock at all—hence he had advised this precise line of questions.

The judge noted something down and when he had ascertained that the hastily prepared case for the prosecution apparently rested entirely with the constable, he seemed annoyed before the clerk called Lady Octavia's name.

Exactly as Adam had suggested, and despite her statement already read by the constable, Sir Thomas took her through the events of that night to make sure that the court knew that she was in no doubt about them.

'Is this your earring, my lady?' Finally, Sir Thomas handed her the jewel.

'It is.'

'To be clear, this is the earring that the highwayman snatched from your ears after he yanked off your pearls?'

'Yes.'

'Is it fair to say that you must have been pretty close to your assailant for him to have done that?'

'Too close,' said Lady Octavia, her clever and curious gaze constantly wandering to the man in the dock.

'Is Mr Briggs the man who held a pistol to your father's temple.'

Lady Octavia stared at the accused for the longest time. Levelly and without any fear. Then, with a brief look of resignation, she shook her head. 'No. He is not.'

'Are you certain, Lady Octavia?'

She nodded and then her gaze locked with Adam's. 'Beyond all reasonable doubt. I have never seen this man before in my life.'

That was the final straw as far as the judge was concerned. Adam saw that in the man's exasperated face as he gathered up his papers and left the court to ponder his verdict, which none of them expected to take very long. Certainly not long enough for him to risk nipping down the road to Trym's to prostrate himself at Gwen's feet, convince her that he had been lying and beg her to take him back.

'This is for you.' The clerk of the court handed him a note. 'From someone in the gallery.'

Intrigued, Adam unfolded it and stared at Gwen's neat, sloping handwriting.

Thanks to some new and disturbing evidence, I have revised my Specific Criteria for a Husband

1. He must be proud and principled (preferably not good at taking orders).

2. He must drive me to distraction—both in the bedchamber and out of it.

3. He must uphold each and every one of his wedding vows until death do us part.

4. He must be someone that I love with all of my heart (and I do!) despite his penchant for garish waistcoats.

5. He must—and this one is non-negotiable—be a barrister and not a lackey at the War Office. I want our children (plural) to be as proud of you as I am.

If you think that you match these criteria without exception, and if you can assure me that you did not ever seek comfort in your key witness's

arms as you *claimed, I would be happy to reconsider you for the post.*
Gwen

His heart in his mouth, he sensed her before he
spied her seated in the furthest corner of the public gallery. Their eyes locked and her half-smile was
enough to give him hope that, with some compromise,
they could fix things. He stood, ready to dash to her
and plead his case, only to have to remain where he
was, while the judge returned and took his sweet time
announcing William's not guilty verdict.

It was a full half an hour later when he finally hovered on the threshold of the public gallery. 'Hello,
Gwen.' It was bizarre, but he had never been so nervous around her as he was now. Not even on their
wedding night when she had insisted they have one.
'How did you know where to find me?'

'Phillip told me after I marched back to Hereford
Street cap in hand, ready to beg you to forgive me and
come back.' She gestured to the now silent courtroom.
'Why didn't you tell me, or anyone for that matter,
about this?'

He shrugged, embarrassed. 'I knew I would have to
give up the pupillage to earn a living thanks to Phillip's predicament, so it seemed easier all around to
keep my own counsel.' He took a step closer. 'I am
sorry I kept it a secret from you.'

'I am sorry for keeping all those secrets of my own.' Her gaze dipped. 'And for not letting you in or for writing that awful list. I thought I wanted something that it turned out I didn't. For the record, I knew straight away that you matched none of my specific and idiotic criteria—but for some inexplicable reason I married you anyway. I am still not entirely sure why, because you vex me exponentially, beyond there being something about you that called to my soul.'

He lowered himself into the chair next to her. 'Well, seeing as we are being entirely honest with one another, something about you called to my soul too.' He risked reaching for her hand and she did not pull hers away. 'I also, much to my shame, lied about being unfaithful to you because you vex me exponentially. I couldn't...wouldn't.'

'I worked that out when you called Lady Octavia to the stand. I feel wretched for accusing you of it now. But—in our new spirit of honesty—you should also know that you hit a raw nerve when you sneaked into her house. The night I fled Gretna...' She stared at their cautiously intertwined fingers. 'I had just caught my fiancé *within* his lover, joking about me being the gullible, frigid milksop with all the money so... I realise I overreacted.'

Adam sighed. 'I think it is fair to say we both did that.'

'He broke my heart and, until you came along and

ruined all my carefully laid plans, I did not think I was capable of giving it to anyone again, nor did I want to. But here we are.'

'Here we are.' He nudged her with his shoulder. 'I love you too, by the way. Pretty much have since the start. Was planning on coming to you cap in hand after the trial to tell you as much.'

'That's good to know.'

'I want to be your husband again in every sense of the word, Gwen, but I cannot—will not—be a kept man. Not even for you.'

'Yes you can,' she said standing and plonking her hands on her hips. 'If I can swallow all of my pride and all of my fears to lay my heart on the line and beg you to take me back, the least you can do is swallow yours enough to honour the contract we signed. It states that I would pay all the household bills for the duration of our marriage.'

His own hands went to his hips as he stood too. 'I have stated repeatedly that there is no way I am letting you do that forever!'

'Two years isn't forever, darling,' she said grinning. 'Not that you have any contractual say on how I choose to spend my money. But even so, according to your brother, who is as peeved about your secrecy as I am, you saved enough to pay for your own pupillage so you can still keep yourself.'

He went to argue again and she silenced him with a kiss. 'You once told me that you had no idea why the universe saved you. What it considered so special about you that it kept you alive—and in case it has escaped your notice it is this.' She swept both arms about the room before she looped them around his neck. 'Using the law to save lives, like you just did William Briggs', is your destiny, Adam. That is the debt it wants you to repay. Today was as clear an omen on that as it is possible to be so it is time you embraced that instead of feeling guilty about it. Just as it is apparently my destiny as your beloved, besotted and hopelessly devoted wife to use whatever means I can—including outright blackmail—to force you into doing it.'

He absorbed that for a moment, which was all it took for him to realise that this clever, controlling, conniving, confounding woman that he had married was absolutely right. This was his destiny. It always had been. She was too. 'Blackmail is a crime, you know. A capital offence.'

'Is it?' She grabbed his hand and tugged him towards the door. 'Then you should put me at the top of your list of criminals to prosecute once you pass the bar. But in the meantime, why don't you practice your cross-examination skills on the carriage ride home?' She shot him a look of pure, unadulterated sin as she dragged him down the stairs. 'Only thanks to you I have become a shamelessly wanton and totally brazen hussy and I think it is about to rain…'

* * * * *

*If you enjoyed this story,
make sure to read
Virginia Heath's
A Very Village Scandal miniseries*

The Earl's Inconvenient Houseguest
His Maddening Matchmaker
A Wedding to Stop a Scandal

*And why not pick up her instalment in our
Society's Most Scandalous collection?*

How to Woo a Wallflower
by Virginia Heath

How to Cheat the Marriage Mart
by Millie Adams

How to Survive a Scandal
by Christine Merrill

MILLS & BOON®

HOW TO COURT A RAKE
Bronwyn Scott

Book 1 of Wed Within a Year
The brand-new regency trilogy
from Bronwyn Scott

It was a quick waltz and Caine wasted no time getting them up to pace, taking her through turns with a rapidity that left Mary breathless, her cheeks flushed from the exertion and the sheer thrill of waltzing at top speed. 'I've never dared to dance so fast,' she said with a laugh as he guided them through a sharp turn, expertly avoiding another couple.

'You're a good dancer.' She managed to catch her breath long enough to make conversation. Caine had a keen sense of navigation on a crowded floor and an innate confidence in his own skill. She was struck once more by the agility and enjoyment on display when he danced.

'You seem surprised by that.' Caine took them through a corner using a reverse turn as if on cue to illustrate the point.

'Big men aren't usually so gifted with such grace,' she managed to say, still somewhat in awe of the reverse he'd just executed. It was one of the most difficult parts of the dance and he'd managed it effortlessly.

'Aren't we?' He raised a dark brow, his gaze fixed on her, the hint of a sinful smile teasing his lips. 'Are you an expert on big men, Mary?' A low purl of naughtiness rippled through his words and her breath caught for entirely different reasons than the speed of their dance. She didn't understand his reference entirely—no decent girl would—but she understood enough to know his innuendo was wicked. While she wasn't an expert on big men, she suddenly wished she was, especially if that big man was him.

'It's only that you don't dance much. I assumed it was because you didn't enjoy it or lacked skill,' she confessed openly, smartly letting his innuendo go untended. That was a battle of words she hadn't the experience to win. She cocked her head and took in the dark gaze, the smiling lips. 'Surely you see the contradiction. If you love to dance so much, why do you do it so seldom?'

His gaze lingered on her, meltingly warm. 'Perhaps because there are so few partners worthy of my efforts.'

She felt the heat rise in her cheeks yet again at the implied compliment—that *she* was worthy.

Continue reading

HOW TO COURT A RAKE
Bronwyn Scott

Available next month
millsandboon.co.uk

COMING SOON!

We really hope you enjoyed reading this book.
If you're looking for more romance
be sure to head to the shops when
new books are available on

Thursday 27th March

To see which titles are coming soon, please visit

millsandboon.co.uk/nextmonth

MILLS & BOON

LET'S TALK

Romance

For exclusive extracts, competitions and special offers, find us online:

f MillsandBoon

X @MillsandBoon

O @MillsandBoonUK

♪ @MillsandBoonUK

Get in touch on 01413 063 232

afterglow BOOKS

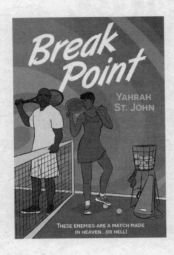

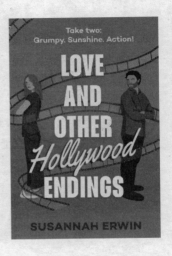

 Second chance

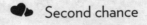 Second chance

 Sports romance

Workplace romance

Enemies to lovers

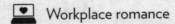 Grumpy/sunshine

OUT NOW

Two stories published every month. Discover more at:
Afterglowbooks.co.uk